LOVE IS A PIE

"And I imagined love as a pie, a slice for each, chacun à son goût."

NOEL in *A Diary of Love*

By Maude Hutchins

GEORGIANA

DIAGRAMATICS

with Mortimer Adler

A DIARY OF LOVE

LOVE

IS

A

PIE *by*

Maude Hutchins

A NEW DIRECTIONS BOOK

Acknowledgment is made to the following publications for permission to republish the indicated stories and plays:

Accent, for "The Marriage of Toto."

Circle, for "Soliloquy at Dinner."

Epoch, for "The Fifth Commandment."

Foreground, for "From Morning Till Night."

Kenyon Review, for "Innocents."

Mademoiselle, for "French Wife in America" (reprinted from *Mademoiselle,* Copyright by Street and Smith Publications, Inc., 1947).

New Directions, for "Joseph Smith, Jr.," "The Case of Astrolabe," "Aunt Julia's Caesar," and "The Wandering Jew."

The Quarterly Review of Literature, for "Mary Play."

First published as New Directions
paperbook in 2010.

ISBN: 97808112897-9

Table of Contents

LOVE IS A PIE

Joseph Smith, Jr.

"Joseph Smith . . . (1805-1844), the founder, in April, 1830, of the Church of Jesus Christ of Later-Day Saints, was born in Sharon, Vermont, on the 23rd of December 1805. He was killed by a mob in a jail at Carthage, Illinois, on the 27th of June 1844."

Encyclopaedia Britannica, Eleventh Edition

"There shall not any man have save it be one wife, and concubines he shall have none, for I the Lord God delighteth in the chastity of women. . . . For if I will, saith the Lord of Hosts, raise up seed unto me, I will command my people, otherwise they shall harken unto these things."

> *The Book of Mormon* (which is a translation, dictated by Joseph Smith with the aid of a pair of supernatural spectacles, of the golden plates dug up by him after three conversations with the Angel Moroni).

Coffee and tea are forbidden in the *Book* but Joseph Smith recognizes expediency.

IDEA

The play should consist of many wives and Joseph Smith. By their conversation and behavior his story should be told. He is warmly and gratefully loved by them all. A lack of passion is noticeable, however. It is a friendly love they have for him. It is straight and just and forgiving without patronage or jealousy. It is neither maternal nor childish but it is satisfactory. The presence of one sweetheart-wife, very recent, very young and very romantic, should not disturb the impression of satisfaction and womanly appeal of the play, but act as a reminder and foil for the audience without annoying it.

The very recent sweetheart-wife, Dierdre, cannot understand what she thinks of as the attitude of the many wives. She does not understand or appreciate or desire their peace and everyday contentment. She is amazed that they are not jealous of each other and that they do not envy her. She is amazed especially at their lack of envy of her although she is constantly unhappy, frightened and dissatisfied.

Joseph Smith is courteous and good to his many wives. Each of them appears to receive his undivided attention although it is not obvious or studied. He pets and plays with his recent sweetheart-wife but at no time is he overcome by his emotion for her. Her own emotion makes him shine in her eyes, and his speech and gestures she thinks belong to her, making her momentarily happy in his presence, but to the audience it is clear that he has no preference. It is also clear that his life at home does not interfere with his life as a prophet and that his many wives do not object to his special calling; neither are they impressed by it.

THE PROLOGUE

The scene is a winter landscape, with a brown house in the foreground, a hill in the background. Joseph Smith is surrounded by some children and some neighbors.

FIRST NEIGHBOR:
Hi, Joe.

JOSEPH SMITH:

Hi.

CHILDREN:

Uncle Joe, don't go in.

JOSEPH SMITH:

Lunch.

SECOND NEIGHBOR:

Been slidin'?

CHILDREN:

It's wonderful today. It's wonderful today.

JOSEPH SMITH:

We had fun.

FIRST NEIGHBOR:

I thought you was a prophet.

SECOND NEIGHBOR:

Do prophets slide downhill with the children?

JOSEPH SMITH:

I am a prophet only when acting as such. [*He goes in — there is a general dispersal.*]

THE PLAY

SCENE: *The dining room in the brown house. There is a refectory table in the center. About the room are chairs of many designs — one or two rockers, a couple of slipper chairs with footstools, a handsome antique or two, a ladder back, a Windsor, a painted Sheraton, some ordinary kitchen chairs and even a love seat.*

As Joseph Smith comes in the wives are in motion. One is pouring water into glasses, one is arranging a few flowers, one is coming through the swinging door from the pantry. Three are seated talking animatedly, one is standing behind her chair embroidering inside a little hoop; one is stooping trying to see herself in a tiny mirror on the wall. There seems to be plenty to do but it is being done without confusion. The sweetheart-wife is sitting very straight in her own special chair. She is the only one who appears to be tense with wait-

*ing. Her cheeks are very pink. The others notice Joseph Smith's
arrival slowly, but Deirdre jumps to her feet and quickly steps up
to him.*

DEIRDRE [*in a high sweet voice*]:
My love.
    JOSEPH SMITH [*touching her cheek but looking evenly at all*]:
Hello.
    ALL THE WIVES:
Hello, Joe.
Hello, Joseph.
How d'ye do, Joseph.
Mr. Smith.
God bless you, Joseph.
Well, Joe.
    DEIRDRE [*feeling him*]:
So cold.
    MARY [*taking his gloves*]:
There'll be some hot soup.
    ELLEN [*taking his coat*]:
Was it good sliding today?
    LOUISA [*taking his scarf*]:
Your neck is wet; you'll catch your death.
    JANE [*picking up his galoshes as he kicks them off*]:
Nasty things — they're soaking wet. I'll put them in the oven.
    DEIRDRE:
No — I!
    JANE [*with a laugh*]:
You've just manicured your nails.
    DEIRDRE [*placing the backs of her hands close to his face*]:
Smell — Jinny.
    JOSEPH SMITH [*kissing them neatly*]:
Pretty . . . What happened to Frieda?
    A WIFE:
A headache, Mr. Smith.

4

JOSEPH SMITH:
And Katherine?
ANOTHER WIFE:
Shopping, Joseph.
DEIRDRE [*flushed and impatient*]:
Please, Jinny.
JOSEPH SMITH [*kindly*]:
Five minutes, Deirdre. I'm hungry.
DEIRDRE [*angrily*]:
You don't love me. [*The other wives continue as before and do not appear to notice the conversation. Deirdre and Joseph Smith might be alone.*]
JOSEPH SMITH:
Yes I do.
DEIRDRE:
No you don't.
JOSEPH SMITH:
I love my Deirdre.
DEIRDRE [*insistently*]:
Best?
JOSEPH SMITH:
Best.
DEIRDRE [*insistently*]:
Of all?
JOSEPH SMITH:
All.
DEIRDRE:
All all?
JOSEPH SMITH [*laughing*]:
Baby.
DEIRDRE:
Tell me. All all?
JOSEPH SMITH:
All all.
DEIRDRE [*standing so that he cannot reach or see the others*]:
Jinny.

JOSEPH SMITH:

I've been so busy.

DEIRDRE:

You went to Jane last night.

JOSEPH SMITH:

I couldn't have.

DEIRDRE:

I heard you.

JOSEPH SMITH:

Then I must have, but I thought I was writing a sermon.

DEIRDRE [*almost in tears*]:

You're laughing at me.

JOSEPH SMITH:

No, little one.

DEIRDRE:

Tonight.

JOSEPH SMITH:

I must write my sermon tonight if I didn't write it last night, and you tell me I didn't write it last night.

DEIRDRE [*in tears, running into the pantry*]:

Oh!

JOSEPH SMITH [*sorry but not affected*]:

Ellen — how are the children?

ELLEN:

Well, Joseph. Only Henry has the croup again.

JOSEPH SMITH:

Did you use the kettle?

ELLEN:

Oh, yes.

MARY [*interrupting*]:

Kathleen is a darling, Joseph. Couldn't you stop in our wing this evening and see her?

JOSEPH SMITH:

Of course, Mary.

JANE:

I didn't have quite enough muslin for my frock, Joseph. May I?

JOSEPH SMITH:

Speak to me tomorrow, Jane. [*A snowball hits the window with a thwack and flattens out.*]

LOUISA [*jumping up*]:

That'll be Victor. [*She opens the window and calls.*] Victor! Go in with the others. Don't do that, Victor! [*to Joseph Smith*] If you would please speak to him, Joseph. He really is getting unmanageable.

JOSEPH SMITH [*placidly*]:

I will, Louisa.

[*The wives are about seated, some by agreement serving the others, when the street door is pushed open by Katherine, her arms full of bundles, her face happy. She lets go her packages, leans over Joseph Smith and kisses him while her eyes look over the table.*]

KATHERINE:

I am exhausted. I am hungry.

JOSEPH SMITH [*fondly, with his arm around her waist*]:

My greedy wife. My smart girl.

KATHERINE:

Let go, Mr. Smith. I am starving.

JOSEPH SMITH [*not letting go*]:

How much did you spend, Cricket? Must I have a revelation to pay the bills? [*The others smile at what appears to be an old joke.*]

KATHERINE:

Let go.

[*There is a slight scuffle. Joseph Smith lets go her waist and flips her bottom with his napkin as she turns away; he holds it in his right hand and snaps it through his left like a boy in school.*]

KATHERINE [*to Jane*]:

I found you some beautiful muslin, Janey.

ELLEN:

Did you get me my cotton thread No. 22?

KATHERINE [*to Ellen*]:

Yes, I did and a spool of silk. It was not so dear. [*to Mary*] I didn't

have time to look for you know what, Mary.
    MARY:
But I need them.
    JOSEPH SMITH:
Need them?
    KATHERINE *and* MARY [*together*]:
Joseph Smith, don't be curious.
    JOSEPH SMITH:
What is a them?
    LOUISA:
He knows perfectly well.
    JOSEPH SMITH:
Show me, Louisa
    LOUISA [*looking as if she would*]:
I shall!
    JOSEPH SMITH [*delighted*]:
Show me, Louisa. Show me what Mary needs so badly and Katherine
didn't have time for.
    LOUISA [*jumping up, blushing and excited*]:
I shall, Joseph Smith, I shall! [*The wives are all laughing like a lot of
little birds.*]
    JOSEPH SMITH:
One to . . .
Two to . . .
Three to . . .
And four to show!
[*Louisa raises her skirts high and from the pantry door comes a wail.
Deirdre is standing there.*]
    DEIRDRE:
Jinny! [*Everyone more or less shrugs. The fun is over but Deirdre is
not criticized.*]
    JOSEPH SMITH [*quieting down*]:
Deirdre, baby. Come and eat something.
    DEIRDRE [*sobbing with her face in her hands*]:
No, no, no! Oh, how disgusting. Oh, how disgusting. You are all

8

disgusting.
[*No one replies; things are being passed. Steps are heard coming down the uncarpeted stairs, and Frieda appears. She is pale.*]
FRIEDA:
What is all the noise? My poor head.
JOSEPH SMITH:
Good day, Frieda. What ails my tall girl — are you better?
FRIEDA [*kissing him in a frail manner*]:
I'm awful, Joey, but what is happening?
MARY:
I fixed you, Frieda, and pulled the shades and now you get up. No wonder you always have a headache, no wonder at all.
JOSEPH SMITH:
You aren't fat enough, Frieda.
FRIEDA:
I can't help it.
JOSEPH SMITH [*going about his meal*]:
Eat.
FRIEDA [*restless*]:
What was happening?
ELLEN [*raising her eyebrows toward Deirdre who still stands in the door*]:
Nothing.
[*Joseph Smith finishes a mouthful, wipes his mouth, sits back and looks at Frieda.*]
JOSEPH SMITH:
Come here, Frieda.
FRIEDA [*coming to him and standing listlessly between his knees*]:
Don't make me eat, Joey.
JOSEPH SMITH:
I promised your father I'd fatten you up. What does she weigh, Mary?
MARY:
Practically nothing, Mr. Smith, in her shift.
JOSEPH SMITH [*making love to her*]:
My pale and lovely Frieda. [*Frieda bends her head and whispers in*

his ear. Then she speaks to the others.]

JOSEPH SMITH [*continuing his meal*]:

FRIEDA:

I am going up again if nothing is going on. [*She glances at Deirdre in the doorway who is staring at her in misery, and then she wanders out.*]

JOSEPH SMITH [*continuing his meal*]:

I'll bring you a cup of tea.

THE WIVES [*mildly shocked*]:

Tea!

JOSEPH SMITH:

It is expedient, my dears. [*Perhaps he feels a little guilty about Deirdre because he goes on.*] Deirdre, baby, you shall have a cup, too. [*Deirdre gives up her post in the pantry door and comes and kneels beside him. He lifts her face, looks into her eyes and kisses her mouth. She is happy.*]

DEIRDRE [*gently*]:

Jinny.

JOSEPH SMITH:

Yes.

DEIRDRE:

Do you love me?

JOSEPH SMITH:

Yes, silly.

DEIRDRE:

Then don't go to Frieda.

JOSEPH SMITH:

What?

DEIRDRE [*pleading*]:

Please don't, Jinny.

JOSEPH SMITH:

Don't what?

DEIRDRE:

Go to Frieda.

JOSEPH SMITH [*kissing her*]:

Frieda needs me.

10

DEIRDRE [*wildly*]:

I need you!

JOSEPH SMITH [*soothingly*]:

Deirdre needs me.

DEIRDRE [*calmer*]:

I love you.

JOSEPH SMITH [*absently*]:

Deirdre loves me.

[*Deirdre is happy for a while. Her head is on his knee. He is stroking her hair. The meal is about over, things become quiet and Joseph stares out into space. As the feel and rhythm of his hand changes Deirdre looks up at him without raising her head. The others are quietly gossiping. Joseph Smith looks as if he saw a vision. The many wives are quiet but not impressed. Deirdre loves him with her eyes now as she sits back on her thighs. Then Joseph Smith gets up, looks vaguely around and speaks in a businesslike way.*]

JOSEPH SMITH:

I shall go to the temple now. I may be a little late this evening for supper, Mary. [*He starts to go, then murmers.*] Frieda's tea.

DEIRDRE [*jumping to her feet*]:

I'll take Frieda's tea to her, Jinny. I'll make it now. I'll take it to her, Jinny.

[*Mary and Ellen interrupt his rapt walk to the door.*]

ELLEN:

Oh, Mr. Smith.

JOSEPH SMITH:

Yes? Yes, Ellen.

ELLEN:

If the general store is open, please bring me five pounds of stewing apples.

MARY:

Sour ones.

JOSEPH SMITH [*writing in a little book*]:

Yes? Yes, Ellen, Mary, apples. [*There is a pause.*] But there is a probability I may be called out of town tonight. [*He goes out.*]

Good-bye, Joe.
Good-bye, Joseph.
Good-bye, Mr. Smith.
God bless you, Joseph.
Good-bye, Joey.

Innocents

Beginning with nothing, except of course the prerequisites of breeding: bone and tendency, light rations of calcium and such for her physical possibility, she emerged as I say, with nothing. Rudely slapped by a medico whom later on in life she would bewilder with her complicated ego, tossed in a sterile basket, bathed, swathed, pinched, poked, rolled and so on. Thus I say: from warmth and satisfaction, irresponsibility, peace and quiet, solitude, look what she had to face: notoriety, daylight, indignities, vulgarities, obscenities, sterile bandaging. Torn from the stem of her parent, bleeding and angry, pried open like a flower too soon, forced to straighten out, as she would be forced hence and once again in death.

Ave atque vale. She came unheralded and went the same. We regret to say her talents perished with her as undeveloped and pristine on the day of her death as at her birth. Born like any other, not a monster, with the invisible sign of Free Will stamped upon her buttocks, this female child supposedly had not the vitality to exercise her right; she might as well have been born with a fishing rod as with that imaginary diploma: This entitles N or M to do as he chooses, to

13

exercise his reason, to make decisions, to know good from evil, to inherit the earth (weather permitting) and to enter the kingdom of Heaven; signed by the Word himself, by God. All this to a babe, no favored child, simply no monster. Nothing was asked of her the first day. And yet by night a cloud hung over this child, a misunderstanding of some sort, an expectancy, a nostalgia for the past which had been in the morning, a fear of consequences, a chilly sensation followed by a too warm one, a tightness in the throat, a racing of the heart, a short ambitious interlude, restlessness, irritation physical and mental, a wish to be alone, a desire to be loved, a horror of criticism, a distaste for vulgarity, a thought that she was unappreciated, even unwanted, a critical condescension for her nurses, a fleeting desire for the hands of an interne, hunger, thirst, the terror of examinations, modesty, a hatred for those who saw her in the nude and anger for those who witnessed her weaknesses. Altogether it had been a bad day, her first; and the thought of the interminable future appalled her and suddenly filled her with such nightmarish terror that she screamed "I cannot bear it" and turned blue in an attempt at self-destruction.

But this suicidal attempt, her first decision and her last, was frustrated by a smarty-pants nurse who had been sneaking through the otherwise sterile nursery looking for just that sort of thing, and seeking to circumvent, in her ignorance, freedom of will. Thwarted thus, she spent the next day in irresolution and remorse. Remorse for the frightened face of the little ignoramus nurse and the general disturbance and uproar which ensued in the nursery, but mostly remorse at the bright innocent face of her mother, from whom of course the knowledge of this attempted suicide must always be kept. This increased her deep feeling of responsibility for her mother which had been almost overwhelming from the start, and led her to feel a slight but loving contempt for her father, who seemed so ignorant of the facts of life, so innocent of catastrophe and the imminence of things and so proud and sure of himself. Decisive was the word for him, and she envied and disliked his strength of purpose and his vitality and ability to choose and decide and maintain. Her first curiosity, therefore, about the difference between the sexes was a purely intellectual one. She was much later to learn from a frightened lover that the male, too, as such, has his fear of responsibility which encourages procrastination and the instinct to say no.

In one day she had been born and wished to die. What a small world it was in point of time, then, how microcosmic. Would anything else happen to her in her whole life more shattering, discouraging, or character destroying, than the sequence of things past? What was the subject matter of her life to be, now that she knew its design? She already knew fear, love, hunger, contempt, arrogance, pity, concern, passion, thirst, heat, cold, fatigue, remorse, but most of all she had exercised in spite of her early age and frailty, her will, only to be prevented from witnessing the results of her action, as it were, by a symbol dressed up as a nurse, by a human monkey wrench. As one day passed into the next, therefore, this female child was an experienced child; there was not much she did not know, the notorious instinct for self-preservation having been denied her. That terrible, humiliating desire to change one's mind she had been so far spared. If one wished to consider this child fortunate, then, one might say with truth that she was, because she had not witnessed in herself that terrifying struggle for balance in the midst of a fall, unhappy though she might be and wishing to fall, that struggle with nature in which nature, the animal, wins, leaving one with unfulfilled intellectual desire and disgusted with the power of the purely physical. How much worse, indeed, it is, than accidental intervention, in which at least one may not blame oneself, animal or otherwise, but forever bear a handy grudge in time of need and "but for that I should have made my mark and carved my name indisputably upon an oak."

But unaware of her good fortune in having escaped the nightmare of self-preservation, the awful conflict of mind and body, the baby opened her large brown eyes still stinging from silver nitrate and still refusing to focus, upon the morning of her second day, gloomy and preoccupied, melancholy and introspective with a distinct feeling that she was unwell, a slight but real hypochondria. She was to learn on this new day, if nothing much else, because of her propensity to live in the past, the importance of something to eat, but unfortunately for her and for her friends in later life it was a knowledge that might be called *a posteriori*: she only knew it after each meal and never before. So that often her mother was frightened, her friends less admiring, her lovers disconsolate, her husband morose, the cook taken aback, her father disgusted and herself speechless and unhappy, spreading unhappiness like a fever, because she was hungry. Oddly enough, no one that was close to her ever found it out by himself and she herself never told anyone of her simple observation, not so much because of chagrin as from a desire that it not be so, and annoyance that it appeared to be, nevertheless. From birth she chose to believe that the soul was superior to the body and that large things happened for large reasons. That her overwhelming melancholy on the first day of life could have possibly been caused by hunger, she did not choose to believe. It is not clear how this choice came about and why it remained so strong a need to maintain throughout her life, but it no doubt was responsible for much of her spiritual charm and everlasting innocence, as well as for much unhappiness and misunderstanding. Before she was born, the day before yesterday, that is, she had been comfortable, warm, and contented. She remembered her content-ment. Almost immediately at birth she had felt disgust for physical things and a decided preference for the abstract. So that young as she was, and nostalgic as she was for her recent contentment, she seemed to recognize that it was but contentment and not happiness. A subtle use, then, as it were, under the gift of free will, therefore, was this desire for happiness rather than comfort, this distinguished choice that our small female made without hesitation. So that it seemed that she herself had accomplished her birth by choice and had deliberately torn herself from comfort and contentment, to real-ization, responsibility and the desire for happiness. You have heard of the results of her precocious use of the gift of free will in the first place and its consequences and also of her early good fortune, and thus on her second day how she was an advanced, experienced and melancholy child.

An almost complete fast up to this time had dangerously sharpened her wits but had left her with a low blood sugar count increasing to a degree her sombre mood. Eating by mouth, which she was now forced to do, against the will she was fast developing, made everyone connected with this event extremely unhappy and nervous, but especially disgusted this aloof and spiritually determined baby. Even in the animal comfort and security of her protected will-less past nothing so creature-like as this had been asked of her. Eating by mouth was vulgar; eating on purpose of your own accord was disgusting. And eating like this from your mother was a great horror that caused shuddering and near convulsions, so great was this small baby's repulsion. Sixteen years later this same baby refused, after her first real kiss, to eat for four days because she felt that the kiss was a spiritual thing of beauty and to satisfy her desire for food with the same mouth was horrible. Any thoughts that came to her astute mind in later years that the desire for food and the desire for kissing might be related she dismissed as untrue and as at the most, merely analogous.

Nevertheless it was clear that this little female, aged twenty-four hours was part animal and lacked the vitality to be all soul, so that it shortly, having exhausted its mother, said, "Yes, I will take the bottle." It had said a large no and a small yes. It had refused at least to humiliate its mother as well as itself, it had refused her beautiful breast, the lovelier uses of which she came to understand later, but had agreed, as its first compromise in life, to make people shut up, to the synthetic glass bosom enhanced and somewhat mollified by a soft rubber nipple. Exhausted, sobbing, angry, disgusted and red, she had allowed the insertion of the glistening object, forever after something she turned away her eyes from, whether it were seen in a drugstore window or on the nursery shelves of her young matron friends, an object of humiliation and weakness, a disgraceful kind of unnatural perversity, beloved, desired, and despised. Never, in her right mind, did she like milk again, that chalk-like, sweetish stuff and when as a child she was promoted to the dignity of a bowl and spoon, her parents watched with anxiety her finicky disgust and her careful separation and drainage of her bread and milk. Neither could she tolerate cream or butter which resulted in a spindly kind of lovely elf-like child it is true, but one who spent long wakeful nights and day-dreaming days. For no good scientific reason, in the second week of her marriage, after a day on skis in the Adirondacks she stuffed three pats of sweet butter into a popover and ate it in three bites and after that always wanted popovers and sweet butter whether it was available or not. But it never in her seemed like healthy, vulgar appetite. It was always, "Look, what fun, three pieces of sweet butter in a popover. Surprise!" and people were affectionately amused. She was mildly amazed to find that she knew what to do and the rhythmic sucking on the nipple was quieting her nerves and also those of those around her. The harassed look on her nurse's face disappeared, the interne was grinning in a knowing way that reminded her of her sex and his and made her angry, but she was exhausted and she let it pass. She was falling asleep; she let go the nipple and smiled; the interne laughed out loud with pleasure and the nurse hugged her: she had charm, she felt it, gave in to it, slept.

And so she learned that she would be loved for her weaknesses which made her arrogant and superior and only charming when she felt the need to be loved. This need however she felt often, and for prolonged periods, because she was sensitive and beautiful and looking at her own reflection in the mirror made her wish to impress it upon another without actually giving it away or allowing it to be handled.

She became used to many things on her second day, and learned so quickly how to handle the nurses that it seemed almost politic. Her poise and bearing impressed everyone in the nursery to the extent that they said, "She is queer," and once when a handy, muscular little nurse grasped her by the legs and flipped her over two other nurses said in unison, "Don't treat that one like that," and the red-headed head nurse said only, "She is a witch." She accepted much with the thought, "It is temporary," and it was pleasant to please as long as one held in reserve the right to independence at a more propitious time. Never, as a matter of fact, in her whole life was she more agreeable, cooperative, tolerant, accessible, amenable, open-minded, altruistic, a sort of good-for-a-fourth-at-bridge kind of child, than on her third day of life. She might have been the author of such spiritless axioms as "The Good Die Young" and "Handsome Is As Handsome Does" and "One must live," although at twenty her anger at a person who shrugged at one of her enthusiastic criticisms of worldly ambition was such, that she looked at him coldly and said candidly, "Why?" when he made just that last remark.

The third day passed, and she had made certain compromises; she knew how and when to behave; she knew how to get ahead; she avoided issues; she made comparisons but held her tongue; she treated her mother with respect and her father indulgently; she thought the doctor was a liar, but accepted the possibility that he might have some good in him that she had no way of knowing about.

The staff decided that she would live. They went so far, and why not, as to say, "She is a normal, healthy child."

People lost interest and she noticed it, but I cannot in fairness to her say that she took advantage of her observation, or of the careless optimism of those around her. There was nothing to it except that she just was not that kind of person at all, and it was extremely bad for her health to be treated as if she were, the result being that on the fourth day, just when everyone was beginning to think of something else, her mother of how nice it was to have a lovely figure again and a new black slinky dress for dinner, her father about how to catch up with his work, the doctor about the next baby, and the whole world going about its business as usual—she upchucked all of her meals just as fast as they gave them to her, her blood sugar count fell rapidly, and she became again the charming, sporadically melancholy child that she was to remain throughout her life.

She felt much better like this and began to use to advantage her senses. She knew for instance that early morning was blue and that it came and went quietly, and that evening was mauve and had a buzzing sound. There was no smell that did not give her pleasure: soap, oil, hair, skin, ether in the dead of night creeping under the door of the nursery, rolls going by to hungry mothers, coffee, tea, visitors, linen, electric light bulbs both hot and cold, fingernail polish, the strange smell on the interne's fingers that she was to recognize later as nicotine, the cold smell of just plain fresh air that sometimes clung to the doctor making a late call, and that other smell that sometimes came in late at night with the same doctor as he bent over her, whiskey. She inhaled deeply; all of it was nice and an education to her senses. When she was seven she could tell people by their smell like a dog and did not know for a long time that it was unusual or that there were smells she wasn't expected to like. In love she could not wait to bury her nose in the neck of her lover, to smell his wrists, his coat, the breath of his mouth, his eyelids. She could distinguish but was not critical. She went to a fire to smell the smoke, the rubber hoses, even the water. She loved the approach to the sea because of the seaweed, the clams, the sand, and the sand fleas; the fields because of the hay, the earth, the rabbits and the holes they lived in, and if she picked up a feather lost by a pheasant she held it to her nose and knew the difference between the smell of the end that had been in its body and the end that had not. She might have devoted her whole life to smells. She was very good at smells. Perfume, that is, synthetic odors, irritated her and shocked her nervous system as if she were a bee. She lost her bearings, as it were, and couldn't recognize directions correctly any more than a bee in turmoil. She scolded her roommate at school and said, "Don't use perfume, you smell better without it" and "Don't bathe so often, you smell like nothing much only a bath tub." She knew and liked the smell of herself and recognized the graduations when she was angry, sad, happy, in love. She learned as she grew older to keep these observations to herself, however, and only secretly whispered to the one she loved, "You smell good." In fact there was a slight flurry in the nursery on the fourth day when our baby, entranced at the smell of banana oil in the corridor, inhaled deeply and held its breath so long that its face began to turn blue as it had on the first day when it had sought to destroy itself. She meant to hang on until she could place the smell: lying as it did somewhere between one of the nurse's highly polished nails and the doctor's wristwatch, the latter smelling a bit metallic however and the former deep, sweet and haunting: a variable might of course be that the nurse had been holding hands with the doctor. A horde of Jewish relatives passing through the corridor at this moment chased ahead of them the lovely smell and gave her nose and brain a real workout, distinguishing, tabulating, specifying and determining. A little Jewish child marked "Isaac Lowenstein, male," was lifted from his crib and taken away. He came back later, his face very red, an expression of humiliation, dejection, and anger in his eyes, and smelling of disinfectant and orthodox kisses. The female Christian child was impressed by the fact that no Jewish male child was allowed to grow up in peace, but was always whisked out of the nursery, sometimes in the middle of a nap, immediately upon the stomping arrival of bearded Jews and plump Jewesses, to return soon with that fury in its face and bearing and not wanting to discuss it with anyone. Years later, in the Piazzale Michelangelo overlooking Florence, she stood with her husband and, with her chin caressed by the soft Italian air, stared with wholehearted pleasure at the huge, white, undulating *David* of Michelangelo. She missed nothing. Her candid look took him in. Her eyes were like twin searchlights. He was beautiful and pure; she loved his large hands, bent so gracefully at the wrists, and his listless weighty pose, she watched the easy turn of his head on his straight round neck and liked his aloof cool face. She looked and looked. A man came up to her husband, not noticing or paying any attention to her, and said strangely, "Excuse me, David was a Jew, wasn't he?" Her husband replied. The man looked at the huge statue and then at her husband and frowned, "Why hasn't he been circumcized, then?" This incident and the continual *sorti*, as it were, of male babies from the nursery, constituted the extent of this girl's information on this subject. In the Piazzale she remembered her nursery observation and that was all. She was extremely, intellectually curious from birth, but she did not choose to go into this matter and she did not allow her appreciation of the lovely *David* to be harmed by the discourteous and extracurricular question of the puny-eyed gentleman on the hill. She only, to close the subject, it seemed, asked herself the question, "Is it a superstition, the answer to which I could find in Frazer's *The Golden Bough*, or is it a medical precaution of some sort, the answer to which is no doubt in the *Encyclo-paedia Britannica?*" But she let it drop; it was not in her line. And this choice is, and was, characteristic of her. She did not dislike the subject matter so much, which she realized could not rationally be disliked, as such, as she did the strange person who had asked the question, and she felt the same contempt for him as she felt for the gentleman who had written to the London *Times* to ask why Adam was always depicted by artists with a navel, when he was not, as far as is known by believers, born of woman.

Not only with an exceptional sense of smell, but with the other four senses, this baby, I should think, was unusually equipped and highly developed. She never, even in her first week, confused the senses but with a surety isolated them correctly and without hesitation. Discriminating and discerning, she received and perceived. She knew the variety which existed between hearing, smell, sight, taste and touch and her experience became intuitive. Precise in her senses, she did not, as many older than she, and as I have said, confuse them; she did not, that is, smell the perfume of a flower when she was looking at it, nor did she see it when she was smelling it. She savored each sense by itself, in isolation, and consequently received the highest reward from each. I do not mean that she could not imagine sensations. She could, at will, and this power grew as she grew and gave her much pleasure in the solitude she chose to inhabit for long periods. Her acute sense of hearing caused her more pain and nervous exhaustion than it sometimes seemed to be worth, however. She felt that everything, as a matter of fact, was too loud. She loved sounds but she hated noise. And just as I have described her as being uncritical of smells, so she was of sounds; she appreciated them all, from a mouse in the wall to the booming of cannon, but the cannon must be far enough away so that it is not much louder than the mouse. As this could not always be managed for her, even by her lovers, she learned to interchange, to an extent, her senses, deliberately, of course. It was quite easy, for instance, in the case of fireworks. She liked best of all the sounds of things in people's pockets, especially if she were sentimentally attached to the person. She could hear the ink changing its level in his fountain pen, and the doctor she always loved never quite lost interest in her because of her ability to tell him as he approached her bed how many little hard white sleeping pills were in the white paper box in his left trouser pocket for her. This doctor was not the kind of man she could tell, however, that she heard the sound of his knee against his left trouser leg or that she lay in bed sniffing the paper pillbox a long time because it smelled of his hands, and of his pocket, as well as the clinic where he worked. A symphony she could not endure: it frightened and irritated her and she shocked her friends by saying coldly, "My God, what a racket," at a Beethoven festival. As a result this poor baby suffered during her first week, in spite of what is advertised as a noiseproof nursery. The noise inside it deafened her and made her eyelids flutter nervously, as they did afterwards, when that over-confident young man thought that he whispered, "I love you." The noise of that first "I love you" so shocked her that she anticipated uneasily the second man in her life. And of course she heard hospital noises in the corridor. Hospital noises she compared later in life with Hindu music and vice versa. There were thumps, bumps, whines, sobs, cries, names called, slippings, slidings, cleaning noises, rhythmic pacing, uneven galloping, creaks, ringing of bells, glasses jumping up and down on trays, bed springs, coughing, draughts, windows going up and down, sudden crashes, giggles, ejaculations, nurses' starched aprons, dishwashing, radios, telephone conversations, and a constant sound of women like birds in a zoo. Our baby suffered, jumped, twitched and controlled the wish to go mad and join the hubbub. The trip through the hall to her mother was a great din to her but there was more to see and smell, so that she deliberately sublimated the sounds. One of the nurses used to rock her in her arms and hum to her when she could find the time, because she felt sorry for the strained look on the baby's face (it was controlling itself) and this experience was quite awful: the nurse's uniform let out shrieks in her ears; the ear pressed to the nurse's bosom heard everything going on inside the nurse: humming noises, splashes, tickings; the great thump of her heart was as terrifying as an Indian drum, and over all could be heard the coarse moaning buzz of "Rock-a-bye-baby-on-the tree-top" that began in her throat, went down into her lungs, overcoming obstacles of sound as it went, and then came rushing and roaring out, smacking against her teeth and interrupted by her palate and tongue. And besides all this commotion the nurse tapped her foot if you can imagine that.

The visits to her mother, where she also saw her father, were pleasanter as the memory of her insult to them, her attempt to rid herself of the responsibility of them, to exercise her free will, and return to unconsciousness and oblivion, became less vivid, as she, with all her strength, attempted to forget her action. Nevertheless she obtained an important feeling of security, alone as she felt she was in her young superiority, in the definite assurance in her own mind that she might quit when she chose to quit. "All this I may leave," she thought, "when it becomes too difficult." In this thought, she held her peace, her tongue, and endured much. Death to her would always be voluntary, in other words, not death at all, but choice: a decision, the decision, an ultimate use of the gift of God.

The young baby enjoyed its mother and father, then. It seemed to sense relationship, that queer sophisticated love, which is incest; that very special pleasure, which is never granted one again in life because, oddly enough, it becomes as one grows up, illegal. The innocence of parents astonished this baby. Their caresses and fondling of her were public and unashamed. Was it deliberate camouflage, pretense, did they really not know, were they playing at being children? Were they not in the presence of each other and sometimes a nurse, a doctor, ashamed of her nudity, her soft skin, her small breasts, her smooth thighs, her cheeks and her mouth? What absurd innocence and how quickly she learned, herself, to use it! Until it became, in a sense, real, so that her charm itself seemed almost to depend upon it; so that as she grew up and was loved and loved she chose the innocence her father and mother taught her, in their innocence, as it seemed to her. The sophisticated baby learned to be innocent, paradoxical as that may seem, and chose it as her theme. Her everlasting innocence protected her throughout her life and made her beloved by many who loved innocence, and who does not? It was a natural, in the sense of logical, choice for our child, a choice again of the abstract and to her mind the real, and it must be distinguished from ignorance which it definitely was not. She was as physically alert as any specimen in the nursery and I might say more so, sensuous to a degree, as I have described. Her innocence, then, let us say, was an abstract quality, an aloof decision, although there is no doubt that it was practicable: it worked, in the sense that it protected her all her life from sensuous creatures who had not made the choice of innocence but who recognized and respected it in our little female. I mean by respect: did not harm it, though desiring it; loved it without accepting it and marveled at it constantly. This sophisticated innocence, added to the aloof and reckless character of the baby, later gave to the young girl a reputation for physical bravery and intellectual courage. Because of her early experience she seemed not attached to life and this seemed to add much to what was described as "vague unattainable charm." It preserved in her all her life a youngness that was not childish but Eve-like; mature, but the maturity of youth. She knew that she possessed it because she had chosen it. It was not synthetic, neither was it in the least a perversion to attract erotic attention. It was simply a part of her preference for the abstract; a choice of the intellectual as against the physical, a happy selfish choice amounting to a denial, a decisive blindness, a sort of myopia, a single-minded, sure-footed career in character. I do not mean that she was at all preoccupied with the formation of her character or in the creation of her personality. She had no end in view, she was not ambitious in the least, she was not building a house or a monument; she was not an orator and persuasion was not part of her make-up; she did not seek converts or proselytes, parasitic friendships, or symbiosis among her acquaintances. She did not ask for sympathy or advice and gave neither; she was like a tulip rather than a morning glory and grew straight up without tendrils. I think I should add that her choice of innocence was not by definition a moral choice. To her, choice was an act without subject matter.

And so the babe in its first week advanced in perspicacity and innocence, using the first to enhance and develop the second and watching and classifying the innocence of others. She could not decide however and never did, what with the many diversions of growing up, whether the innocence of her parents was naivete, ignorance, lack of sensibility, or on the other hand a kind of supreme, nth power sophistication, more subtle and less precise than her own. She did decide in her first week, however, that whichever it was, it no longer concerned them actively, they accepted their own attitude without question, *sans doute*, and made no comparisons, as she was doing. This, she decided, was what made them characteristically, parents. Neither did they observe her new innocence any more than did the doctor, the interne, the nurses. She did not mind their lack of attentiveness, she only wondered at it. The nurses were undoubtedly ignorant, but both the doctor, who smelled so nicely of fresh air and whiskey, and the interne, whose large practical right hand would have reminded her, if time were reversible, of the fitted metal seat of the haying machine which had been warmed by the sun and the hired man, on which she used to sit, her legs hanging, after the horses had been unhitched and the sun was setting, with a feeling of guilt because it was so pleasant and sweet and cozy—but both the doctor and the interne, she was sure, possessed innocence of a high order, deliberate, educated, chosen, cultivated, refined, developed, polished, encouraged, depended upon, exercised hourly, desperately clung to, the first and last guiding principal, practical ethic, and protective insurance of their profession; a kind of look-but-don't-see, touch-but-don't-feel, keep-your-mind-on-medicine innocence which she delightedly appreciated and which made her feel with her related innocence, even closer to the members of the medical profession, than she naturally felt from propinquity. It was a spiritual as well as a physical response at the age of one week. At the age of twenty-five it had become, with practice, almost entirely spiritual, because, as I have said, at the age of forty-eight hours she had chosen the abstract and with her acute senses and powerful imagination it soon became apparent to her that her choice had been wise. And as she became preoccupied with abstraction she found it better and better and more real and rewarding than things themselves, objects and results. And that is how she came to choose unrequited love as a career because in the field of love she decided that unrequited love was the best, and in unfulfilled love she found she was best fitted to practice her innocence.

And so at twenty-five she was the highly developed baby of one week and the choices and observations made in the hospital led her to choose a doctor to be the victim of her unrequited love and on whom she would practice until death her innocence.

It should be clear that she could not practice unrequited love on her father. This girl was spiritually determined but she was not pig-headed or unreasonable. She walked lightly because it was pleasanter that way. She chose, always, an oblique approach rather than a headlong one. She did not care to break the major rules of behavior and although she was very much charmed by her father she did not tarry a moment with the idea of practicing unfulfilled love upon him. The vivid thought that his innocence and hers, different in description, but alike in essence and each deliberate, could make them exciting lovers, she sublimated. Her alternative then was the doctor. She could not have made a better choice, or reached a happier conclusion. If it was unrequited love that she wanted, that is what she got and to a degree beyond her hopes and even her strength. Her unrequited love blossomed and flourished through tears, laughter, arguments, near anger, whisperings, plans, reminiscences, renunciations, involved daydreaming, plain daydreaming, and almost constant sensuous pleasure. She found that unrequited love lasts forever and she made a note of it. She learned much as she stood on the brink, as it were, danced on the crater, and never got burned by the fire, because she depended upon that which is most dependable: innocence. Conscious in her because she was the kind of person who was conscious and unconscious in him because it was unconscionable, and as with her father, it was choice not so much as chosen, as inconceivable. With her father also it was a moral choice inherited from Moses, the difference itself, as it were, between right and wrong. As for her, she not only chose innocence in love because it was an abstraction but because, deeply interested as she was in free will, grateful for it, and proud to be distinguished from the animals, she chose in order to choose, to make use of her birthright, to feel her power. She felt that her father and the doctor were innocent in a less intelligent way than she and perhaps she was right. Her father and the doctor did not do things, because they were inconceivable, and she did not do them because she chose to do otherwise. She would have liked them to know that Moses was a pragmatist, making laws because they were practicable not because they were right and that the touch-not-thy-patient of the American Medical Association was no more than an ethic designed to protect the Association, not the patient. Nevertheless she felt fortunate in the doctor's innocence, and told him nothing. Without it, and with her beauty, on whom might she have practiced unrequited love? She did not, at any age, from the nursery, through her school days, into maturity, ever feel a thing for a woman that was pleasurable. Not ignorant, on the contrary very observing, she wondered why. Discerning, precise, intellectually careful, she did not inter-confuse her senses when she was older anymore than when she was in the nursery. She recognized the beauty of women with her eyes but with her eyes alone. The touch of one disgusted her, and the kiss of a woman she could not endure. If her infant experience of horror at her mother's breast was the cause of her everlasting disgust, she was angry that it should have happened to her, because she did not like to think she was to miss anything; and it might have been pleasant to have loved, unsuccessfully, a woman of sensibility.

As I have said, however, her choice of the doctor for a lover was a *succès fou*. I do not mean it did not have its bad moments. It was so bad at times, so difficult not to be loved that she wished to die, because it is impossible to remember in all conditions and under all circumstances, that unrequited love is the best love, and this girl was susceptible, dramatic, enthusiastic, and brave. Their two innocences were the cause of unrequited love, but she chose him because of his, and he refused her for the same reason.

It was definitely a refusal.

She took the initiative from the beginning and she soon found to her delight, not perverse, but pleased with her correct deductions, (her insight, if it had not been so cumulatively conscious), that he would be adamant: he would not love her.

This gave her every advantage.

Her innocence and consequent denial, first to himself, and then to her, that he loved her, was in the beginning unspoken, just as her love for him was silent, and preoccupied, according to her nature, with the past and the future, so that the present moment seemed suspended and waiting to happen.

This suspended present became her whole life in the subject matter of love. She prized it and appreciated it with her intelligence and with her senses. This constant waiting for the present and not letting it overtake her, these descriptive sentences in her mind that led up to and away from the moment, kept her alert and keen and she never felt that inertia during love-making that resembles fatigue and gives the heart a rest.

The history of her love can be traced to her first week in the hospital when she felt the eyes of the doctor upon her. That single-minded look, that gaze that has dismissed all else but you, can only be compared to the searching eyes of an artist upon his model. The layman, child or grown-up recognizes in that look devotion, and sometimes confuses it with love. It is love, in that it resembles it so closely, and lacking only its essence: the doctor's gaze is synthetic love, the response it provokes is love itself. The baby responded because it was a sensitive baby and its first love and its last were identical and everlasting, innocent and unrequited. In the interim, the girl and woman this baby became was loved and returned the love she inspired but always she sustained the image of her first love and she made it her last. As a baby the doctor's eyes influenced her to love him. His concentration upon her warmed her small body as the circling light of a lamp and his caressing hands warm at the palms and cool at the fingertips pleased her beyond her powers. This attention several times a day was the big content of her emotional life and as I have said she practiced the abstract innocence of her choice and that which she so admired in the doctor and was puzzled by in her parents.

The true and unfulfilled love of her maturity began in much the same way as her infant passion. And her experience and knowledge of love, her ability to sustain an image and suspend the present, began from the date of his first bright gaze upon her to make her the happiest of lovers who do not gain and consequently lose their darlings. She was ready and equipped for unrequited love and so she said without hesitation, "I love you," and the woman who has never taken the initiative in love, who has never said it first, cannot know the suppressed excitement, the neat pleasure of that short sentence, containing as it does the contained and the containing. The doctor was a man of ability and imagination and some insight, but being a person of wide contact with average people of both sexes and having little or no time to find the answers to problems other than prophylactic ones for the comfort of his patients he made the mistake of responding to this statement automatically and morally, according to his mother's teachings, rather than innocently, from his medical innocence, which if it had been as sophisticated as hers would have replied, "Yes." If he had replied, "Yes, I love you too," the heroine of our story would have experienced perhaps unrequited love, but unrequited love plus the pleasure of continuous love-making, no. What more could there have been for these two innocences after her statement if he had accepted it? As it was, his refusal gave her the upper hand, a headstart which she took advantage of, and her campaign consisted of tents in unexpected places, forced marches, feints, excursions, ultimatums, proposals, armistices, fourteen points, strategic camouflage, cruelties, atrocities, advances, retreats, calls to arms, and tears.

He held out.

Her confidence in him grew with each failure of a new plan. He watched her with amazement, admiration, amusement and horror. His negation, his denial that he loved her, astounded and delighted her, while in parenthesis, as it were, she suffered violently from his deliberate callousness. The pain of his words, "I do not love you," was intrinsic, extrinsic, physical, psychic and measurable. Her eyes stung with tears, her body ached inside and out, she was doubled up with pain in her bed at the recollection of his cruelty, but her intelligence told her that this was the best love of all and that it would last forever.

She did not cheat or flirt; she made every effort and with all her strength attempted to seduce him. Well armed with her powerful innocence and her recognition and confidence in his, she had no need of artifice or pretense. She was never coy, shy, or artful. She was not coquettish or consciously enticing. On the contrary but successfully, her innocent candor, her naive immodesty, interested him as she boldly approached something she anticipated but did not expect. In the beginning, as I have said, he repulsed her instinctively, but gradually he accepted her love and love-making with only sporadic attempts, which irritated her and slowed up her progress, to persuade her that she did not love him. Her endurance was extraordinary and as unrequited love was not his career as it was hers, and as he consequently had not the talent or ability to pursue it, he sometimes became as exhausted and lacking in imagination as if he had possessed her, with the result that he was definitely not at his best and hardly a fit companion for an indefatigable lover such as she. This made her unhappy and led to quarrels similar to the quarrels of ordinary, less intelligent lovers, spoiling to an extent, temporarily, her dream. It was at times like these that she, for the moment, appeared to lose sight of her unattainable goal and became so human, so miserable, so insecure, and so terrified at the conviction that she was not loved that she behaved like a person in a like position: she wept bitterly, tears flowing from wide-open eyes, and making no decent effort to hide her face or her feelings. This behavior was unfortunate. As a man of feeling his reaction was frigid. As a doctor it was doubly so with an added disgraceful curiosity as if she were a rabbit being teased for the good of mankind including herself. As an exceptionally intelligent and observing person she knew these things, and that her tears were repellent, but nevertheless she continued to experience these fits and breakdowns as regularly as if she had planned them, spoiling her own pleasure and his, and making him skittish and hard to handle for days afterwards. Like any foolish mistress she persisted in asking, "Do you love me?" Like any foolish mistress she asked this most foolish of all foolish questions at the time when it was foolishest to ask it: with his arms enfolding her, for instance, or immediately after a caress that called for silence. She did not get the petulant affirmative, however, that most mistresses get. She got an almost jubilant denial because in this way and at those moments when he felt himself lost, this statement confirmed his innocence and strengthened his purpose. His cheerful, heartless, "I do not love you," the first time she heard it, stung and hurt her almost beyond endurance and, taking her breath away with its shocking unexpectedness, made her wish to die. She felt the shame, humiliation and insult that any woman feels at the actual statement, "I do not love you," as if, silly thing, she were good for nothing else and this was the end. It may seem strange to the reader that this particular girl, however, could not bear to hear spoken the unrequited love she encouraged and desired and without which her own love could not exist and progress, but it was one of those natural paroxysms, another parenthesis, that nearly put an end at first to her career. She learned at last not to ask the foolish question when she was feeling feminine and weak but only at times when she could look him in the face and smile at his reply. And so her "I love you" and his "I do not love you" became the double motto of their innocence, each said out of deliberate innocence and each characteristic of each and each interchangeable to each, a dialectic to their love.

The wisdom of her choice, when she was not indulging herself in parenthetical behavior, became more and more apparent to her. She was a fortunate girl to have chosen exactly the right man not to be loved by. He would never fail her; she presented him with her happiness, as it were, and said, "Here, hold it for me." That she might use all her powers, all her charm, her wit, her appeal, and subtle use of words, and that he would not fail her, she was sure of. His will was as strong as hers and she knew that the seduction she sought would not take place because of her happy choice in men. Her behavior built up in him a resolve not to harm her; she became the woman he would not accept, the ideal person who must not be defiled. All his former disgust with love, his guilty conscience at having loved only women whom he cared for, fed his resolve and she became, in a way, his opportunity, a chance to make good. She became his first love in the sense that she would never be his and the queer charm of an ever present first love, like a photograph in his pocket, his own virgin through his own strength and goodness, appealed to him strongly without his having the time to know, quite, that that was it. Women had flirted with him but no woman had ever made love to him. Her sincerity cured him almost at once of embarrassment; "I love your face," "Your hands are so beautiful," and "Your skin is so smooth," and, "You smell good," he accepted. He understood, as a male, the conventionally feminine woman who did everything in accordance with her alleged passivity and his wife's dearest friends had sometimes astonished him with their cute retreats, which did not feed his imagination, but this girl in her innocence pursued him as brightly as a novice and as bravely as a captain. She played as if his *no's* were *yes's*. She answered her own questions, laughed at her own sallies, teased him, lifted his chin, begged him, harassed him, like placing pins along a map to hang up at the end of the day and continue in the morning. Her initiative, her audacity, and his resistance began to result in some strange interchange of state, a juxtaposition with highlights, semi-colons, as it were, and little perversities: neither changed his sex in symptom but there was a coloration, a differentiation that seemed to ring little graded bells in each and please each, and heighten the senses of each through long evenings, as if they were in costume and changing their masks. Each watched. Not as capable as she, unwilling to accept unexplained pleasure without guilt, he often interfered, spoiled an interlude, evaded a small climactic if, changed the subject, placed his heel upon a flower, said good night. Disappointed but by no means discouraged she began again the next time, and her energy, faith, and fearlessness, combined with constant watchfulness and resourcefulness, gave her a foothold and a claim. He began to feel, without knowing it, responsible. This, if it is the essence of male love, may have caused his capitulation, although, until the last, he denied his love. Her innocence was so true, so real, that her sophistication and wantonness appeared to him to be his guilty male doing, and so his unacknowledged love for her became the love of a man for a woman; the caretaker, the father, the shamed, unwilling Oedipus, in this case unknowing, but restless, uneasy, irrational, argumentative, unjust and cruel. Only her positive state made her put up with him; only his moments of unguarded adoration made up to her, during her series of parentheses, for the knife-like pain of his obvious desire to be free of her. Her thrashings about, his want to escape the responsibility of her, frustrated her girl-like, deep dark wish to be his own love, his little one, his wicked forgiven child, his little love, his small heart, his baby. These parentheses were hard and sickening and painful, and exhausted them both to a degree. Completely confused, he at one time, late in their everlasting love, forgetting his resistance which was in the first place, instinctively, a natural, accused her of inhibitions as if she were refusing his advances. This maze, this cumulative error of his was due probably to his not understanding that she did not want what she wanted; he in his turn wanting so badly what he did not want, could not understand why nothing climactic or real and evident ever happened. His accusation, however, seemed at the time merely an anachronism of love, an unchronological, almost flighty observance, unrelated to anything and, seeming such, neither noted it very much, except that she thought he was criticizing her, which he did frequently, in a loving observing way that she liked. His critical attention, his medical stare, affected her pleasantly and of the two more so than her compliments did him.

I have said that only her positive state made her put up with him. It is true that her intellectual assurance, her abstract course, her daily homework in his absence, her strength of purpose and powerful personality kept her on the straight and narrow path of her choice. But I do not mean that even in the parentheses this man was ordinary. He behaved, it is true, like a man who is pursued, but it was in his own parentheses, as it were, that he behaved according to Hoyle, at other times he was as preoccupied as she with the abstract; his imagination responded to hers and he was capable of invention and play; his doctor's education had not robbed him of spiritual appreciation, and her nicely articulated body did not remind him of a cadaver. She had picked her man for pleasure of two kinds. The excitement of unrequited but not unrewarded love was her prize for patience that seemed at times almost beyond human endurance. But she did not give him up during the dry spells, the hard times, the exasperating, common, anybody's interludes, because just when she thought he was selfish, he would be generous; just when she felt sick with cruelty, he would be sweet-and-low as a kitten; just when he was stubborn and a man who would never give in, he gave in; just when he was too proud to say he was sorry, he was sorry.

"I'm sorry."

"Darling."

It was one thing to have no hope. It stabilized things for her; it made her strong. To have no hope was very important and she would have been sorry for herself if she had been hopeful; the uncertainty of hope at least she was spared. She considered, in his absence, after a particularly difficult evening in which he had treated her as if she had been a flighty girl, or, if not that, something immoral out of Hardy—an evening when his resistance seemed to her out of all proportion to the attack, when his somewhat holier-than-thou attitude had been unbecoming, insulting, illogical and unsuited to any occasion among friends—that in any event, in spite of her temporary discouragement and genuine grief, she was without hope. Consequently the evening should be canceled in her memory as meaning nothing, adding nothing to the sum total which was after all by her own wish to be nothing itself. The evening, painful as it was, and he unjust and ungallant, was less than a phrase in the subject matter of her course and without such evenings, in fact, could she have honestly called her love unrequited? And neither could the course of unrequited love run smooth. She found as time went on that their quarrels could be as violent and shocking as if they were conventional lovers, and this interested her as an eager observer of all the phenomena of love. As their unfulfilled love took on the color and characteristics of plain love she felt the scientific pleasure of a man with a test tube: to see the mixture in one tube resemble so almost exactly the mixture in the other, when, as she alone (in this

metaphor) knew, that the essence (supposedly [supposed essence])
was absent (wilfully) excited her as a physicist, and let her imagination play with inventing something, "just as good," synthetic and
ersatz. In spite of her abstract approach to everything by choice
from babyhood she was too wise and matter-of-fact in matter-of-fact
things, and candid, to believe, with some, that the physical act was
not the most important part of human love. She knew on the contrary that all affection between all persons of all sexes and all relationships was obviously based on it and it alone. That, in fact, was why
she chose to choose the choice she chose. She did not at any time
say, nor could she be quoted as saying, that unrequited love was
illogical. She simply, as I made clear in the beginning, preferred the
abstract almost from birth, happiness to contentment, innocence
(chosen) especially, and as a theme for her life among men she
therefore chose, unerringly and brilliantly, unrequited love, and either
from observation in babyhood or intuition or gambler's luck, as a
partner without sin, she chose the doctor of her choice. The time
she spent after her particularly difficult evening in congratulating
herself on being spared the uncertainty of hope was well spent and
strengthened her morale. Her vivid imagination and sympathetic
interest and feeling for unhappy lovers pictured to her the awfulness
of hope. She imagined the pathos and horror of expectancy, the
cold intentness of probability, the sickliness of depending on the
undependable, of taking heart in the unlikely, to be sure and not
sure, to fail, the anticipatory shock, the waste of forewarning, the
doubtful intuition, the daily curse of being let down, the constant
ghastly insecurity of not knowing the answer to that tight little statement which is only a question in grammar books, "Does he love me?"
   None of this was hers, fortunate girl and happy discontented lover.
Always sure of herself but doubtful of being able to bear it she made
sounds like:
   "I cannot stand it."
   "I won't take it."
   "I cannot take it."
   "It is humiliating."

"I am desperate."
"I want to be loved."
"I wish I were dead."
But these were automatic sentences from her perfectly normal subconscious, not to be taken too seriously when confronted by the beautiful expression of free will which was her most prized gift from God: "I love him and he does not love me. I want it like that. His innocence and mine make us everlasting unrequited lovers."

Expecting nothing, she got much. She found that it is not true that a man loves his part and will not relinquish his prerogative: she took the initiative and the responsibility, in so far of course as there can be responsibility in the love of a woman for a man. It was a make-believe responsibility, a synthetic article, without doubt, but she played the game and he accepted it without losing his stance, his footing, his man's appeal to her senses, nor did he on his part feel ridiculous, effeminate or cold. He loved the queer peace of being pursued (except in parentheses when he behaved like his mother's son), the security of being loved under all circumstances, the charm of resisting in place of insisting; he liked accepting her girl-like compliments; it was restful just to take it and not dish it out. Never having been loved, only loving, and not often enough to have become at all expert, he began to see how incompetent he had been, how inadequate, unimaginative, clumsy, solemn, important, arrogant, domineering, platitudinous and without vocabulary he had pursued the women of his choice. This girl made him feel what a fool he had been and how pathetic his own love-making was in comparison with his present funny little love's past-master-like lover's behavior in the face of his adamant refusal to accept her.

"Men have no perseverance," she said to him, "they take 'no' for an answer."
"But isn't it?"
"No."
Their love-making seemed sometimes like playing a game of who could hold his breath the longest and her feminine endurance was greater than his. His innocence was superior to hers in strength only

in that hers depended on his, and even that was apparent rather than real, a conventional truism, a combination of words. He most certainly wanted to quit. He considered himself a realist and this girl's room was no place for him; neither could he bring himself in fairness to stalk out of the place as if she were a prostitute, a bad woman, or even one of his wife's friends. She forced her little world upon him and it was pleasant and exciting but she was making a slave of him, a kind of chief-black-eunuch and he did not care for the metaphor or the fact. He began to feel himself on the spot and he was not inclined nor built for active activity such as she desired. He recognized however that the circumstantial spiritual evidence was in her favor and that his objection to their joint behavior would call for the inevitable, because it was perfectly true that what she was doing was deliberately avoiding the inevitable, denying it with a strength and purpose beyond his own and although he did not want to give in and say uncle to her choice, neither would he consider the inevitable: he would not love her. But in her presence, in her eyes, in her arms, in the pleasanter parenthesis, in the long hours of dalliance just exactly as sweet as if they were real lovers, he began to take a stand: afterwards. He did his homework, then, just as she did, but it was characteristic of him to plan conclusions and of her to design sequences. It may have been that she had more time (she did nothing else) than he, or that considering the nature of their love a conclusion of any kind would be absurd and illogical. His outbursts of anger against her, which she feared, but which she preserved her strength for and which she made every effort to meet with equanimity, failing always, were the only "conclusions" he ever made. She was always fresh and he was always fatigued because it was her idea, not his; she was the artist. Unrequited love only comes to those who want it and even then it is not simple. She found it did not come for the asking; it was unpredictable as a colt and in her eagerness to have it and her greediness, and an unconscious desire to have it over with, which is characteristic of wilful persons, she often came near messing the whole thing up, overstepping her mark, and ruining her career. She had constantly to remind herself, "I do not want it," "It must last

forever," "I shall always have it to do," "It cannot be finished." She
held his attention as if she were a sleight-of-hand artist and he could
not leave her, her funny ways giving him the impression that she
was standing on her head and saying "look" and he did not want to
miss it. She was domineering without losing her childlike dependence, she was wilful, spoiled, without ever having been spoiled to his
knowledge, and thoroughly impossible and unfeminine according to
his bringing up, but she was weak, sweet, loving, sorrowful, gentle,
forgiving, pleasingly silly and by her prestidigitation she held her man.

And so he never left her. And without distraction, interruption or
avocation, she pursued him, to her credit, being her choice of a liveli-
hood, as it were, her career. And nowhere in a successful career such
as hers is there a place for that word *assez*.

There is no record of what actually happened except that it is
obvious that her death took place in one of those parentheses of
which I have spoken; one of those parentheses she dreaded and had
taught herself to forget as soon as they were over; he too never mentioned them, whether from guilt or from natural anesthesia following
an outburst, I do not know. Their love had lost none of its queer
vitality that was like language rather than fact, like thought rather
than things; its abstract quality being like a highly polished pane of
glass, like a word that cannot be sounded; everlasting. The parenthesis was no more than any other; she was in good health, and it is
not clear what variable sent the weight off, broke the camel's back,
and the spirit of our child. She did not awaken, and he did not, as
he stood over her, show to her family, or when he was alone with her
as she was unconsciously dying, any different behavior than he did in
her living presence. He did not ask her forgiveness, he did not weep,
he did not call her the gentle names she had always begged him to
call her. He sat by her side and bent upon her his medical stare; his
aloofness, his perfection, not deserting him. The fright, the horror,
the tenderness of human nature did not appear. This abstract being,
the physician *par excellence*, did not eat or sleep and why should he?
He did his best to save a life without asking if it should be saved, as a
doctor he was no moralist, and his little love no longer able to take

the initiative died quietly without any more love-making at all. Not a kiss, not a caress, no pet name (little monkey), and it was quite in keeping, completely natural because she had been the lover, not he, and he could not change because this was her parenthesis, not his. She left no notes, no platitudes, none of the wishful proof, the want to hurt those or that she loved. To believe therefore, the lack of evidence not being against her, that she was an ordinary human being who, when hurt, fought and bit and hated her lover, to the point of wishing to harm him by her death, natural and usual in court and in domicile as that is, would be stupid and incompatible. Her death, then, is a mystery and should not be accepted as suicide at all, because (1) what reason had she for suicide, and (2) what did she wish to accomplish by suicide; whom did she wish to hurt? These being the worldly, almost rhetorical, questions.

Those of us who know her from these pages remember her early childhood and her second-day attempted suicide, her self-infanticide, her first decision and her last, it was called, because I do not believe that this death could be called decisive. A reasonable and responsible child such as she would not have repeated that effort, that supreme and last effort as such an effort may, by definition, be called: people only commit suicide once. She did it; being saved only, as is recollected, by a young unthinking monkey-wrench of a nurse, trained only to do her duty for a certain number of hours a day. Having made her decision and used her free will, and being prevented from accomplishing her wish only by accidental intervention, having been spared as you remember the horror of self-preservation, that change of mind and direction in the midst of a well-defined, powerful course, like a horse gone berserk and dashing for the paddock in the middle of the race, she returned to her everyday life, spared, not only the above horror, but the necessity, if forthcoming, of having to decide again to die. Only those, let us say then, who have experienced self-preservation, try to die again, having failed to see the thing through intellectually the first time, having been unsuccessful in expressing their will. She also remembered her remorse and her mother's face and her sickening sense of responsibility for her parents, as certainly she would have felt now, for him, her unrequited lover. It is true that she reserved through life a feeling that there was always later a more propitious time which made her, if you remember, more amenable in the hospital that first week and through her girlhood too, but with all her awareness, her consciousness, she did not notice that that protective aura, that helpful crutch, that laughing gas, good fairy, was just that and no more and only those who have not made the decision are entitled to make it, "A more propitious time" meaning "I do not have to put up with it always," "I may die when I no longer care to endure it." "Not now, later" means "Later, if I don't like it I may die if I choose." The habitual sing-song, "Tomorrow," therefore, means, "When I am dead." This love of death, in that death means the end of freedom, and the necessity no longer to make decisions or accept responsibility, was also unconscious in our child, being the person we have described, proud of her choices and eager to make decisions. Decisive then, in all things else but death, the end of deciding. More rational, then, in this indecisive death than in her early wilful and mistaken one. It is a good thing, or more precisely, a pleasant thing, that she did not lose this helpful aura because without it she would have been headstrong, less attractive, unloved, a lonely being doing only what she believed to be right. As it was, of these two innocents, these lovers, she appeared less sure of herself than he, as is perhaps proved by this parenthesis as she lies now quietly, making no move to entice him, nor to touch his hand, and he does what is right, damned unamenable, headstrong, deliberate and cruel, in other words, her choice, her love, her unrequited, unfulfilled darling. The fact that, as realists, we must defend, that she is white and still and quite dead, makes me insist upon the observation that her death took place in a parenthesis, because by using this literary metaphor there is a possible insight into her suicide, which we can find no explanation for otherwise, having analyzed the thing thoroughly and exhaustively, have we not? Only in a parenthesis could she have been unhappy, discouraged, humiliated beyond feminine endurance, so that she desired and automatically sought oblivion, sleep, everlasting unconsciousness, which is now hers. And he, as I have said, does not desert their stronghold, their fort: he does nothing in gesture or speech that would make this parenthesis an everlasting eternal parenthesis, in time cancelling the power of the original sentence, if only by its infinite length. Let us gratefully maintain, therefore, that this love story has a happy ending; these innocents making the most of the best, the female child, with the help of an imaginary diploma and that invisible sign which I have mentioned, and the doctor, her love not alone by propinquity or coincidence, fortified by his mother's advice and medical ethics, each preferring the abstract to the physical and she happiness to contentment.

A metaphorical P.S. to our little female's career might be, "Her life was a speech and when she was breathless she died."

French Wife in America

Je suis Madeleine. Mon mari est Paul. En France Paul m'a donné deux poupons très jolis et maintenant en Amérique il m'a donné sa mère, son père, sa sœur charmante et aussi son *pal*, George. L'Amérique n'est pas comme la France. Bien, alors, j'arrive en Amérique. D'abord, je vois des *skyscrapers* et j'explore le Centre de Monsieur Rockefeller. Paul dit, "Que pensez-vous, Madeleine?" (il ne parle pas très bien le français) et je lui réponds, "Merveilleux, mon petit; je t'aime, Paul." Après Madame de la Liberté, Paul me présent à sa mère qui dit, "Elle est charmante," à son père qui dit, "Ello," et à sa sœur qui dit, "Hi." Paul dit, "J'ai faim," et tout le monde dit, "*Let's eat.*" C'est très amusante, cette famille de Paul. Mama dit, "*Have some more*" et le père de Paul dit, riant beaucoup, "*What's a big idea?*" "*Take it from me*" et "*Youra locky dog.*" Le dîner est magnifique; d'abord la grande soupe du jour (soupe "toutes les choses" Paul a dit [il est très amusant]), ensuite bœuf rôti au jus et pommes de terre Irene Castle, et pour le dessert—*pie!* "*Pie* à la mode," Paul dit. "Pourquoi riez-vous, Madeleine?" "C'est plus que drôle, votre *pie* à la mode," je réponds. "Je ne comprends pas," disent le père et la mère de Paul. Paul dit, "Au revoir, chouchou," et sort. "Où va

Paul?" je dis et la mère dit, "*Out.*" "Oui, je comprends, mais où?" "Chez George," tous les deux répondent. "George?" "Oui, Madeleine. George est le *pal* de Paul," dit la mama.

Le jour prochain Paul me présent à George. George est l'image de Paul, très gentil et très drôle. George dit, "Comment allez-vous, Mademoiselle, je vous aime, je vous adore, que voulez-vous encore, ha, ha, ha." Tout le monde rit et Paul dit, "George parle français très bien, n'est-ce pas, Madeleine?" "Oh, oui," je dis et George dit, "Oo-la-la, *somme babay, youra locky guy*, c'est la guerre." Alors, George et Paul et Mary Lou (c'est la sœur charmante de Paul qui dit "Hi") et le fiancé de la sœur charmante et la *blind date* (en français, je ne sais quoi: la surprise) nous avons tous beaucoup de badinage, beaucoup de joie. George me donne des leçons en anglais, et moi je donne à George des leçons en français. C'est très drôle *an I laff*. George dit "je compris" et, moi, je dis "*I unnerstan.*" Tout le monde rit. Mama appele, "Silence, donc, Papa dors," et Paul appele, "*Tell the ole man to* dormez bien." George me baisait et je regarde Paul. Paul dit, "George est mon *pal. Go right ahead.*" L'Amérique n'est pas comme la France. Paul embrasse "la surprise" et la sœur est disparue avec son fiancé. Paul et "La surprise" sont sortis. George est charmant, plus que drôle, l'image de Paul. Il dit, "Comprenez-vous, Mademoiselle?" et je réponds, "*I unnerstan.*" J'aime bien le *pal* de Paul. Le jour prochain Paul n'est pas à la maison et George *telephone me.* Je dis, "Oui," et George arrive. Il est beau et il me donne beaucoup de roses et dit en très bon français, très gravement, "Je t'aime, Madeleine," et je dis, "*I lohve you, George*" en très bon anglais, aussi. Parce que George est le *pal* de Paul il me fait la cour et c'est comme en France; mais exactement, le même chose. "Mon ami," je dis, et George ne dit rien. Je regarde George. "Pourquoi ne parle-tu pas; mais pas un mot, George?" George ne parle pas. "George, *why you no spik to Madeleine?*" "Il n'y a plus rien à dire." "Oh, George, tu parle français très, très bien; c'est merveilleux! Continus," *an I clap.* "Merci, Madeleine, pour me donner des leçons charmantes." "*You are wonnerful, George.*" "Et tu apprends vite, toi-méme, Madeleine, et très docile, ma petite; la petite maîtresse

Madeleine. Félicitations!" "Oh, George, merci; *thank you ver much, George.*" "Adieu," dit George.

George ne revient pas. *I done unnerstan. I am scare now. What is?*

Three months gone now and George not write me, pas un mot en français ou anglais. Paul est très occupé, *bizzy; ver bizzy an hardly look at Madeleine,* mais Mama *see* et dit, "Félicitations, Madeleine." *I am ver scare.*

Enfin Mama *tease Paul an laff and say,* "Félicitations, mon fils. Encore une fois." "Pourquoi?" demande Paul. "Trois poupons est *just right,*" dit Mama, "très chic." "Bravo!" dit Papa en latin et, "*Whoops,*" dit Mary Lou. "Ce n'est pas vrai," dit Paul, et il ne me regarde pas, "deux poupons est suffisant; assez." "Mais, oui, Paul, Chéri, *it is true.*" Paul arrizes, *ver angry,* "Que dis-tu, Madeleine, tu sais très bien ce n'est pas possible. Deux poupons est assez pour moi." "*Pleez my Paul,* oui, oui. Calme-toi. Tu as raison. *The* bébé *is not to you, Paul, it is the* bébé *of George. It is to George, who does not write me* un mot *an I am ver sad.*" Tout le monde me regarde. *I know that Paul is ver estonish because he say nothing.* "*I done unnerstan,*" I say. "*All the world has said 'George is the pal of Paul.' Paul give me his pal, George,* n'est-ce pas? *Have you not said, Paul, 'Go ahead, done mind me.' 'This is a free country'?* Alors, George me donne des leçons, oui, et moi, je donne des leçons à George. Où est George? Pourquoi George ne . . . ?" "Silence donc!" *cries Paul.* "George, George, George! *The dirty rat!*" "Oui, George est très charmant," *I say.* "Fi, donc!" *cries Mama.* "Moi, je suis sans voix," *say Papa.* Toute la famille parle français maintenant, *ackcep* Mary Lou, qui dit, "*Dope!*" "Que vous parlez tous très bien français!" je dit. "J————C—————!" *cry my Paul; he is now ver ver mad; he forget his good French.* "J————C——————, *your nuts!*" *he scream at me.* "*You done deserve my son!*" *cry Mama.* "*Get out of my house!*" *yell Papa. All the good French is gone.*

Now Madeleine go home to France. She speak English ver well but not unnerstan any. Madeleine est désolée. Adieu, Madame la Statue de la Liberté, et le Centre de Rockefeller. Adieu, *everbody. So long.*

The Case of Astrolabe

IDEA

Astrolabe, which I would like pronounced sounding the final e, was the son of Heloise and Abelard. This play shall concern the arrival of Astrolabe in Heaven and his rights in that place according to the Angels. Their discussion of him is the play itself. Anything that may be said of Heloise and Abelard shall be based on the "Historia Calamitatum" written by Abelard and on the letters of Heloise and Abelard. Astrolabe is mentioned once in the former and a very few times in the letters. I think therefore that all that is known of Astrolabe is that which will become known in this play. The discussion of the Angels shall consist therefore of their doubts, impressions, prejudices. There are no facts; there is no record. Astrolabe stands before them but he is dead. They attempt to judge him according to his actions and deeds on earth, but he appears scarcely to have existed. They gather and surmise. They think that he must have been a complete failure on earth: he had no human love and consequently no earthly ties; on earth he behaved as if he were in Heaven; he could not love because he was not loved; he married, but, unable to recall his mother, his choice of a wife is unsuccessful. It is I who become aware of these things from the discussion of the Angels. The Angels do not necessarily understand the significance of what they are saying. The Angels are not very bright. Some facts are brought out: he was a lutanist, probably a daydreamer; he says that he went to the Holy Land as a child with many other children to sing to and play for the soldiers in order that the Sepulchre might be saved from the Infidel. The Angels insist there is no record. They call it a daydream or an excuse perhaps for his unsuccessful life; they point out that many men, and their friends for them, gave the Holy Land as an alibi for failure: if a man did not come home to his wife — he was in the Holy Land no doubt, fighting the Infidel.

As I have said the discussion by the Angels is the play itself. Astrolabe waits. God is. The Angels appear by their conversation to be the only worldly things in Heaven. Their discussion is like a discussion on earth. Some are informed; others not. Some have insight; others have not. Wit is unlikely. Humor appears to be lacking but no more so than on earth. There may be a little wise-cracking. None seems to have become more reasonable during his stay in Heaven with the exception that logic is an accepted technique and no angel is quite so crude as to say, "I see what you mean but I don't agree." The Angels appear to have learned that to accept a premise is to accept a conclusion when between the two you have logic. The Angel discussion therefore is not as embarrassing as an earthly one and no Angel in the presence of God ever begins a sentence, "In my opinion."

The meeting will probably adjourn without a vote being taken as there is plenty of time, but not before Astrolabe, by his modesty and charm, shall persuade God to let him speak. It is not yet clear to me what Astrolabe shall say but it will not be an excuse, an explanation or an appeal for mercy.

SCENE

Blue Heaven.

CHARACTERS:

God . . . Messenger Angel . . . Astrolabe and Angels.

GOD

Everyone is standing and none moves from his place. God appears to have momentarily arrived however; as if He had been somewhere else and will soon return. He is the only One who is a little restless; a trifle absent-minded. The others are wrapt in the immediate circumstance. He is abstract. He knows that Astrolabe is as nothing in the Infinite, but His manners are perfect; He shows neither arrogance nor superiority. Now and then He bends His look upon Astrolabe and the rest of the time appears to wait for the angels to finish so that He may be gone.

ASTROLABE

Astrolabe is unwittingly like God in that he takes no deep interest in the proceedings. Upon entering with the Messenger Angel he stares gently at everything: the blueness, the differently colored angels each in his place like candles in candlesticks and God. His glance is neither critical nor snobbish.

ANGELS

The Angels do not move about but remain each in his place as one day Astrolabe shall, God willing. The Angels are sexless; the term "he" being used generically. In appearance they are male, however, which is traditional. The Angels have no identity. Each is an individual and behaves accordingly. The Angels do not know and God is not interested in who they were on earth. Each has been judged as Astrolabe is now being judged and given his place. If it occurs to the reader that Heloise and Abelard may be present, it is an amusing suggestion but illogical.

MESSENGER ANGEL

The Messenger Angel is pleasant, practical and has obviously made friends with Astrolabe on the way. This does not prejudice him however. He is honest, capable, dependable.

MESSENGER ANGEL [*rhyming*]:
The natural son of Abelard
The bastard son of Heloise
If you please.
Astrolabe

48

SEVERAL ANGELS:
His story?
GOD:
Yes.
MESSENGER ANGEL:
Begotten in Paris
Gestated so they say
Among the wolves
And on the way
To Orléans
There born
In Brittany bred.
SEVERAL ANGELS:
And then?
MESSENGER ANGEL:
They wed.
MANY ANGELS:
Against her will!
Against her will — so it is said.
ANGELS:
She wanted glory not a husband
Glory for her lover
She gave no thought to Astrolabe
Glory for her lover
Her desire was for Abelard
Glory for her lover
Her love was sure — his glory not
Thus Astrolabe was begot
Thus Astrolabe was forgot.

ANGEL:
She gave no thought for Astrolabe.
ANGEL:
But glory for Abelard.
ANGEL:
Glory.

ANGEL:
Glory.
ANGEL:
She dreamed him Pope.
ANGEL:
She would have him Pope.
ANGEL:
Glory!
ANGEL:
His Holiness!
[*The blueness pales slightly.*]
MANY ANGELS:
God Forbid!
[*God does not mind.*]
ANGEL:
She gave no thought to Astrolabe.
[*There is a pause.*]
INFORMED ANGEL:
There have been Popes and will be Popes
But there is only one of Abelard
Is what her lover said
And you would have mine enemies
Destroy me — lest we wed.
GOD:
Hmmmmmmm.
ANGELS:
Ambitious Heloise.
Ambitious Abelard.
It was love.
And still no thought for Astrolabe.
GOD:
Yet he is here — waiting.
Have I said that he must suffer?
ANGEL:
You said it Lord.

MANY ANGELS:
For I the Lord Thy God am a jealous God visiting the iniquity of the
fathers upon the children unto the third and fourth generation.
GOD:
Ah me.
AN ANGEL:
None has proved his parents evil
They lie together even now in Père Lachaise
Proof of honesty in wedlock
Astrolabe is no bastard.
INFORMED ANGEL:
Doubly so
I say he is
First in fact
And secondly of her free will
Voluntarily I say
She took the veil
Ex Post Facto
Astrolabe
Born in sin — recalled — denied
By lustful Heloise.
AN ANGEL [*crossly*]:
Who are you to use so many I's?
INFORMED ANGEL:
I know the facts
It was a plain case of lust
Lustful Heloise.
MANY ANGELS [*a little pleased*]:
Lustful Heloise.
INFORMED ANGEL: [*Quoting from the letters of Heloise. The blue
turns slightly purple.*]
"To her master, nay father, to her husband, nay brother; his hand-
maid, nay daughter, his spouse, nay sister: to Abelard, Heloise . . .
For it is thou alone that canst make me sad, canst make me joyful or
canst comfort me . . . I had the strength to lose myself at thy behest.

And what is more . . . to such madness did my love turn that what alone it sought it cast from itself without hope of recovery when, straight way obeying thy command, I changed both my habit and my heart, that I might show thee to be the one possessor both of my body and of my mind . . . And if the name of wife appears more sacred and more valid, sweeter to me is ever the word friend, or, if thou be not ashamed, concubine or whore . . . I preferred love to wedlock . . . I call God to witness, if Augustus, ruling over the whole world, were to deem me worthy of the honor of marriage, and to confirm the whole world to me, to be ruled by me forever, dearer to me and of greater dignity would it seem to be called thy strumpet than his empress . . . what wife, what maiden did not yearn for thee in thine absence, nor burn in thy presence? What queen or powerful lady did not envy me my joys and my bed? There were two things, I confess, in thee especially wherewith thou couldst at once captivate the heart of any woman; namely the arts of making songs and of singing them . . . thou hast left many songs . . . And as the greater part of thy songs descanted of our love, they spread my fame . . . and inflamed the jealousy of many women against me . . . what woman who envied me then does not my calamity now compel to pity one deprived of such delights? . . . wherein if I deserve naught from thee, thou mayest judge my labor to have been in vain. No reward for this may I expect from God, for the love of whom it is well known that I did not anything . . . Would that thy love, beloved, had less trust in me, that it might be more anxious! . . . Remember, I beseech thee, what I have done, and pay heed to what thou owest me. While with thee I enjoyed carnal pleasures, many were uncertain whether I did so from love or from desire. But now the end shows in what spirit I began. I have forbidden myself all pleasures that I might obey thy will. I have reserved nothing for myself, save this, to be now entirely thine . . ."

[*There is a pause and a silence.*]

"So that the more genuine my love was for thee, the further it was removed from error."

ANGELS [*admiringly*]:
What logic!

AN ANGEL:
Ahhh.
MANY ANGELS:
Ahhhhhhhh.
GOD [*who has not appeared to be listening but who brings them
back now to the discussion*]:
And Abelard?
I seem to remember he proved my existence
Or was that my dear Thomas?
[*It is blue again.*]
ANGEL:
Thomas did it five ways, Lord.
GOD [*absently*]:
Why?
[*The angels do not answer God when He asks questions that cannot
be answered. They always behave as if He had made a statement.*]
AN ANGEL:
Abelard was the first "Protestant."
GOD:
I forgive him that do I not?
AN ANGEL [*stuffily*]:
I personally owe my conscience to Abelard.
AN ANGEL [*Pleased with himself. It is the first wisecrack. The blue
light shimmers a little.*]:
And conscience hath made angels of us all.
GOD [*who does not recognize jokes*]:
Messenger, my child, where did you find this lad, this Astrolabe? Did
you find him under any particular circumstances? Was he hungry? He
is young, is he not? Did you find him in a burning bush, or where? eh?
ASTROLABE [*looks at God and smiles*]:
Sire!
ANGELS [*annoyed*]:
Watch your manners
Do not address the Lord as if He were a knight!

[*They mutter.*]
The little bastard.

ASTROLABE:
My Father which art in Heaven.

GOD:
Yes, little love.

ASTROLABE [*shy*]:
Nothing.

GOD:
Nothing.

SOME ANGELS:
He is rational.
He has insight.

MESSENGER [*reading from a notebook*]:
I found him, Lord, in a little house. He looked as he looks now; he did not hesitate or mind coming with me; he said no farewells; he wrote no letters; he waited quietly while I took inventory.

SOME ANGELS [*curious*]:
What were his effects?

MESSENGER [*Reads. During the reading there is the sound of instruments very quiet at first but growing louder.*]:
A lute, a lyre, an organistrum, a violin, a pipe and a bag pipe, a syrinx, a harp, a gigue, a gittern, a symphony, a psaltery, a single and a double regal and a tabor.

[*Heaven is very blue.*]

GOD:
How nice.

AN ANGEL:
. . . his father was a great lutanist; often a gleeman and a trouvère, when he became weary of being a philosopher.

AN ANGEL:
Astrolabe was taught by an old lutanist who would have been eaten by wolves had not the Nuns let him into the convent.

GOD:
How very nice.

Did he have no other worldly goods?

MESSENGER [*continues reading*]:

A copy of Virgil, some fairy tales, a bad translation into Latin of Plato, much used, and a copy of Aristotle's *Ethics*, barely fingered.

INFORMED ANGEL:

A Platonist!

GOD:

I like him too.

INFORMED ANGEL:

But, Lord, it was Aristotle who gave us dialectic without which — without which . . .

[*He looks embarrassed.*]

GOD:

Without which

Just so.

ASTROLABE:

My Father which art.

GOD:

Yes — yes — very nice, little love.

AN ANGEL:

Let us not get into that old argument — Plato or Aristotle

Let us be happy that we exist.

GOD [*gently*]:

Five ways.

AN ANGEL [*sputtering*]:

Aristotle! Humph.

AN ANGEL [*sputtering*]:

Plato! Phaugh.

ANGELS:

Shsssshhh.

MESSENGER [*hopefully*]:

He told me on the way that he had been to the Holy Land.

GOD [*interrupting*]:

May I just take a look at that Plato?

MESSENGER [*embarrassed*]:
Er — I always strip them — Lord.
Moth and dust you know.
GOD:
Me again?
ANGELS:
Yes, Lord.
ASTROLABE:
It's quite all right.
AN ANGEL:
Shall we go on?
A KIND ANGEL:
They sleep in Père Lachaise
Shall we disinter them thus
While Astrolabe waits
Shall he be Godless
As well as motherless — fatherless?
ANGELS:
It looks like it.
He has no rights.
He is scarcely a generation from sin.
ANGEL [*bored*]:
Let us hear some more of Heloise's letters.
GOD:
Some music would be nice.
[*The sound of instruments is heard again.*]
ANOTHER ANGEL [*who has not spoken before*]:
We have not mentioned Abelard's misfortune
His calamity.
ANGEL [*the stuffy one*]:
That sort of thing is of no consequence here.
OTHER ANGEL [*angrily*]:
I beg your pardon — it is of canonical consequence; it is of ecclesi-
astical consequence; it is therefore of consequence here and to us.

56

ANGELS:

Hear Hear.

OTHER ANGEL:

May I quote you, Lord?

GOD [*He is interested*]:

Yes do.

ANGEL [*quotes*]:

"He that is wounded in the stones or hath his privy member cut off, shall not enter into the congregation of the Lord."

GOD:

That's Deuteronomy.

ANGEL [*patronizing*]:

Your word — dear Lord, all the same
Revealed truth as it were.

GOD:

Hmmmmmm. Silly.

SAME ANGEL:

And again "Ye shall not offer unto the Lord that which is bruised, or crushed, or broken or cut."

GOD:

Leviticus?

SAME ANGEL:

Yes, Lord.

GOD:

Mighty foolish.

OTHER ANGEL:

And then Heresy! Is Heresy of no consequence either! Have we no Ethics anymore? Are we Nominalists or Realists! Is this Plato's Heaven or Aristotle's!

[*The blue light is getting a little muddy.*]

GOD [*with some show of authority*]:

It is mine!

[*Heaven shakes. There is lightning. He is scarcely heard however in the angelic hubbub. Angel faces are flushed.*]

Thou shalt have no other gods before Me!

Deuteronomy!
   [*There is a pause.*]
It is mine.
   OTHER ANGEL:
Your forgiveness, Lord.
   GOD [*singsong*]:
I say not unto thee until seven times; but until seventy times seven.
   SAME ANGEL:
Heresy.
Not convicted but suspected
It is all one with the church
And it must be all one with us.
   ANGELS:
Go on.
   SAME ANGEL [*all genuflect*]:
He spoke of the Holy Ghost
as of equal consequence . . .
   ANGEL [*joking*]:
Are we going to play consequences again?
   ANGELS:
Sssshhhhh.
   A NEW ANGEL:
But we speak now of God the Father
God the Son and God the Holy Ghost.
   [*He makes as many genuflections as possible.*]
   SAME ANGEL [*irritably*]:
But we didn't then. Abelard was a heretic in Time. Is that clear?
   [*It seems to be, as no one says anything.*]
   GOD [*smiles encouragingly at Astrolabe*]:
A little more of this.
It concerns me does it not?
   SAME ANGEL [*proudly*]:
After Abelard was threatened with excommunication . . . following
his trial for Heresy at which time his book was burned . . .

   58

GOD:

Excommunication?

SAME ANGEL:

Yes — Lord — due to his showing to some brethren, *quasi jocando*, a saying of Bede who asserted that Denys — or shall we say Dionysius — the Areopagite was Bishop of Corinth, and not of Athens as maintained by Hilduin. Hilduin being, as we all know, their Abbot; of whom it is recorded that he spent much of his time and travelled extensively in Greece to acquaint and ground himself with and in the facts and the Acts of the Saint, compiling which facts and acts, as I say, it was said he removed all doubt.

[*He pauses, pleased.*]

AN ANGEL:

All doubt of what?

INFORMED ANGEL [*patiently*]:

Dionysius the Areopagite was Bishop of Athens according to Hilduin. According to Bede he was Bishop of Corinth. Abelard, *quasi jocando*, to tease the brethren, as it were, showed them the saying of Bede upon whose writings he well knew the entire body of the Latin Churches depended and consulted. Hilduin, however was their Abbot; they were incensed. Hilduin, they said, had proved without doubt . . .

GOD [*kindly but insistently*]:

The Heresy please
I am so interested in the Trinity you know.

SAME ANGEL [*gladly*]:

Where was I — oh yes after that he founded a place, founded and dedicated it and named it Paraclete. His action was denounced, naturally enough, it being unlawful that any church should be assigned to the Holy Ghost, rather than to God the Father, [*genuflexion*] rather than to the Son, [*genuflexion*] rather than to the whole Trinity. [*Genuflecting, he sighs, but goes on energetically.*] Abelard held them to be in error; their error being that they did not see the distinction between the Paraclete and the Ghost Paraclete.

ANGEL [*interrupts*]:

As we all do no doubt.

SAME ANGEL [*continues*]:

Whereas: Abelard said that the Trinity itself also, and any Person of the Trinity, as He is called God or Helper, so may rightly be named Paraclete, that is Comforter, as is said by the Apostle: "Blessed be God, even the Father of our Lord Jesus Christ, the Father of Mercies, and the God of all comfort; who comforteth us in all our tribulation" . . . Why then, continued Abelard, when the whole Church is consecrated alike in the Name of the Father and of the Son and of the Holy Ghost, [*rhythmic genuflexions*] possessing nothing separately, should not the house of the Lord be so ascribed to the Father, or to the Holy Ghost as to the Son?

GOD [*honestly*]:

It's very complicated isn't it?

SOME ANGELS:

He was a heretic we guess all right.

[*There is a pause.*]

AN ANGEL:

I would rather hear some more about Heloise.

ANGELS [*murmur*]:

Heloise Heloise Heloise.

AN ANGEL [*willingly*]:

It appears that Heloise took the veil but kept her love for Abelard as well . . .

[*Heaven turns blue, then slightly purple again.*]

AN ANGEL [*continues*]:

While Abelard incapable of love and desiring a rational and holy life was denied the priesthood.

GOD:

Silly.

ANGEL [*repeats and continues*]:

Abelard, incapable of love . . .

[*Angels recite in unison the declension of Calamitas.*]

AN ANGEL [*as if to himself*]:

Heloise.

SEVERAL ANGELS:

Heloise, Heloise.

LOTS OF ANGELS [*loudly*]:

We want Heloise!

[*Heaven changes color. Astrolabe waits. God is thinking. The Angels cannot leave their places but they seem as one as they listen.*]

AN ANGEL [*surreptitiously*]:

There is the story of the refectory.

ANGELS [*eagerly*]:

Yes?

AN ANGEL [*same*]:

No sooner had he left his beautiful Heloise in the convent, than he returned. No sooner returned than he persuaded her into the refectory. No sooner in the refectory than they kissed.

ANGELS [*weakly*]:

Ah.

SAME ANGEL [*getting confused*]:

And then they sinned.

ANGELS [*already exhausted*]:

They sinned.

SAME ANGEL:

Once more.

ANGELS [*losing interest*]:

Once more.

INFORMED ANGEL [*who has been intellectually restless*]:

I want to quote.

ANGELS [*wearily*]:

Enough.

INFORMED ANGEL [*insists brightly*]:

"So sweet to me were those delights of lovers which we enjoyed in common that they cannot either displease me nor hardly pass from my memory. Whithersoever I turn, always they bring themselves before my eyes with the desire for them. Nor even when I am asleep do they spare me their illusions. In the very solemnities of the Mass, when prayer ought to be more pure, the obscure phantoms of those

delights so thoroughly captivate my wretched soul to themselves that
I pay heed to their vileness rather than to my prayers. And when I
ought to lament for what I have done I sigh rather for what I have
had to forego."

AN ANGEL:

Disgusting.

AN ANGEL:

Skip it.

AN ANGEL:

Let him finish; we will never get through.

INFORMED ANGEL [*continues*]:

"Not only the things that we did, but the places and times in which
we did them are so fixed with thee in my mind that in the same times
and places I re-enact them all with thee . . . [*He looks around for en-
couragement which he does not get.*] At times by the very motion of
my body the thoughts of my mind are disclosed, nor can I restrain the
utterance of unguarded words."

[*The angels aren't even listening except one who speaks, as if to get
it in the record and over with.*]

AN ANGEL:

What was Abelard's reply?

INFORMED ANGEL [*immediately*]:

"Farewell in Christ, Bride of Christ, in Christ farewell, and in Christ
dwell. Amen."

ANGELS [*from habit*]:

Amen.

GOD [*gently*]:

I would like to hear about Astrolabe. [*Adding a little sternly*] Aye.
Verily.

[*When God reverts to biblical language he at once gains the attention of the Angels.*]

ASTROLABE:

My Father which art in Heaven.

LOTS OF ANGELS:

Silence!

ASTROLABE:

Dear God.

LOTS OF ANGELS:

Be still. You may not speak. It is by your deeds you shall be judged.

ASTROLABE:

Now I lay me down to sleep.

GOD [*looks up*]:

Aye.

ASTROLABE:

I never did a deed
But I can sing.

[*There is instrumental music and Astrolabe sings one of Abelard's
love songs, a famous one.*]

But ah the dawn — it comes too soon . . .
But ah the dawn — it comes too soon

[*After each chorus there is the sound of distant clapping. Heaven
gently changes colors — pink, blue, lavender, yellow to blue again.*]

But ah the dawn — it comes too soon
But ah the dawn — it comes too soon

[*The Angels look happy but quickly recover their various characters.*]

GOD:

I am well pleased.

AN ANGEL:

It was a love song.

GOD:

Verily.

AN ANGEL:

On earth he was a failure — he was definitely not a success.

ANGEL:

He was a daydreamer.

ANGEL:

There is no record of anything he ever did. His birth alone seems to
be certain and there is some authority for his having lived a while
with his mother at the convent of Argenteuil.

ANGEL:

She was no mother but a Nun
She took the veil and by her act Astrolabe became
A bastard and motherless.
He had no earthly love or ties.

ANGEL:

He behaved as if he were in Heaven
He was not loved nor could he love.

ANGEL:

His mother was a Nun — he did not love her.

ANGEL:

He never loved another.

ANGEL:

I have heard it said he took a wife
But she left him.

AN ANGEL [*one with more than average intelligence*]:
Motherless sons make phantom lovers.

ANGEL:

He was a lutanist when he was eight.

MESSENGER ANGEL [*hopefully*]:
He told me on the way that he had been to the Holy Land; that he
went when he was ten.

ASTROLABE [*it is his longest speech and he appears exhausted*]:
I did, I did go. I remember the sailors. I remember the cart and all
the other children. I remember all the mothers crying hard along the
road for miles and miles. I remember the children singing and singing
and singing.

[*There is the sound of children's voices from "The Children's
Crusade." God listens.*]

ANGEL [*impatiently*]:
There is no record.

ANGEL:

Many children went it is true.

ANGEL:

To save the Sepulchre.

64

ANGEL:

To fight the Infidel.

KIND ANGEL:

They surely are in their places now
While Astrolabe waits.

GOD:

My Sepulchre you say? Was my Sepulchre in danger? And did the
little lad save it for me? [*God turns to Astrolabe.*] But you say you did
no deed!

ASTROLABE:

It was no deed, my Father which art in Heaven, I played my lute and
my organistrum. I sang Abelard's love songs.

ANGEL:

There is no record.
It was a daydream.

[*Astrolabe smiles and waits and does not mind.*]

INTELLIGENT ANGEL:

There seems to be nothing to say about Astrolabe. Did he never
then commit a sin?

A BRIGHT ANGEL:

Look out! Don't answer that one.

INTELLIGENT ANGEL:

The sins of Heloise and Abelard made history of them. Everyone
knows in Heaven and on Earth of Abelard's seduction, Heloise's sinful joy, and Abelard's calamity. The fact that Abelard was a great
logician, the first to deal with the essence of universality, a master of
dialectic, the young man of twenty who confounded the great Wil-
liam de Champeaux, is secondary knowledge. Is there no sin, I say,
to recommend this boy to our attention?

MESSENGER [*uneasily*]:

He told me on the way he loved a Nun.

LOTS OF ANGELS:

Ahhhhh.

LOTS OF ANGELS:

So.

ASTROLABE [*gently corrects the messenger*]:
Some Nuns.

LOTS OF ANGELS:
Oh! Some Nuns.

GOD [*who has not been listening lately*]:
I never heard of Heloise and Abelard. Queer isn't it?
[*The Angels do not appear to have heard him.*]

ASTROLABE [*happily*]:
May I speak of my beautiful Nuns, good Angels?

STUFFY ANGEL [*obviously curious; with restraint*]:
You may say a few words about the Nuns whom you — admired — at
a distance.

ASTROLABE [*poetic*]:
Distanced by the cloth and cloche
Awhile
But I outwitted both
Lovely eyes admitted me.

STUFFY ANGEL [*really horrified*]:
Sssshhhhh.

AN ANGEL:
You were only eight.

AN ANGEL [*sarcastic*]:
That was his wit.

AN ANGEL [*repeats*]:
You were only eight.

ASTROLABE [*happy*]:
Then I am still eight. It is the same. No Convent closes its doors to
me. And no sister her heart. I am Astrolabe.

AN ANGEL [*sternly*]:
You are no one. You are dead.

ASTROLABE [*pays no attention*]:
No Sister summer or winter. I know the way. I have loved a hundred
Nuns.

MESSENGER [*very worried*]:
Astrolabe — don't.

ASTROLABE [*continues*]:
But I will sing to one at a time.
AN ANGEL:
He is daydreaming.
SOME ANGELS:
Let him go on.
AN ANGEL:
It is sinful.
SOME ANGELS:
It is our unpleasant duty to listen.*
ASTROLABE [*sings*]:
Oh Beautiful enclosed and safe
Tell me with your lifted eyes
Show me the way with lovely hands
To love you
I am Astrolabe

Oh warm in white
And cold in black
Keep such perversity for God
And love me
I am Astrolabe.
AN ANGEL [*one who has been speechless collects himself and actually hollers*]:
Censored!
GOD:
I like music very much.
MESSENGER [*gently*]:
Astrolabe, wake up.
AN ANGEL [*kindly*]:
Pull yourself together — you are dead.
ASTROLABE [*wants to go on and does*]:
When I returned from the Holy Land I was thin and white; my legs
were long and my knees knobby but I wore my hat with a feather and

---

*Note: I think they mean it; the angels are not virile in a physical sense and the
letters of Heloise may have exhausted them.

I had my lute. I played it on the street and people blessed me and gave me pennies. A Sister came along and I lifted my head in the middle of a line because I know when there is one of them about. She appeared to be passing me in profile but she suddenly looked at me and I entered into her eyes. It was a cold day and I could smell and taste her skin as if she were an apple. "You do not have to beg" she said. I went with her and she bathed me herself without smiling. I knew how to love her and I did. I had to leave her but I shall always remember my lovely unsmiling one. She could open and close her eyes without lowering the lids and I went into them so often I was tired.

[Heaven appears to spin a little. God alone remains unaffected. He likes the sound of Astrolabe's voice but he does not appear to listen to his words. Astrolabe rests and there is no sound in Heaven. It is as blue as ever and God seems to be enjoying the stillness. There is no hurry.]

ASTROLABE [*beginning again*]:

I sang and played. My heart beat with happiness; I was at a loss for nothing. When I was hungry I was fed as if I were a bird. A blue-eyed Sister let me feed from her hand. I licked it and kissed it and then it lay along my cheek while I slept. None knows like me the joy and beauty of Nuns; the separateness of their hands; and the look of their bare feet like vases alone in a black room. A face like a mask cut off at the chin and capped by white clouds is preferable to one that is merely used to terminate a body. (Yes I am sure of that.) And I know other things because I am Astrolabe whom the Nuns love.

[There is quiet.]

ASTROLABE [*continuing*]:

Of course I was sorry when my wife left me but she was no friend of mine. I wanted someone to talk to about my Nuns. I wanted a companion who would listen. I did not want a lover; I had so many and not a friend to tell it to. At the turn in every street I came upon my Sisters with tilted chins and deep eyes. I loved them all singly and in two's and three's. I had them in stillness and with music; I had them in the dark and in the bright consistent sun. One with the light in my eyes and her face in the shadow and one gold with the sun making her eyes white and me in the dark. I don't remember about my wife. Wife is a strange word. It is a sound I never sing. I am telling the truth: I did not marry; I was married. With Nuns dancing in my head as in a frieze I was asked to perform that which I was unable to perform. I am not a clown! Someone said my wife was beautiful. I don't know, I only saw that she was naked and boring; immodest and demanding; cruel and importunate. I asked her to cover her feet and hands and she laughed at me. I asked her to dress herself and leave her hands and feet bare and she was angry. I asked her to be my friend. I told her I wanted to tell her some beautiful things and when I began she struck me. I begged her finally in an attempt to please her to let me dress her as a Nun. I told her I would get her a lovely coif and veil and wimple of the kind that the Sisters wore at Argenteuil when I was a little boy. I told her that she should wear a rosary around her waist with the cross at her knees and that I myself would remove it when she chose. I promised to teach her everything. I said she should pass me in profile in the street as I sang and when she turned her face to me I would leap into her eyes like lightning. She said I was mad. She ran out of the house. She left me; she was no friend of mine. And it is just as well I did not spoil my real Sisters by playing with a false one. I returned to my beautiful ones and they laughed at me and stroked me and rubbed their faces to me; their long hands slid down my neck and I tasted them again like apples. I confess that I do not feel quite the man with them but I am young. One day I shall be stern and cruel; one day I shall . . . [*He looks about.*]

AN ANGEL [*faintly*]:
You are dead.

ASTROLABE [*smiling*]:
Never.

GOD [*to Astrolabe*]:
Possess thou thy soul.

ANGEL [*startled*]:
Lord!

GOD:

I love thee, Astrolabe.

ANGELS [*to have the last word*]:

Whom the Lord loveth He chasteneth.

GOD [*firmly*]:

Possess thou thy soul, Astrolabe.

[*God gives His usual blessing to all, turns as if to go, and the Angels without more ado sing the Doxology.*]

An Affair of Honor

That French engraving has haunted me, at least followed me, kept within calling distance of me for so long, as long as I have lived, that it is time it made sense. It certainly didn't make sense in the extra-staid New England house in which I didn't exactly blossom. Neither am I as puny as, when in all kinds of weather, because weather was bad for me, it appeared, I was semi-solaced by the box-like rooms of a house that seemed like a series of cupboards to me then as it does now as I recall it. I grudgingly admit I loved the house, however, as only a monster repudiates his first domicile, and fostered my resentment against the relatives, the cupboards housed in genteel frugality as is also expected, I believe, of a normal brat of decent lineage but so-so appetite. (The appetite is no longer so-so, [*un peu façonnier*] as any of my hostesses will bear witness to as well as to the physique many of them also know.) Housed as I say in a box of a house divided into more boxes, each box lined prettily enough with perpendicular garlands of prim unopened rosebuds, and down the narrow unevenly floored hall another little box, *cabinet*, added in my time which contained anachronistically enough in this old house inside plumbing,

I soon got used and sentimentally attached to everything that enclosed and surrounded me, excepting the French engraving that I never got used to and neither was its attraction exactly sentimental. Now that I am a man-about-town, a gentleman of leisure, *homme de bon ton, amateur,* now that I have become a bachelor through seniority, as it were, simply by growing up, and a bachelor who is in constant demand in the best society, an extra man, so indispensable that I have to carry a little black book, rude as it is, as well as a watch in the evening, not *comme il faut,* either, I know that there were many valuable pieces in our funny New England house: the outsized Queen Anne chair that made my Aunt look as if she were wearing a huge wooden comb, rather rakish, the Windsors, the ladderbacks in the kitchen, the inlaid Sheraton sideboard, my granddad's desk, flocks of footstools under foot, little embroidered schoolgirl platitudes and childish clichés in red, white, and blue, Mount Vernon in French knots, *Mon Dieu,* paintings of relatives that unfortunately looked exactly like them but "quaint" now, as you know, American primitives, awfully good. All these things come back to me when I hear a couple of old girls comparing their successes with antique dealers, smart bargains, stylish gallery openings, relative value of refugee decorators, or when in the gentlemen's washroom in Sutton Place I notice, "God Bless Our Home Mary Ann Elizabeth Welch," looking frightfully chic, I can tell you, holding its own with a Pruna gouache. But fine art or useful, good taste or bad, *comme il faut ou gauche,* elegant or crude as these objects which I remember may have been, aside from the fact that I might clean up, vulgarly speaking, if I could lay my hands on them now, they could not as everyday accepted periphery ever excite me or arouse my curiosity. But the French engraving is a different matter. That engraving has had the honor of educating me. *Elle m'a elevé très bien, je vous assure.* And like a good book, a continued story, I can't put it down; it leads me on, holds my interest, and to it goes the credit of my sophisticated successful bachelorhood, my good taste in women, my *sangfroid, savoir vivre,* my reputation as a connoisseur, slightly untouchable but sensitive imaginative gentleman, lover, good sport, extra man, *un fin.* Imagine a small boy with big eyes, *la!* awakening to that French engraving and losing sight of it as he was put to bed only because the twilight gradually obscured it but first enhanced it, turning it blue, *séduisante.* Why my relations hung that particular picture, *cette gravure douce,* in my bedroom I don't know but as I remember that as long as I lived in that house which was from my birth until I entered Groton, nothing ever moved from its place, I suppose the picture had been hanging there in another generation; perhaps the room had belonged to one of the uncles whose taste was more like mine has become. Don't think the picture was obscene or even indelicate, certainly not. It was a well-known engraving with a certain style, strength of character, even lacking in *nuance,* rather cold, detailed, factual: *An Affair of Honor* (Une Affaire d'Honneur). The dualists are women. They stand in the traditional clearing; in the background are their seconds, I think, and if I remember, a saddle horse or perhaps a Victoria, *je ne suis pas sûr.* Well in the foreground stand the two women facing each other; they are naked to the waist. Each, with one hand, holds up her skirts and petticoats from behind; there are ruffles, ribbons, stylish high-buttoned shoes; I think each lady wears her hat and each has curls escaping. Each is earnest, plump, feminine, soft; each is *délicieuse, digne d' amour.* I shuddered at the wounds each would inflict on an identical body. I guessed at the flesh I could not see when I was shut up with the dualists too long but usually the picture gave me as it stood more than I could comprehend, more than I could take. From too much looking at that *assaut d'armes* I became different. I walked among my innocent relatives with something extra, something special both in my insides and in my exterior bearing, in my visible make-up. I had spells of temporary oblivion: I imagined winged horses with jade necklaces, little girls fastened together like cut-outs, and a woman with six interchangeable faces, a talking cat, and a tune that followed me around, as the French say, *humeur,* very *à propos.* When I was empty of things I could imagine after a good look at *An Affair of Honor* I would bolt my food to get rid of it, drink a big glass of ice water and go up for another look. I decided I was an orphan and the answer to my parentage could be found in the picture. I held it up-

side down and sideways to discover an extra face as if it were a puzzle.
I imagined my mother behind the clump of trees to the left and my
own name hidden in the French words proclaiming the engraver
which I did not then understand. I lay on my back squinting at the
picture and watched the tremulous torsos of my friends as they
lunged, the foils quivering, causing me exquisite pain, at twin nipples,
violet; *riposte*, parry and thrust, return; *en guarde! de retour, en avant
. . .* ahh, *touché du sang?* One of them sways with bent head clasping
her wounded bosom; her hat falls off; her curls leap out; she sinks to
the ground slowly, gracefully, silently, soporifically, *mais non, c'est
une victoire non sanglante, grâce à Dieu, mais ravissante, si jolie,
une amourette, n'est-ce pas? j'étais ravi en extase,* and I too sink
into a spindly kind of jumpy sleep, (good Lord where am I?). In
broad daylight I imagined that behind the picture on the wall there
was a tunnel, the tunnel led to a pasture, across the pasture a cowpath
took me to a wood (someone had marked the trees and made signals
with leaves), on the other side of the wood there was a train, the
train delivered me to a boat, a fast one, no one spoke, we docked; I
walked down the dock and got on a bicycle . . . By these diverse and
stubborn means of locomotion, some fast, some slow, abortive, I anticipated for hours my French girl friends with bare breasts, finally
arriving on foot too exhausted to enjoy them. (I still like to go on
foot, as it were, to a particularly desirable assignation; this placing
myself at a distance from the thing I wanted most and then approach-
ing it slowly became my personal technique and a very good one with
endless possibilities and much reward; I always feel complete confidence in myself from the moment I have made my choice; my lovely
prey seems rooted to the spot, Eurydice, and with infinite patience,
sweet calm, awaits my meandering, triangular approach; stumbling
blocks are precious to me, of my own invention, strategically placed.
I have never lost a woman or an *objet d'art* this way. And like a good
hostess I am extremely annoyed at people who arrive on time and
God forgive the one who is early, before she [the hostess] or I, as it
were, am dressed. In other words let me miss you, Ma'am, before you
come as well as after you leave. *C'est ça.*) I sometimes wonder what

74

sort of a lout, simple-minded rustic, *benêt*, I might have become if I had not been initiated by these charming ladies into, if not the facts of life, the possibilities. My mother had hid herself all the way from her pretty jaw to the soles of her foot (there were little bones besides in her collar that kept her continually tugging and in a continuous blush from constriction and shame), and her good night kisses were self-conscious and cool; once when I spontaneously hugged her, her whole body felt like a waffle-iron, a criss-cross grill, the soft places not an inch square; I had no lascivious little sister with beckoning impudent tongue; the hired girl was not for me. And so the sweet myth of bare ladies on the wall taught me physical modesty, intellectual censorship, the penurious anticipatory pleasure that feminine beauty everlastingly offers if properly approached, which I never would have had cause to learn without the French engraving, and as dividends to my thesis upon which I have spent my entire life, perfecting my periods, eliminating commas, tastefully arranging the asterisks, and gently adding *fin* at just the right moment, I received the rewards willingly bestowed upon me by the subject matter itself: those lovely women, more or less naked to the waist, not without curls, blushes, tremulous bosoms, who fence, and quite well. (*Touché! du sang? mais non.*) In every other drawing room I stand by, intense but preoccupied, exactly as I did as a little boy, *poupon*, waiting for my reward; *et je sais, maintenant, d'ailleurs, que je suis la bonne fortune (le prix), du reste,* and worth scrapping for, *je vous assure encore, le petit monsieur très gentil aux grands yeux qui crois: une belle femme a une belle âme et son coeur saigne pour moi. Au contraire,* if my love is "consumed by that which it is nourished by" (Shakespeare), *j'ai ma récompense à jamais, toutefois. Célibataire? du sang? mais non, pas vraiment, mais figurément, une façon de parler, pour ainsi dire. Assez, assez, mes enfants, dormez bien.*

Fin

The Help Gets the Legs

I never liked Dr. S., one of those analysts who gets around, you
know, who has patients in stylish places and comes and goes where
some of the rest of us get snubbed. There's something funny going
on when a doctor succeeds where a lover doesn't, except, I suppose
convention gives him *carte blanche*, as it were, and he'd be a fool
and no man if he didn't take advantage of his position in some way.
Having trained himself not to spend the night with a woman he has
just undressed I suppose one can hardly blame him for coming to
her dinner parties. As for me, however, I have always thought that
Hippocrates should have added to his well-known oath* the following: I pledge myself to refuse invitations to dine at the house of my
patient. I suppose I am jealous; I feel he has a decided edge; I do

---

*I swear by Apollo the physician, and Aesculapius, and Health, and All-heal, and
all the gods and goddesses, that, according to my ability and judgment, I will keep
this Oath and this stipulation—to reckon him who has taught me this Art equally
dear to me as my parents, to share my substance with him, and relieve his neces-
sities if required; to look upon his offspring in the same footing as my own brothers, and to teach them this art, if they shall wish to learn it, without fee or stipulation; and that by precept, lecture, and every other mode of instruction, I will
impart a knowledge of the Art to my own sons, and those of my teachers, and to
disciples bound by a stipulation and oath according to the law of medicine, but to
none others. I will follow that system of regimen which, according to my ability

things the hard way: I am good looking, I've had experience, I fall
in love easily, but I don't understand women. Dr. S. does. I've seen
women lower their eyes before Dr. S's bland gaze when I can stare
to no avail. I've seen lovely women hate to leave the dining room
after dinner when Dr. S. was one of the gentlemen to stay behind;
I've seen one hesitate as if to say, "Please, I have to tell you something," and I've seen him continue as if he said to himself, "Later,
there is plenty of time, and there are others ahead of you."

This particular woman I've seen do just that but no one noticed
it at first but me; I suppose because I loved her. Please notice the
past tense: I couldn't tell this story if it weren't in the past tense. I
no longer love her. I had a powerful rival as you have guessed, Dr. S.
Until she met him she was as well balanced a young woman as I in
my libidinous wanderings about town in the best places had seen.
So well balanced that I thought of her as a friend, don't laugh, a
sister, or even a brother; she seemed secure in whatever little world
it was she inhabited, liked her husband, got along with people, didn't
seem to be on the hunt for anything in particular. Her name was
Pamela and I called her Pal. That's how sentimental I can be when
I am not in love; Pal is a dog's name not a sweetheart's; I liked her
and said so; nobody minded because she wasn't anybody's rival. Not
being the least afraid of her my hostesses tried to interest me, teased
me, told me how seductive she was, as a matter of fact she was, but I
didn't see it until I intercepted a look that was meant for Dr. S. I

and judgment I consider for the benefit of my patients, and abstain from whatever
is deleterious and mischievous. I will give no deadly medicine to anyone if asked,
nor suggest any such counsel; and in like manner I will not give to a woman a
pessary to produce abortion. With purity and with holiness I will pass my life and
practice my Art. I will not cut persons laboring under the stone, but will leave
this to be done by men who are practitioners of this work. Into whatever houses I
enter, I will go into them for the benefit of the sick, and will abstain from every
voluntary act of mischief and corruption; and, further, from the seduction of
females or males, of freemen and slaves. Whatever, in connection with my pro-
fessional practice or not in connection with it, I see or hear, in the life of men,
which ought not to be spoken of abroad, I will not divulge, as reckoning that all
such should be kept secret. While I continue to keep this Oath unviolated, may it
be granted to me to enjoy life and the practice of the Art, respected by all men, in
all times! But should I trespass and violate this Oath, may the reverse be my lot!

saw him take the look as if someone had said, "Will you have some more peas?" when just the bit of it I got, because I was in the line of fire, practically knocked me out for the evening. I suddenly saw her as she really was, or was not, as you like. I felt as if I had picked up a message that was not intended for me, but as Dr. S. seemed to have left his antennae behind along with his stethoscope I decided on the spot to decode the girl.

But I am going too fast. Before I capitulated I got a good look at her (afterwards I forgot what she looked like, as usual) and she was very beautiful, especially when she felt like it. She always felt like it when that moron Dr. S. was within shouting distance so I suppose I should have been grateful for his bringing her into focus, as it were, lighting up the landing field for me if nothing else. I wasn't the only one after a while who felt the vibrations; the woman began to look like an old photograph that has been restored; she began to glow and shine and jingle and she looked just as well when she was miserable as when she was happy; it began to be quite a show for the lot of us, painful for me, and Pamela became the envy of all the old girls who formerly thought she was "such a dear." They were just as jealous when she was in despair as when she was happy if you can say she was ever happy; well, not exactly. The men were jealous of Dr. S. and very curious about the whole thing. One evening when my Pamela was nearly swooning in public, her big dark eyes trying to swallow up the doctor, as if she were a female spider, a wit asked, "Isn't it time for him to saw her in half?" "Can you imagine anything more wonderful," sang out my hostess. "Could anything be more wonderful than waiting to be put together again by the man you love. Oh!" "It's very simple why you feel like that," somebody said, "you women want so badly to be dependent on the man you love that it is quite true the situation you mention would be wonderful and very exciting." "When really," my hostess agreed, "it's such a bore to be dependent, I really am filled with chagrin every time." "Men, too, want to be dependent," I added, feeling quite solemn, "and they are when they are in love; no free man is in love." "Hear. Hear."

But I have got to go back still farther. Dr. S., as I have said, was a society analyst. Like some priests who concentrate on the great, seeking their conversion, feeling evidently that God is a snob, or perhaps to do the priest justice, that the great, in proportion, must be subject to greater temptation than the unknown, making them wickeder, therefore more desirable in Heaven, quite a *coup*, solid gold lambs, each one, so did Dr. S., in evening dress, frequent the best drawing rooms looking for patients and finding plenty of material. He worked nights all right and I suppose he deducted his white ties from his income tax; quite a few, I could guess, were ruined by very expensive lipstick. Whenever I think of Pamela, even now when I am no longer in love with her, weeping and sighing for the monetary benefit of that cold fish, that gigolo Midas who could turn women's tears into gold and did, I feel sick. And that happy look when he smiled at her sometimes, just to keep her from jumping out the window until he had finished, was worse. Pamela, two inches taller than he, linking her arm in his, oblivious of everyone else, shining and glowing and jingling, humiliating me the one who loved her, to whom she began to tell her troubles, more than I can express in printable language! All I got from Pamela was the excitement of her love for Dr. S., who never gave her anything but advice and sent her a bill for that. There is no doubt, however, that the doctor recognized in her something extra special, a real beauty, a very desirable woman, and any decent man would have torn up his membership in the A.M.A., spit on the callow oath of Hippocrates, that Mother Goose of the medical profession, and married the girl; but I think I have made it clear that Dr. S. was no idealist and neither, as I have said, did it ever enter his crass old dome to refuse an invitation to dine with his patients. He had not, in other words, the nice integrity of the artist who likes his model to dress during rest periods and practically never serves her tea in the nude. Oh well, the doctor was a bastard. Pamela loved him. I loved Pamela. Now everything is finished; Pamela has become a very ordinary person, quite a bore; lost her happy expectant looks, her sad and yearning desirability; Dr. S. is rich but sleeps badly I hear and hope, and I am in that

nervous interim between love affairs when I am no good to myself
or anyone else, a man without a country, not to mention five o'clock
shadow, good Lord.

I don't know how Pamela got started with Dr. S.; I think she told
me it was "vague pains." One of her friends who was enjoying a
bout of unravelment with her analyst persuaded her to get herself
one, too. "They're imaginary pains," she said and, "Psychoanalysis
is such an *experience*, my dear." Like homosexuals, people who are
being analyzed, I gather, seek converts. They like the cozy knowledge that they are not alone and they love besides to talk about
themselves, the sing-song confidences of the disenchanted. That, by
the way, is the trouble with Pamela now: she's a bore (how can I
say it!); she talks and talks. From a mysterious and haunting woman
she has turned into a bore; there isn't anything about Pamela I don't
know. Everybody knows all about Pamela. She's that monstrous
thing to a man of my sensibilities who adores women, a female bore.
And besides that, having loved her modesty which I had hoped to
seduce, how I squirm now at the personal attack, the searching gaze,
the intimate indecent approach of a woman who has been psycho-
analyzed, the gulping possessive stare of a woman who knows all,
my Pamela! But right up until that night that she passed out at
dinner I adored her, I humbly ate the pie that Dr. S., in his perversity,
refused. He had been treating her according to Freudian Hoyle, more
and more cruelly, and Pamela was his hamburger (the edible meta-
phors are due to the fact that I haven't had lunch). He was excited
at his success; on his toes; it's quite a game for a man, (man?!)
psychoanalysis; if for some reason you are afraid of your fellow beings,
afraid of women especially but afraid even of men, sexually afraid,
by all means take up psychoanalysis. It has its rewards; it has the
design, follows the pattern of a love affair, but it gives you a feeling
of power which a genuine love affair never does—just the opposite.
You may exercise the cruelty, however, of a lover who knows he is
loved; you can see men and women desperately in love with you, at
your feet; the smartest, the prettiest, the ones who never would have
given you a glance if I was around to take orders, but you are well

armed with the Hippocratic oath and you need take, therefore, no responsibility; you are not *allowed* to. That which you fear most you are protected from by medical law. You see, Dr. S. can't fool me and I despise him.

The collapse of Pamela at dinner, quite a gay little dinner, the kind that this particular hostess, a favorite of mine, always gives, was a shock to everyone but Dr. S. As for him, I distinctly saw him glance at his watch (an expensive one, a gift from a patient) just before it happened. I don't say he knew what the trigger was or why Pamela would pass out but I am ready to swear he knew it was time and that she would. He had fondled her psyche for the given time, she was hypersensitive, ready, and subtracting daylight saving time, a few healthy setbacks such as having won at tennis that afternoon and a new hat, something was due to happen and the old bastard (excuse the repetition) knew it. Pamela was trying to look after the gentlemen on either side of her but was staring across at Dr. S. at every pause. The doctor was looking rather well for him; it was as if the invitations had read, "decorations will be worn," while as a matter of fact we were all in business dress, the ladies in street clothes, our hostess having made a point of the informality of the dinner. Dr. S., nevertheless, wore a white tie (to be smeared later with lipstick) and actually, besides, the discreet but obvious little ribbon of the *legion d'honneur* (*La Comtesse de* ———————— followed him all over Europe in '41), ready for the kill, as it proved, dressed for the occasion; he even wore some male perfume that makes you smell the way women think you ought to.

Our hostess stood up; people stopped talking and mildly clapped. It was just before the *pièce de résistance* and we were hungry; we hadn't expected a speech so early. She looked very lovely and she turned her head from side to side, lifting her glass. The table shone with silver and smelled of tube roses and carnations, there was a servant for every three guests, Muzak was turned low. She made the following speech: "Listen *all* of you, this is a speech, please listen. This isn't like most of my parties, I am very serious. I have been reading so much in the newspapers and I am so sad, all of us are sad, aren't we, it makes me very unhappy to read the newspapers lately because people are hungry. Yes people are hungry, they are starving, really they are, and so I decided to do something for our poor starving neighbors, they are our neighbors. I think we should do something for poor unfortunate starving Europe and so (to the maid) wait a minute, Mason, I am going to do something unusual and I want to explain, I am sure you will agree with me. *Wait* Mason. I know you always think my little dinners are good but tonight I decided to do something different. I have guinea hen for you (cheers) but wait, I know it's perfectly awful but it's wicked in these times to waste anything and besides it's not *patriotic* and I thought it would help our starving friends in Europe so I told cook to serve the *legs*." Pause: we looked at each other. "The legs you know," my hostess went on, "the legs, too, and yes I think a guinea hen has second joints, not just the breast, we aren't having breast of guinea hen (proudly) we're going to eat *the whole bird!*" My hostess sat down blushing prettily; patriotism, generosity, was very becoming. The servants lowered the silver platters, turning aside their heads, decorously refraining from mingling their breath with the tantalizing odor of sherry, hot butter, sizzling plump flesh. The guests responded, with some grumbling from Mr. ———— who was seated in that neutral section of the table where one is neither loved nor respected by the hostess, who muttered something about thinking up his own charities and not having them thrust down his throat (legs! Ha, ha.), and licked the platters clean, as it were. My hostess was congratulated on her pretty speech, her Hattie Carnegie frock, and her cook. The lady on my right began to be jealous and decided to take her down a peg. "Really," she said, waiting for everyone's attention, "really, dear (to our hostess) but don't you think that this is the time to look our *best*, don't you think we should dine well and look our best to *encourage* those poor people, it encourages them, you know, what would *happen* to *Charity*, I mean if Society *starved* itself?" "That's true," said the lady on my left, "that silly affected Gandhi, what possible good did he do, he's neurotic, positively neurotic." "You mustn't kill the fatted *calf*" shouted someone from down the table. "It's a duck I think that laid the golden egg, or maybe a goose or something." Grumbler: "Sure it wasn't the jewelled toad?" At which the lady on my right clapped her hands, "Oh I *remember*, he was a darling, a big toad with a jewel on his forehead when I was a little girl!" We all looked at her queerly as if we were thinking the same thing, that she must have identified herself with the poor beast, she so successfully resembled him. But as I have said we devoured the guinea hen, thighs and all (they had pretty pink frilled panties on them); my hostess's cook, as a matter of fact, was such a clever thing she could have made door knobs palatable with a bit of amandine and I think she could have served buttered Chinamen and got away with it. Such was our sacrifice for starving Europe; and I looked around at the flushed cheeks of the ladies and secretly let out an inch in my belt. *Petite noblesse oblige.*

Pamela!

I was on my feet but the doctor reached her first. Her head lay sideways beside her plate, the only plate, I noticed, that had left its quota of guinea hen untouched; two guinea hen legs were neatly crossed like part of a coat of arms; a little bright currant jelly shimmered in the candlelight like congealed blood.

"Pamela!" "Pamela!" "Pamela!"

"Shut up," said Dr. S. and every last one of us did.

We must have looked like a ballet, suspended as we were; Dr. S., spotlighted, lifted our Pamela from the white cloth, a hand under each breast, and her head gently and gracefully fell against his shoulder, her bright red mouth kissing, it seemed, the *legion d'honneur.* He looked so pleased, so successful, so about ready to send in his bill that I would have liked to bash his goddam head in.

Well, Pamela's story follows; I shan't write it down as a case, undoubtedly as Dr. S. had it in his little black book, I'll simply tell it quickly as it was told to me: Pamela had been a lady's maid; had learned, unfortunately, ambivalent, as it were, ways; my lady's tastes and finicky pleasures she practiced, but she had the organs, one might say, of a servant. This, according to the doctor, caused a serious, miserable conflict in the girl (named oddly enough after that same

Pamela whose history was somewhat like her own). Her sufferings began in the servants' dining room. Leaving each evening her mistress's perfumed rooms, smoothing the linen sheets, brushing her sparkling hair, loved a little bit by her, in her confidence, mailing her lavender letters, pressing with a warm iron her precious panties, sniffing her high-toned flesh, mending tiny rents in fragile bits of this and that, making excuses for her over the telephone, teased a little by her beaux, putting away blesséd high-heeled pumps and curling up damp ends of her hair, folding her stockings and shading her night light—well—from that to the loud noises and vulgar camaraderie of the servants' hall, the butler in suspenders, the cook drunk on cheap sauterne and inhalations of onion and garlic! She never forgot the butler's snorting, silly, everlasting, "The Help Gets The Legs," when guinea hen was served. Need I go on? She could not eat; the dishes, the food, disgusted her. This very starvation enhanced her looks and, like that Pamela I have mentioned, she attracted the indecent attention of one of her lady's boyfriends; but she was virtuous and he married her. There is nothing much more to say; until, having bravely put it all aside, with the assistance finally (quite expensive) of Dr. S. she drew it out again and painfully, sorrowfully collapsed that night at the beautiful sweet smelling table of our hostess. "The Help Gets The Legs." Poor darling. But she is quite well now, quite well and quite a bore; we all know the details and Dr. S., being a good psychoanalyst, has cured her completely of her very becoming love for himself, the bastard; she's a plain girl now and I can't get over that look she has of wearing a little white cap.

A Tale

It might as well be told in the beginning that she was black. And she had other tendencies, too, if you know what I mean; anyone who has seen a number of colored girls knows that no white woman has that past-description, certain something, not exactly out of proportion, only to be described with the hands tenderly, gently; well, a Virginian great-aunt would call it a "behind" and an Elizabethan something worse. I refuse to call anything as beguiling anything at all, and the reader must imagine a dark girl with that certain something, not obvious, but peculiar, elegant, precise even, in that it was never out of bounds, never anything else but just it, the common denominator among colored girls, always charming regardless of the rest of the girl and worn amongst them, sometimes proudly, sometimes innocently, like a lovely little stern on a lovely little boat. Ready About! and it might take your aesthetic breath away.

The observer of such has seen it in an otherwise unattractive place going through a swinging door and the other everyday ugliness has been eclipsed. While no white woman likes to think, and understandably, that she is being followed by that unavoidable something, a dark girl will get into a closed car very bravely, the more willingly if she has a crazy savage little face; she happily takes her time, her best foot forward as it were, while her white comrade in consciousness tries, almost hysterically, to tuck herself in and sometimes gets in backwards, her fair face taking the glare and the applause.

This black girl had no heed to hide her face; she was beautiful, as anyone, even the most conventionally minded, would agree. She was black, yes; but forget it, everyone does. I can not say she was mauve or yellow. She was a negress. Call her a nigger if you are a Yankee and let me get on. Discover her anywhere and watch. Look, here she is: Sullen? No. Gay? No. Sad? Desperate? Irresponsible? Loving? Crazy? Wild? Innocent? Generous? Superstitious? Yes and no. Physically, she was, let us say, medium tall; one can't be sure; to judge height there must be comparison and when she was present no one else existed. I know her waist was small because I have seen it ahead of me in the street and the huge black hand of her escort nearly surrounds it, and besides a bright ribbon encircles it. I noticed at the same time that the backs of her knees were small and her calves high and round and shining, and her heels as they left her sandals were pink, believe it or not. And on top of all this, or shall I say behind it, that certain something, that extra-light syllable. What about her face? Look at me, don't smirk, I am describing you to a lot of ignorant unbelievers. Need I say it is black? I can not insist on that enough. Her eyes are bright and flaming as she laughs her wild colored-girl's laugh, and shows her shining teeth and red tongue, but in a moment they are filmed like a dog's; a little lavender curtain creeps over them before the final curtain with its fringe like a row of tacks, crashes down, and she is crying hard, complaining, moaning, swaying her body; her hands at her breasts.

Her hands? Her breasts? Why go on? She is beautiful and I can't say she was deceived either. How can you deceive a wily, knowing, courageous, soft-hearted, happy little bitch just because she is black? And he white? How can you say he took advantage of her innocence when she was born knowing and hoping and slept with her brothers and her cousins and all her kinfolk from babyhood whenever it was convenient or the nights chilly, or warm for that matter?

And besides she did it. She wanted him the minute she saw him; he reminded her of a blond girl she had seen her grandmother spit after in the street in uncontrolled hatred, and her quick feeling for him was a dizzy loving hatred, a kind of female-spider-love, a desire to get him over with. And her crazy gay laugh won his attention, and other things besides that I have mentioned, and together they looked like a sandwich, as wonderful for a third person to watch as anything in the world.

Of course he left her, you can't live in a crazy make-believe world for long when you're as blond and Anglo-Saxon as he was, and he hated her all the rest of his life, even more than he hated his wife, whom he later married, because she did the same thing to him in a mild way. And he chiefly hated her because he had loved her so, and it was that certain something that he held responsible, that extra-light syllable, that past-all-description, tenderly described with the hands as he described it to me and as I leave it to you to imagine if you want to.

What's in Two Names

Today's name reminded me of another and each, now, reminds me of each, so that it is not so much that the new love, the new name, has erased the old love, the old name, but has on the contrary revived it, reanimated it, set it humming and skipping through my head, turning little screws, putting on forgotten lights, bringing into focus, side by side with the new, the old, the nostalgic; that fragrant name: Consuelo Daly. And here is the new one: Angel O'Hara. My mind had wandered, perhaps in its own defense, from the news, but as my eyes had not left the page, after a while that name: Angel O'Hara looked out at me like a pair of eyes. I was probably daydreaming, unconscious of my subject matter, and the new name for some reason recalled to me the old one, as I have said, and the name of Consuelo brought quickly to my mind the person of Consuelo: that lovely girl; scenes, poses, turns of her head started slipping across my forehead like a movie film until, of an orderly disposition in spite of a certain absent-mindedness upon occasion, I had to cry halt. Wait a minute. Let's take it slower. A little order here. And finally, "Why Consuelo for Angel and vice versa?" But I gave up the latter question as too hard for the present and returned to Consuelo as very easy indeed, in fact a pleasure. "Consuelo had the delicate manners of a doll and did not mind my staring at her feet." But I must go even slower than that. "Consuelo lived in a bungalow on a grand canal (not Venice)." But wait a minute. "Consuelo, fragile but expert, swimming at my side disappeared and walked on the bottom of the sea talking with fishes." I was young and impressionable, who isn't?; I had my faults, who hasn't?; I was very imaginative and still am; all this sounds very stuffy to me in the middle of a reminiscence of Consuelo. I am probably excusing myself in some idiotic way when I need no defense. I loved her. I haven't loved anyone since I loved her. *Angel O'Hara?* I was twenty-six, now I am forty-two; is it possible I shall take up Angel where I left off Consuelo? It's quite possible. Consuelo Daly was a name to me at first, in fact for a long time I heard that nice, sweet, pretty name in the conversation of my elders on the beach, at the golf course, at the bridge table, I even saw it printed in the local newspaper. Consuelo was an actress, the only one of that profession who vacationed and finally settled down, commuting into town, scenting in a heavenly way the awful 8:15 and the frightful 5:02; in our part rustic, part spa-like strip of pleasant seaside on Long Island. Everyone else was respectable. Everybody could swim well, most of the girls got prettier every summer, went away to school in Connecticut in the winter, but no one ever changed. Consuelo was the only change for me and from loving her name I loved her person; her person, her queer free association mind that didn't use punctuation, her everlasting soul, I think, although that is debatable, I may be mistaken. I went away to school, myself, to camps in summer and to Harvard. I got to be twenty-six and the year was the same, '26. Consuelo who was my change remained the same, nevertheless and paradoxically. I have never known her age but she was certainly younger than I at twenty-six, although she had been older when I was fourteen. This sort of error is perfectly possible in arithmetic, which is at best not so precise a symbol of number as we presume and capable of mistake and impossibility* Consuelo reigned alone and supreme; all

---

*A child born a day before another is twice as old but does not remain so. It is impossible to trisect an angle.

the boys, and the girls as well, loved her, but I am positive that I, alone, became her lover. I do not say I was one in a million and I do not know what she did in other places, neither do I care who the men were who sometimes came to her bungalow for week-ends from somewhere else, but I repeat I am positive that I was one in a hundred-and-two which was the census (male and female) of eligibles to Consuelo's regard and confidence at Summer-Sea. Chronological as I would like to be for the reader's sake, I see now in technicolor that mauve July evening when she and I fought for breath and temporary supremacy over each other in an atmosphere almost devoid of oxygen, it seemed, so that we were angry and uncomfortable and wanted to quarrel when we had finished. Three giggling girls, I could count their heads as they passed the window, crept up the steps to the porch and ran away. Later, hopefully seeking a change of wind, a little breeze, we found at the screen door a drooping bunch of dahlias, pale pink, with a note, "We love you," signed: "The Mysterious Three." Not a bit vain, not curious, taking all things without comment, Consuelo felt most for the ugly pink dahlias, took the trouble to fill a big vase at the kitchen sink and gave them a drink on such a stifling night. The girls kept coming back in between the thunder showers that followed, hoping for a glimpse, I suppose, of my little mistress but she slept in the cooling night as quiet as death, on her back, her arms and legs apart like a March kite in a pink chemise. There was no room for me and I took a walk along Consuelo's Grand Canal (not Venice), got a brief nap at home and it was already hot again as I caught the 8:15 for town, still dreaming of Consuelo and smelling of her too, so much so that I thought people looked up as I passed.

I remember her as I first saw her actually with my eyes, not in a daydream, at twenty-six, no longer a lovely name by itself but a girl or perhaps a doll; she *was* like a doll with long, smooth, calcimined legs, pink ones (I am afraid I saw them first); they were the longest, the least hinged, the nicest on the beach. The other girls' suits I think were called "dressmaker," hers was in one brief piece and did not cover her thighs at all and the front of each of the latter was rose colored and the back of each calf, too, from the sun, but I stared at her feet. They were so little they were foolish, quite silly. I must have stared very hard and got absent-minded about it, too, because I suddenly felt sand in my eyes. Consuelo had flipped her foolish toes at me. I looked at her face and I thought there must be a triangular pendulum weight (I used to perform autopsies on dolls) in her throat that kept her eyes on the level because it was the level gaze of a doll; or there might be two holes in her face as she stood against the sky because her eyes were the same color and value as it was. Perhaps if she stood with her back to the wall they would be grey, I thought, and if against a tree in the woods, violet, and if I lay her down on the green grass, green, or if, as I soon did, on my pillow at home, a glimpse of bluish white before the little weight in her throat pulled them shut from her change in position; gravity.

I had no plans and it was her idea, although she did not mention it, that we swim out to the big yacht half a mile out. The air and sea were still and there seemed to be space beneath the yacht as if she hung in the sky but when we reached her half an hour later she was no longer suspended but clung to the sea, perspiring a little all over, trembling. Consuelo swam beautifully, if not according to Hoyle, quietly, without any fuss, her chin well out of the water, with arching back, so that only her waist was under water. I could see her round buttocks and pink heels; I wanted to take the two round halves of her in each hand and break her in two the way one firmly breaks an apple. (This was the only violent, but not very, impulse I ever had with her; the rest of the time I was a real sissy, sentimental, good.) I was certainly happy and I let her keep in the lead. But several times on the way she slowed down and let me slide by her, grazing her side, her hip, one long leg, all the way to her toes; once she nestled against my side, breathing easily, and I felt her chin in my neck and twice before we reached the yacht, swimming dead ahead of me, she submerged, turned on her back and I slid neatly over her as if she were a sand bar. I couldn't help laughing out loud. Even under water I could smell her vanilla-flavored perfume and I made a note of it. Then she frightened me; diving under, disappeared for ten minutes (I swear it). Where had she been? It's just as I said, she talked with the fish and when she reappeared a little way off she looked thoughtful, as if she ought to do something about it. She climbed up the ladder to the deck with me close behind her, my face at her waist. Our bodies became quickly cold as we left the water and our skins were so close to the same temperature that we hardly felt each other at all but the motion of our mutual climb was nice and I remember that item best, I don't know why. I can't remember what we did on board although it was the first time and I ought to, I suppose. I could swear, as a matter of fact, that nothing happened at all except that that was not the case. Half way back Consuelo put an arm around my neck and rested, floating lazily while I swam; she gazed nostalgically back at the big yacht and said that when she was rich someday she was going to have a yacht not so much that she really wanted a yacht as that she wanted to call it The Menopause. "It's a lovely lovely name for a yacht," she said. I suppose I ought to say here that Consuelo used words as she pleased but they always made better sense than other people's. Auspices was a tent and gubernatorial was baby talk, and Menopause was a wonderful name for a yacht; there is no doubt of it.

Well, all day long I dreamed of Consuelo Daly but after her name in my brain, sometimes in parenthesis, sometimes bracketed, appeared the new name: Angel O'Hara. Until, having exhausted my memories of the first girl, having fondled her, teased her, dwelt on her all day long, as I have said, I had the horrid ungrateful feeling that I must desert her for Angel, the new girl, and quickly; at once. I wanted to leave home, as it were, for something novel but not for something new. Angel O'Hara and Consuelo Daly were the same and not the same. Let's say I wanted to leave my love at home and look for her somewhere else.

Without much effort I found myself at ———'s where I was always welcome as was everybody else of any interest to ——— and everyone could go to ———'s who had had his name in the paper once or who was an extra man. As I was both and genuinely liked my hostess as well, which she appreciated, I always got kissed on both cheeks besides being called darling as everybody else was as a matter of course. If my hostess had bloomed in the Eighteenth Century she would certainly

92

have been called, without any nonsense or bones about it, a procuress, but all of us accepted her matchmaking in the spirit in which it was intended, whatever that was, and made our own choices. She kissed me as usual but at a distance, as it were, holding back her head, watching my eyes as they roved around the room passing over familiar brows, slim elbows, shiny hair-do's and nods of recognition, bird-like calls; looking for something novel. She waited for them to settle on something and they did. And in that split second, clever thing, she quickly whispered, "You're to sit next to her at dinner." Without any confusion at all she got us all seated just as she chose, to make us all happy, to please us, and thus please herself. "Who knows," her bright eyes seemed to say, "what will come of this; who will be sleeping with whom a week from now!" She stood pointing us into our places until we were all arranged and then sat down, herself, nodding to the servants to begin and beaming on us all as if she had fixed it so that one too many kittens could nurse at their mother's breast at the same time. My heart, in spite of my long experience, slowed to half its usual count and then began steadily pounding faster and faster as I turned (in fact I had not taken my eyes from her) to the girl at my left. *Angel O'Hara.* Tears came to my eyes as my nostrils caught a candy-like perfume and breathed it deeply in. A quick but fleeting remorse shot through me at the blue and level gaze of a doll, the small curved mouth, the same calcimined skin of my first love, my poor darling, as I gazed at my new one: *Angel O'Hara.* Hateful that I am, I am never at a loss for words even in emotion and I said, "Something smells good." "Could it be me?" and I nearly hated her for having the same high, childishly modulated voice as Consuelo. But I gave my sad thoughts, my remorse, a shove, as it were, and I was completely ready for this new girl. What luck! What an astounding, unbelievable coincidence and God bless my hostess! With the insight and confidence of one who has been around I did not hesitate to bend my head and lightly touch the girl's bare, pink shoulder with my lips. "Angel O'Hara," I said, "What a name! *Angel O'Hara.* I recognized you at once; you are lovely." "That Gangster's Moll! You're drunk." She laughed without offense and in five or six tones like a lot of bells until everyone near us looked up and stared with admiration as if it were a trick. "Consuelo" called our hostess. "To you, dear! who are so brave, so lovelier than ever!" and raising her glass she made everyone else do the same. Still I did not wake up and as I stood with the rest as if she were the queen, toasting her, I noticed that the part in her hair wasn't straight just as Consuelo's hadn't been. After a while, however, I became aware of the deception and I determined to ignore it. She is Angel O'Hara I said to myself and the coincidence is amazing. I knew her at once, which is extraordinary and wonderful, something I shall always cherish. If it is not true how explain my insight of this morning, my intuitive linking of the two vanilla-scented names? And what a pleasure it is going to be to renew my past love for Consuelo in this new girl, Angel. How everything, not scattered but continuous, will come back to me, intense, cherished, make-believe and real at the same time. I shall call her first thing in the morning and how nice not to have to guess and flounder around: I know the moment she will awaken expecting my call, no need of television to know that she eats toast burned on one side and white on the other; two pieces, cute; and that she won't wear flowers so I don't have to send them. How cross she would be and call me names ("*Idiot!*"), trying to peel that rubbery stuff off the stems and pulling at the ribbons ("*Stupid!*"). Maybe I will send some, for fun. On the way out (I left immediately after dinner to go home and anticipate my pleasures of tomorrow), later, passing the powder room, I overheard: "She is the famous ballerina; she is dancing her way through the menopause." I went on out. "But that is a yacht," I said out loud, "which is something they don't know. Hi, taxi!"

The Fifth Commandment

The queer thing about the girl was that she was so natural, naive, and gay, except when that dark look came over her; blotting out her blondness, not a blondness of nature but of spirit; transforming her as if she had had a twin sister (negroid) who had died in childbirth, leaving to her the double dejection of self-preservation for two: her sister's nurse, companion, supervisor, confidante, mother and father; doctor.

Don't think all this came from too many martinis (four to one) before dinner or the boredom forcing one back on his imagination which has become a comforting habit that I feel as I find my place after seating my partner at table. I never, either, ever took this especial girl in to dinner; she wasn't my type, my cautious hostesses thought, and so, seated between my sorority, as it were, my cousins, perhaps, blood relations, don't you know, witty, responsive, smarty-pants to right and left, girls with wet lips and dry martinis, I always saw, across the table for an entire season, that blond one. Possessing a slight presbyopia due not so much to age as to fear of proximity, my chosen (by my hostess) companions to right and left, so close that our elbows interfered and our thighs gave each other a certain family comfort, shimmered; the girl across the way was the only one in focus; the others looked rather nice as if under water; which reminds me of the girl I only loved underneath the surface of a super-de-luxe swimming pool which we chose as the one private place in which to confide our common tastes. (On dry land we had nothing in common and we never married because we could not find a pastor who could hold his breath long enough to perform the ceremony.) I stared at her without her seeming to notice or care. I felt that she was too far away to do me any harm; I even thought I could not be seen which as a matter of fact is true, not so much from the phenomenon of the far-sighted as the common reaction of the looked-at to look away. Having stared most of my life without realizing this and feeling the loss of being gazed at I learned only in the second decade to turn away. Then I felt the deep looks, the spade work, the curious return of women's eyes; the questioning, the warmth of their stares, the ticklish feel, almost of eyelashes, down the sides of my face, along my jaw, across my lips. I learned to open my mouth to receive this caress and often raised my handkerchief to see if there wasn't just a bit of mascara there; when I looked up the woman was naturally looking at someone else. But this girl, possessed, as I have said, of a dark look as if the lights in her part of the chandelier had gone out, would suddenly cease her blond give-and-take and at these moments turn her look to me; not to stare but for a change, it seemed, to go somewhere else, to get out of the room, and so our eyes would meet; but only in neutral territory, in the middle of the table, just over the flowers. It happened so often I felt as if I had left my eyes behind and hers too and I began to be curious; I daydreamed about her, began to build her up as if I were a child playing with blocks. One day just before lunch when with the approach of my tray (are there gastric juices in the brain?) I have often received minor insights into prolonged problems of no great importance, I said to myself (my dog always raises her head from a sound sleep when I think), "If I were a doctor she would love me; if I were a doctor she would lie in my arms." At this point, my dog, having been awakened by my thoughts from her slumber, thought she wanted to go out and not understanding me in the least, not following up her strange, instantaneous awakening sensibility, bounced around until I capitulated, let her out and slammed the door. I came back to the same place I had been sitting, assumed the same angles, sniffed my tomato bouillon (hummm: sage), tried to remember, but my insight was gone, at least it did not seem like an insight but merely a statement, and one of no consequence; like a retraction in a newspaper: Yesterday we stated that Francine Jackstraw of 102 High Street was arrested for lascivious carriage; it wasn't Francine Jackstraw but her cousin Francine Jackstraw of the same address. The next day as my luncheon was announced and as my dog (bitch) lay sleeping, the insight returned, but it was more practicable, more sensible, something within my reach (very decent of it). I, after all, could not begin the study of medicine and win that blond girl with the recurring dark look within the time that I could sustain my image of her, my desire for her; eight years would warp her pinkish vitality and bend my compulsion, make us old maids looking at a scrapbook, sisters. "Love her and you heal her; the lover is the doctor; the doctor the lover." The bitch raised her head and squinted at me nearsightedly. "Lie down!" Must I once again play the lover to know a woman? "Lie down!" How much pleasanter if, following my original insight, I could sit beside her bed preoccupied with my profession and accept her avowal, her love for me, in the form of a mysterious tale, satisfying my curiosity but not involving me in the same old love affair with just a change of heads. I remembered a corpulent and portable playwright whose aging talent taught him eccentric tricks to win the attention if not the loving kisses any more of dinner-party ladies; one of these tricks was to go out with the ladies from the dining room instead of remaining behind with the gentlemen. When he first began it people thought he was cute, talented, absent-minded, charming, and the women sustained their feminine eccentricities, gestures, bright eyes and slim ankles, nodding and teasing right through their Sanka and liqueurs, wearing themselves out completely and going home at once when joined by the other men as if they had been to two dinner parties in one night. Soon, however, they must have got used to him, accepted him as one of themselves, gossiped and talked about each other as if he were not there. That is what I would do. And that is what I did. I soon learned that my blond girl had broken one of the commandments; not the pleasantest, the sweetest one, the soonest forgiven, but one without reward of any kind, and these after-dinner ladies treated the subject as if asked what was the one thing they would take with them to a desert island it would be it. I went home after each party without any of the satisfaction I had hoped for. I wondered if with diligence I could read law nights, become a member of the bar, defend her from the charge, sleep with her, kiss her into oblivion. Murder! Would she feel better if I could persuade her it was manslaughter? Wasn't a lawyer somewhat of a doctor and hence a lover, wouldn't she creep into my arms and joyfully confess, linger over the details, retell and embroider it, kiss me, look into my eyes, be glad of her sinful introduction to satisfaction, repeating her story, changing it a little, modifying it, justifying her actions, blaming herself unnecessarily, re-live her childhood sorrows, dressing up for it, wearing her jewels, changing costumes, using her brightest lipstick? Wouldn't I taste her tears, be her accomplice and at the same time hold her in the palm of my hand? Satisfying her again and again without any effort or blame? Let her repeat her tale again and again; see her relaxed and exhausted at my feet after each retelling, my hand on her dark (no blond!) head; feeling so good, (me) so unguilty and loved forever by this funny girl who would never leave me, never shame me? "Lie down!" Case dismissed? What about the priest-hood? How long would that take? Was she a Catholic? Was I too late then? Was that dark look the shadow of the frock; that blond look forgiveness? Holding hands with a beastly priest! Father, am I forgiven; yes my child! Horrid incest of an hour every first of the month celebrating some moon custom, some rhythmic superstition? "For God's sake lie down!" If she isn't a Catholic I certainly haven't time to find a godfather myself, join the faith and pursue her with a prayer book and cross, chasing a skirt with my own skirts trailing (don't be vulgar), convert her.

This is the way I tossed and turned in my thoughts trying to think of a way of having her without making love to her, the only thing I really knew how to do, lacking a Ph.D. Why not? Wasn't she a sweet little murderess? That night she sat across from me again and I stared at her with a purpose. I was on solid ground; my sorority recognized my settling down to work. One stabbed me with her oyster fork; the other dipped two fingers in her *Chateau Margaux* and flipped the drops at my eyes. My hostess was annoyed at me for taking an interest in something at dinner and looked at me reproachfully. "I sent for the scallops all the way to Niantic Bay," she called to me. "Don't you think they're *good*." Mind your manners, her look said, this is a dinner party, I won't ask you again, she pouted. My girl friend on either side of me gave me up and began comparing hairdressers under my chin. The blond girl candidly returned my stare as if it didn't matter but I crossed the line of neutrality, jumped the flowers, joined her look on the other side of the table. This time I felt she went home with my eyes.

I spent all my time on her; I made love to her in the inimitable way for which I am noted and appreciated, and I might add, forgiven. A double row of ladies I had treated to the same enchanting and genuine approach seemed to line the street of my intention watching me with bright and loving eyes, almost cheering me on, but not quite, wondering if just this once I might turn the wrong corner, lose my love in an error of timing, a split second of preoccupation, *petit mal* as it were, loss of concentration. But I was steady; never let fatigue overcome me; I was happy doing my best work well, as usual; and glad I was back in harness headed for the stable door. I was brilliant, charming, intense, made friends everywhere, read a lot of books I had been kicking round, lost my feeling of boredom, regained the affection of a dozen women who had been feeling that my behavior (indifferent) was directed toward them, delighted my select group of hostesses for helping their parties to shine, wrote some letters, found my man some little jobs to do which pulled him out of the sulks and gave a couple of cocktail parties. In other words, I was at my best, in fine order; nothing creaked. But the girl did not behave according to Hoyle. The almost indecent beauty that distinguishes a woman in the first weeks of love was lacking. That nice, immodest glow, the innocent nudity of a woman in love, did not appear. The dark look came oftener and oftener. Still placed by my tactful hostesses (each not wanting to be the first to call attention to something that was perfectly obvious) opposite rather than beside me where I might perhaps have made the blond in her blush, I saw the shadow gain on her. It was not unattractive, outlining as it did the profiles in her face. The other faces in the light looked flat and dish-like, hers as if it were the corner of a little house, one side in the sun, the other in the dark. Only one side of her mouth was round and kissable, the other seemed to recede. I kissed both sides without favor, however. Once I said to her, "One side of your face is always in the shadow no matter where you are, why?" The shadow spread across her face like a blush; I looked at the window to see if the sun had gone under; for the moment she looked like a real brunette and the suspicion came to me that she was in a kind of continuous and willful disguise. I had forgotten my original curiosity. I was making love and busy. I had forgotten the subject matter, at least, of my curiosity; I was just curious. The strong drive of curiosity, the adamantine urge of finding out, intensified my own identity to such an extent that my mistress gradually began to lose hers, became no one in particular, harmless. Always interested in the queer behavior of lovers and constantly doing some research myself I believe that this observation of my own behavior may explain somewhat the behavior of lovers in general, always extraordinary to those who are not in love: the lovers seem to ignore the character and even the identifying features, even *shape* of the loved one; the woman can go to pieces before your eyes, but you seem unaware of what everyone else finds so apparent. I would not like to think that the person on whose existence one seems to depend, in this sense does not exist so I shall pursue this fancy no further for fear of becoming cynical which would hamper my talent as a lover. The moment arrived (naturally!). I was, for a suspended second, about to receive my degree: doctor, lawyer, priest; lover. She put her arms around my neck, her lips to my ear, and did it.

"I am a murderess."

"Yes, I know, darling."

Turning my face towards hers, noticing that her eyelids were so tight over her eyes that her eyeballs seemed flat, I gently opened her lips with my tongue, to make it easier for her to speak. (I couldn't have stopped her!) The sing-song of confession; the weariness of having finished; the fatigue of a fifth act, all having been accomplished, was in her tone. Her body was limp; she forgot to look the way she thought she looked and this is what she said: It is so awful I cannot bear it I am so tired. I did not mean to do it (Ha, manslaughter!). I am not trying to excuse myself and I would gladly give my life for hers but at the time no particular time I mean it was her life or mine (good). But I did not do it on purpose (that's what I mean) I did not know that life was sweet and besides it isn't since I must have done what I did. I simply mean one must know even a little girl that life is perhaps sweet not really but lots of things do you see what I mean? I am not sure about self-preservation I never really felt I suppose it is panic but what I did I did slowly oh very slowly. Nine months! (premeditation; bad) I had no one to advise me (please!) at least not exactly unless perhaps inheritance is advice perhaps that is exactly what it is but if it was good advice I didn't take it. I might as well tell you; I killed my sister. (Jesus!) No no not my sister (thank God) please listen to me I don't know. You will think it is funny (not very) but I don't know no one told me if it was my brother I don't feel so badly but I feel sick just the same my little undercover companion I lay in his embrace he in mine we must have sworn everlasting fidelity uncommon passion. And I took advantage of her I slowly and surely drank her blood stole her bones I took her nourishment the pigment even from her skin no she was the dark one but I have the color in my cheeks I have the blood beneath my skin which rushes to the surface if you so much as touch me that really should have been divided with her. She was jaundiced weak her sex never determined I was pink buxom female child as anyone can see. But they never unfolded her didn't want to bother her she was dead I did it (hmmm) Kiss me (ahh) harder,

longer. Oh when I am hungry I am disgusted; when I lie in your
arms I feel as if she too should be here my dark self my gloomy little
sister invisible, we are inseparable. We were identical, we are identical. Oh darling I feel better now. I never told anyone else; I never
had a lover, even now I am afraid of love and marriage, ultimate
companionship; it is hard to be twins, one of them dead, born dead,
without a single accusing word except identical accusation in one's
own brain; not you did it against which one might take a stand but I
did it which is undeniable. (ssssh, ssssh, my love.) It is so sweet to
talk! when may I do it again?"

"The next time, darling."

Our happiness was perfect and if I had doubts of my sweetheart's
wits I said to myself, "A simple neurosis; I am the doctor." And now I
have to let that idiotic dog out.

Mary Play

IDEA

Mary, in this play, is the mother of Jesus. She never recognizes that she is the instrument of Christ, which is the only way I can express an abstraction, in itself indescribable. God, himself, would forgive Mary her human behavior; let us, therefore, be generous. The action, which is Mary's inability to forgive, if that may be called action, is the content of the play.

Scene

It is the home, not glamorous, not pretentious, but spiritually adequate, of John where Mary in her simpleness, her lack of understanding which may be called sophistication, lack of it, has repaired immediately following the Crucifixion, which she has not understood.

CHARACTERS: MARY
                 MARY THE MOTHER OF THE CHILDREN OF ZEBEDEE
                 MAGDALENE
                 A SYMPATHETIC WOMAN (RACHEL)

There are no men present. (*No man can bear the aftermath, the sentimental throes following an action of cruelty and pain.*)

MARY [*nothing*].

OTHER MARY:
Be calm. It is over.

MAGDALENE:
Over?

OTHER MARY:
Be sensible. Yes, over.

MAGDALENE:
Over?

OTHER MARY [*nods at Mary*]:
This is no time for metaphysics.

MARY [*not sentimental, real*]:
Dear little Jesus, my little Jesus.

OTHER MARY:
How innocent she is.

[*Magdalene crosses herself. It is the first "sign of the cross" and Magdalene, making it, is not so much initiating a symbol as remembering the shape of the body of her Lord and lover. She tilts her chin, languorously raises a curved right arm and with an extended index finger, a becoming gesture, with curled digits, touches first her lovely brow, divided, wrist out, her breasts, then hesitation, a caesural pause, as it were, touches iambically first her right shoulder and, describing a shallow arc, her left. As if weary, then, her arm falls wrist down, fingers following and the expression of her face is bright with recollection.*]

MARY [*doesn't see any of it*]:
The pain is the same in my breast as when his sweet head was there.

OTHER MARY:
Sssh. Let her go on; it will do her good.

MARY:
That great man upon the cross; I thought only of my little lad.

MAGDALENE AND OTHER MARY [*nothing; significant looks*]:

104

MARY:

When he was grown I could not understand him but when he was
little I was everything to him; he came to me; he loved me, the dear
lad.

MAGDALENE [*wise*]:

If she could not understand the full grown man, how could she understand God?

OTHER MARY:

Shame on you with your logic; who taught you to reason at such a
time?

MAGDALENE:

Jesus did. And at such a time.

OTHER MARY [*at a loss*]:

Well, then, be quiet anyway.

MARY [*frustrated*]:

Why, why, why?

MAGDALENE:

I can tell *you.*

OTHER MARY:

Be still.

MARY:

I cannot bear it. He did not look at me. I am his mother but he did
not look at me.

MAGDALENE:

His gaze was on his God, his father.

MARY:

Father!

OTHER MARY [*gently*]:

Yes, dear Mary.

MARY:

But I am his mother.

MAGDALENE [*seriously, persistent*]:

You were. His Father is.

MARY:

Don't humiliate me.

MAGDALENE [*bowing, a little stuffy*]:
I revere you.
MARY [*angry, jealous*]:
You were his mistress!
MAGDALENE:
No, no. It is not so.
OTHER MARY:
Excuse her.
[*A knock; enter a sympathetic woman (Rachel). All the women pull themselves together; even Mary smiles; welcomes the stranger. Other Mary goes out, returns with refreshments. During these few moments each woman is at her best; everything is put aside; each is gentle; each gazes at the newcomer with sympathy, hospitality.*]
SYMPATHETIC WOMAN:
I had to come.
OTHERS:
Of course; sit down; will you have some . . . It is dark out, isn't it? Will you take off your wraps?
SYMPATHETIC WOMAN [*shy*]:
I came about . . . Mary.
OTHERS [*bustle a little; say nothing*].
SYMPATHETIC WOMAN [*intense*]:
Mary, I am your friend.
MARY [*stiffly*]:
Thank you.
SYMPATHETIC WOMAN [*literal*]:
No, don't thank me; what have I done?
OTHERS:
Mary is so polite.
SYMPATHETIC WOMAN:
Oh, I see.
MARY:
I am quite all right.
SYMPATHETIC WOMAN:
Perhaps I had better go.

OTHERS:

Oh, do stay.

SYMPATHETIC WOMAN [*makes effort*]:

Mary, Mary.

MARY [*looks up, her dark eyes miserable*]:

Yes?

SYMPATHETIC WOMAN:

I, too. I, too, forgive me, I was not the mother of such a son; but I, too . . . I also . . .

[*The others look at each other.*]

SYMPATHETIC WOMAN:

But you knew him, yours; loved him, fed him, kissed him, yours; watched him grow up, heard his first words, yours.

MARY [*gloomily*]:

And his last. [*She sobs.*] They were not for me.

ALL [*trying to comfort her*]:

Ssh . . . Ssh . . . Ssh. There, there.

SYMPATHETIC WOMAN [*brave*]:

I have not spoken his name since his death, his murder. My boy, my man, my lover, torn from my two arms. [*She bares them; they are firm and pink; it seems unbelievable that they have been denied anything.*]

ALL [*interrupting*]:

Herod!

SYMPATHETIC WOMAN:

God damn him!

OTHERS:

Ssssh.

MARY:

Don't sssh her.

SYMPATHETIC WOMAN:

My sweet baby [*turning to Mary*] like yours, my dear little love so warm and soft against me, I was his only one, his sweetheart. [*She forgets he is gone and seems happy.*] Oh, Elias, I am not lonely.

[*Others weep for her.*]

MARY [*eager*]:

Go on.

SYMPATHETIC WOMAN:

They came in the night, let's see, it was about, oh, well, let's say it was seven. [*She suddenly remembers.*] Oh my God, Jehovah.

MARY [*leans forward as if eager for more, something else*]:

Finish! What happened?

SYMPATHETIC WOMAN:

He was at my breast, this one. [*She gesticulates; stops.*]

OTHERS:

Yes, yes.

SYMPATHETIC WOMAN [*frantic*]:

I smell their beards, the evil smell of their boots.

ALL:

Tell us! Tell us!

SYMPATHETIC WOMAN:

One big one stooped and kissed me on the mouth.

OTHERS:

No! No!

MARY:

Ahhh.

OTHERS:

Kissed you? Kissed you?

SYMPATHETIC WOMAN:

I feel it now; and he tore my child; ahhh ripped my baby from me as if it were his birth. I bled with his cruelty. My mouth and breast were covered with blood.

OTHERS:

Blood!

MARY [*unlike herself*]:

Women cannot be cured of blood. Blood is their nature. Jesus felt sorry for bleeding women. My son. [*She looks proud.*]

SYMPATHETIC WOMAN [*cannot stop*]:

I heard the confusion in the street and I remember the noise and the shouts; I cannot remember my child and I don't know what the monsters really did. I remember the kiss, the stamping of boots; I smell the dust and the beard of the creature that kissed me but I cannot remember my round white boy. What is the matter with me?

OTHERS:

Never mind, never mind.

SYMPATHETIC WOMAN [*recovers*]:

But I came to help Mary.

MARY:

Me?

SYMPATHETIC WOMAN [*calm*]:

Yes. You at least, my dear, saw the slow, or should I say rapid growth of your beloved child. You saw his hair grow long in ringlets and you cut it sadly off with pleasure in its feel; you watched it change from yellow to brown, bronze to inky black. You watched his looks change from innocent to knowing. You thrilled that he knew. You pitied his wisdom. You saw the baby into boyhood into maturity and you knew that you were his first love. I had none of that.

[*She describes a kind of love Mary never had and Mary grows somber but will not admit anything. She blames God.*]

MARY [*somber*]:

It wasn't like that.

RACHEL [*passionate; feels it must be so*]:

It must have been; it must have been.

MARY [*jealous, cruel, penetrating*]:

You are not thinking of me; you are telling about yourself because you described the color of your own child's hair, not mine. Jesus' hair was red. [*It is as if she had won a point.*]

[*Looks are exchanged; no one loves Mary when she is like this.*]

MAGDALENE:

Rachel's sorrow is greater than yours, Mary.

MARY:

How dare you! How really dare you!

MAGDALENE [*insists*]:

You should be pleased; that's all.

OTHERS:

Magdalene, Magdalene, have pity.

MAGDALENE:

Holy images are made of her and sell like cakes. Jesus said . . .

MARY:

No. No. No. I saw you; I know what you are; don't speak his name to me. You, you who seduced him. [*She hangs her head.*] Ahhh, how angry he would be at me.

MAGDALENE:

Yes, he was often very angry at you.

MARY [*conventional*]:

He should never have spoken of me to you.

MAGDALENE:

He pitied you.

MARY:

Pity! Pity, he had no pity.

OTHERS:

Ssssh. Ssssh. Ssssh.

MARY [*gentle*]:

But it was not his fault; he loved me; he was always at my knee.

MAGDALENE:

As everyone knows. That is how you are represented in all the galleries.

MARY [*ignores her*]:

John took him from me. I hate the memory of John. He made a gentle lad into an ambitious man.

OTHERS:

Jesus? Ambitious!

MARY:

Could he have had his way as he has, without ambition? He insisted. He was willful; he left no stone unturned to fulfill the prophets, to maintain the word. Even on the cross he remembered what to say and said it. And he sacrificed his mother. It was John who led him on with his catchy, "Repent: the Kingdom of Heaven is at hand!" and Jesus, in his sweet voice, his soft ways, repeated John's "Repent: the Kingdom of Heaven is at hand!" My little boy with his big words! I cannot bear it. He was willful and impressionable.

OTHER MARY:
We all must suffer, be calm; all of us must suffer.
MARY:
But I am special!
MAGDALENE [*amused*]:
What?
MARY:
The angel said so.
OTHERS:
Yes, Mary, we all believe you.
MARY:
Why must I suffer if I am special?
MAGDALENE:
That was the price of your halo.
MARY:
I did not ask. I did not ask. If it is true, now, as they say, that he has
returned to his Father, what about me? I will not forgive God for this.
No. Never.
MAGDALENE:
How funny!
MARY:
Stop; you ought to go away; you are evil and you hurt Jesus' reputa-
tion; you really harmed him. You followed him as shamelessly as all
the others and he was easily attracted by women of your sort. They
hung around his house; I was disgusted; I really was disgusted. [*She
looks around.*] I was!
MAGDALENE:
He forgave me my sins.
MARY:
Not I! I won't!
MAGDALENE [*kneels*]:
Hail, Mary.
MARY:
Go away, go away.
OTHERS:
Leave her, some of it is true.

MAGDALENE [*exalted*]:
Jesus made me pure.

MOTHER OF JAMES AND JOSEPH:
It usually goes the other way, you might have corrupted him. Leave
his poor mother alone. You really are quite a hussy you know.

MARY [*is sobbing but lets out little sentences*]:
She is still a harlot; she was fooling him. Ahhh! she slept with him.
Have I not borne enough without the insult of that red-haired woman?
I saw their eyes meet even on Calvary Hill! I looked for his look but
he would not look at me; he looked at her.

MAGDALENE [*proud, learned*]:
It is true. Only St. John places her specifically, by name, at the scene
of the Crucifixion, while I am named by them all as being there:
Matthew; Mark; Luke; John. I could write another Gospel. The Gospel according to Mary Magdalene.

MARY [*very white*]:
I cannot bear it. [*She sleeps.*]

[*As she sleeps, she is outlined in a pinkish light; a plate hanging on
the wall behind her head seems to be a blue halo; her head inclines
until her chin rests in the hollow of her shoulder which is bare.
Sleeping, she uncovers one of her breasts and her long white hand
supports it. This picture is for the audience rather than the women
in the room, with the exception of Magdalene, who steps forward
and quickly arranges the folds of Mary's garments, then as quickly
stepping back, kneels in the shadow, her long hair falling over her
shoulders.*]

RACHEL [*rises, matter of fact*]:
Well, I must go. Let her sleep, poor thing. [*She looks at Magdalene,
who has got up and is folding her hair into the nape of her neck.*]
Where are you going? Are you coming my way; it is so dark.

MAGDALENE:
He will appear to me first; I must look nice. [*She whispers: St. Mark.*]

RACHEL [*curious*]:
It is true that he cast seven devils out of you? What did it feel like?

OTHER MARY [*interrupts, laughs*]:

There are some left.

[*Everyone smiles.*]

MAGDALENE [*intense*]:

I would give anything for it again, just as it was. Nothing ever felt so good, so wonderful. He didn't do it all at once; he held me in his arms seven times. [*She glances at the sleeping Mary.*] Seven times we were lovers. He promised to come back to me first of all. I am going to see him again very soon and I am going to be ready. [*She genuflects to Mary, backs out of the room with grace, is heard laughing happily outside.*]

[*The scene is the same: Other women begin coming into the room; chairs are found for them; the conversation takes on a gossipy tone although many of the women show signs of tears and real fatigue. Through the open door and a window with a white curtain billowing in, the crowd can be seen going back down Calvary Hill. They are noisy; there is argument and some ribaldry; the soldiers go by with a clatter. "The disciple Jesus loved" looks in; (it is his house), says, "Is she all right?" "Oh, yes," say the woman, cheerfully. He withdraws.*]

OTHER MARY [*after a pause*]:

Tell me, is it true that Salome was there?

SOMEONE:

I didn't see her.

SOMEONE ELSE:

I did.

OTHER MARY:

How did she look?

SOMEONE:

She stood to one side.

OTHER MARY:

I should hope so.

ANOTHER:

I only heard someone say, "Salome is here." I didn't see her.

SOMEONE:

I saw her with my own eyes; she was crying.

SOMEONE ELSE:
Was she ever baptized?
SOMEONE ELSE:
That would be too much.
SOMEONE ELSE:
I saw her clearly.
SOMEONE ELSE:
But she is married and rich now. What need has she for Jesus then?
SOMEONE ELSE:
She married Zebedee.
[*Enter Salome and her daughter, Veronica. Veronica comes forward; Salome hangs back.*]
VERONICA [*very young, excited*]:
I lent him my handkerchief!
[*Magdalene re-enters.*]
VERONICA:
It shall be a holy heirloom for my children.
MAGDALENE [*sarcastic, jealous*]:
And a keepsake for the Pope.*
[*Salome moves slowly and voluptuously into the room and everyone is reminded of the part she is supposed to have played. (Music from R. Strauss's Salome.) She moves in hearsay rather than in fact; in the memory; and her audience of women is in direct contrast to the original one so well described by Flaubert. This one is not sympathetic. Mary wakes up and loses her halo and pink light.*]
MARY [*stares; nothing*].
SALOME [*to Mary*]:
I've heard so much about you.
MARY [*dignified, angry*]:
I am of no consequence.
SALOME [*goes on*]:
I feel terribly about what people say I did. I didn't mean to if I did.
MARY [*passionately*]:
Don't apologize. I hate John! He deserved everything.

---

*It is.

114

[Everyone in the room appeals to Mary. Someone shuts the window and the door but Mary is sure of herself and standing, looking tall, she makes the following speech.]

MARY:

I don't know why John was chosen to instruct Jesus; I could have done it myself. I know that everything was written. I know we were all instruments but John was vulgar and coarse; I don't know how Jesus, who was so gentle and well-bred, could put up with him at all. Jesus knew what was to become of him and accepted it like a dove whose destination is planned by another, but John made the most of his position and flaunted it from all the house tops and he did not even bother to wash. *[Magdalene at intervals while Mary gives a horrid description of John: Donatello? Leonardo? Michelangelo?]* He was false. He couldn't fool me; he didn't quite come off, did he? And his dirty boots, his shaggy hair! He fulfilled the law of the prophets but he did it without dignity or submission, without charm. He was vain, boisterous, dirty, rude; he did not have to scream at Herodias and curse her and he deserved her revenge; she was a woman of spirit and John insulted her in public. He was without sympathy, arrogant, too, and he had no real talent; he wasn't genuine. Why did God let Jesus be baptized by such a man? It is another reason why I shall not forgive God, ever. *[Sssshh!]* The company Jesus kept! He was my child but everybody else's companion. I conceived him but I couldn't understand him. I never really had a son any more than I had a husband. Oh, I was terribly fooled. Joseph never got over all the adulation and fuss. *[No, Mary, No.]* At first he was angry and said he wouldn't marry me but then he said he had seen the angel, too, and he was willing—willing! He said, "Until this child is born I shan't touch you," but afterwards I was obliged to submit to his timid manifestations. *[Well, you know, well.]* Joseph was a good man but not an angel so it was quite different, I can assure you. *[The women all hang their heads.]* You are all married to good men and so you know what it is like. *[She pauses; no one says anything. She continues.]* I was a virgin, it is true, betrothed to Joseph; I didn't know any better; I was contented until the angel made me happy! *[Listen!]*

MAGDALENE:

Ahhhh. Why do you complain?

MARY:

Because I was fooled; tricked by an angel.

MAGDALENE:

Was he pretty? Like the pictures? With a skirt on?

MARY [*sweetly, as we know her*]:

Oh, he was beautiful.

MAGDALENE:

How? How was he beautiful? Be specific.

MARY [*softly*]:

Like a girl; like myself as I imagined myself in daydreams; how could
I be afraid, then? There were no trumpets; the Heavens didn't open;
I wasn't a bit startled. It is true he wore a sort of skirt, flowered all
over.

MAGDALENE:

It's called a Botticelli print.

MARY [*continues; silence*]:

He called me Blesséd; I loved him for his voice alone; it had no edges.
Neither did anything that happened; when he touched my shoulder
there was no outline to his touch. I heard him say, "I have been sent
to love you; I am no one in particular. Are you afraid?" I only looked
at him and began to feel my happiness. As he came still closer I felt
I could bear no more than the introduction I already had of love;
tears came into my eyes and I wanted him to wait but I could not
speak. I was surrounded by my feeling and when he placed his hands
on either hip I did not feel his hands, as I have said, but only an
intensification of delight. [*Silence.*] I felt my lips turn up at the
corners; my tears slid aside into my ears as my cheeks rounded out and
I turned up my face. But he did not kiss me. Through a kind of music
in my ears I heard his warning but did not grasp its content. "We may
not play and I may not come again." I continued smiling; how could
I be critical? Or demanding? There were no promises, no pacts; we
did not swear to be true to each other or think of gifts. Again I heard
the angelic voice, "It is just this once," and I did not fret. We did not

lie down because there was not time to plan anything. [*Silence.*] He slid his hands down the inside of my thighs, separated them, and it is impossible to describe to any of you my happiness or my regret as it began to slip away from me. Just before it was finished I felt his curls against my neck although he was taller than I, and as my lowered eyes again came into focus I saw the designs of our two flowered skirts intermingled. [*She sobs.*] So pretty.

MAGDALENE [*in tears*]:

Mary, Mary, darling, how good you are.

[*All the women have listened intently; their expressions changing as Mary's story unfolds. Her description of the Visitation is so palpable and told so sweetly that as she tells it, it is as if she were still the Virgin she describes and all the women remember their own innocence, their own happiness or disappointment, as it may be, and all of them, as Mary finishes, shed a few tears. I cannot emphasize enough the genuine Virgin Mary who appears in Mary's description of herself and hence the absolutely innocent response of all, even Magdalene.*]

SALOME [*as Mary recovers*]:

Tell us some more; it's wonderful.

MARY [*revulsion*]:

It wasn't fair to fool me; I could have been reasoned with; I wasn't stupid, was I?

MAGDALENE [*like Portia*]:

Would you have accepted *tonight*? Can you truthfully say you would have preferred to be reasoned with *at the time*?

RACHEL [*interrupts*]:

Magdalene, ssssh. Mary, tell us about Jesus when he was little.

MARY [*willing, talkative*]:

I tried not to spoil him but what could I do? Everything and everybody conspired against me. I did not want all the presents, all the attention; I didn't want him to think he was different; I wanted him to play with other children but his father liked him to show off with older people. There wasn't anything he didn't know the answer to. He soon sensed that he was not loved for his superiority and although at first he cried, after a while he cherished the antagonism he invited, really cherished it; went off by himself and kept forgiving people which irritated them even more. I liked Bethlehem; I didn't want to leave; then when I got settled in Egypt I had to come back to Nazareth. I should not have let a little boy tell me what to do but he said everything with authority, in spite of a kind mildness, meekness, that made me angry; like his father, like Joseph.

MAGDALENE [*interrupts*]:
What?

MARY:
Yes, Joseph was positively stupid.

MAGDALENE [*quite gently*]:
But what about the pretty angel?

MARY:
You are insulting me!

[*Everyone is confused; Mary seems really to have forgotten her so recent recitation, wants to go on with her present line but Magdalene won't let her.*]

MAGDALENE:
Listen, Mary, are you the mother of God?

MARY:
I am Jesus' mother.

MAGDALENE:
Do you believe in the Virgin birth?

MARY [*stares at her, remembers, is sullen*]:
It happened like that.

MAGDALENE:
Don't you know that Jesus was also Christ, that he is God?

MARY [*genuine*]:
I cannot conceive of it.

MAGDALENE:
But you did!

MARY:
Leave me alone.

MAGDALENE:

You have got to face the abstract.

MARY [*turns on her*]:

You were his lover! I saw you! Is that abstract!

MAGDALENE:

I am proud of it. We were the act on which the symbol of the church
will be based. He shall be called the bridegroom and the lover of all
believers; many women shall leave their husbands and their children
to follow your Jesus, so you might as well get used to it. I've got to.
[*She crossed herself.*]

VERONICA:

May I go to the resurrection with you, Magdalene? Mother, may I go?

MAGDALENE:

You will not be there and it doesn't matter, but I wish Mary would
come although she will not. She cannot come even if she would,
which she won't. Even God cannot change Mary nor give her back
her son. What he has done he cannot undo.

MARY [*like a little girl*]:

I could come if I wanted to but I don't want to.

MAGDALENE [*laughs*].

MARY [*furious, terribly upset*]:

I have no intention of going. I cannot bear it any longer; I can't stand
it; I can't stand the pain. "Woman what have I to do with thee!" I
can't stand it if he comes back! [*Mary suddenly tells the truth.*] *I'm
glad he's dead!*

> [*And with this shocking statement which Mary makes possibly as
> the result of her long autobiographical speech and Magdalene's tor-
> menting insistence, with this catharsis-crisis, the play ends and it is
> Easter.*]
> [*There is the sound of Easter music.*]

From Morning Till Night or

The Daydreamer

She began to be really frightened. She couldn't think of anything
else. By else she meant anything not pertaining to it. And yet so
much pertained to it; all things reminded her and led her so confi-
dently toward it that to say that there was anything at all that didn't
pertain to it might be false. Perhaps she was all right then and besides, even if one thing did fill her mind, what of that? Was there
something outside of it that should be thought of? That ought to
be thought of? Was it then a moral question? Should and ought
suggest a moral must. Must she then? But why? Who was doing
the judging? She herself was doing it. Could she be two people?
How could she judge herself? Well, she was I and she was me. I
judge me. At least it is grammatical. But it isn't sensible. Why must
she appear to be forcing herself to some kind of choice? Why not go
on as she was? Why, when you are sitting in one place, must you get
up and sit somewhere else? Didn't she like what she was thinking

about that she was trying to make trouble for herself this way? How long ago had she begun to be disquieted? And even if she could trace her way back to any period of realization, the exact time, or point, when she began to doubt the wisdom of her course, her mental course, was that a constructive thing to do? Whenever that time had been, it was passed. Much trickling of the stream had gone on since that point, if it actually existed at a given second, when she might have, if she had been aware enough, dammed the flow and the on-slaught which had gathered such force and momentum, that at one high point and watermark only would it have been a powerful and superior thing to do, and not an exhausting search for all the little streams that flowed now into huge fields and swamps and down drainages and even into ant holes. How could she stop them all, dis-integrated like that and spreading and sinking into the ground? She couldn't just yell "Stop!" and expect results. And besides, was there an end to a certain subject matter in the mind? Do you get all you can out of it, exhaust yourself, and it, and quit? Drop it, leave it, go away? She was sure she didn't know. What did other people do? But she wouldn't do what they did in any event; so let's drop that one. Action. Of course she had heard of that. Stop thinking and do something. Well, there was plenty of time for that in a real emer-gency. There was no need to be as drastic as all that and besides, it implied a decision based on the wish to change, to be different, not to do it anymore. And she certainly had not reached by far and away any such conclusion as that. And not do what? What, may I ask? She was not going to answer that one and spoil everything. Why make a statement at this point? For publication, as it were, to yourself, which is certainly unnecessary, if not absurd. Really silly, even. If she didn't know what she was doing, so much so, that she had to eliminate unnecessary data, et cetera, and state explicitly in five hundred words what it was she was doing and then put it up to her-self, present herself with a short and brilliant brief on the subject, well, then what? She'd have to reply to it wouldn't she? Really! And then there would be two minute refutations and finally a decision in favor of one side or the other. Would that end it? She certainly wouldn't give in exactly to either side. How could she when she would do all the work, present all the argument, make all the speeches and listen to them as well? And all the while the subject matter would be developing and increasing and enlarging in her mind. New stimuli would start new avenues of imagination and research. Back over what had happened her thoughts would race while waiting until she had finished the recollection to proceed to a wish or a desire unnamed but delicately seeking fulfillment in her thoughts. And at that hair's breadth of space, where yesterday's doings had been gone over, surveyed in reminiscence, and enhanced by choice and elimination of the doubtful or even unintelligible, because unexplored, being suppositions that could end in the undesirable and even heartbreaking, at that hair's breadth of space, where the past and the deliciously unknown that was already forming in her imagination, would begin to weave the story-like wish, that, too, would walk hand in hand with the reminiscence culled from actual happening, like brother and sister, nostalgic for each other's childhood, lovers without portfolio, down the avenue of her mind, related and beloved, alike and unlike, created by her, in one instance by her strong interest and desire that it be true, and potential and probably in its logical sequence, and in the other (instance) lifted from the actual, chosen bit by bit and artistically and truthfully arranged, eliminating the dangerous and supposititious, and then, in that hair's breadth, in which the past and the future of her mind hesitated, stood on tip-toe, held its breath, in that small space, which was her only present, her only time for a decision, must she make it? In that strangely empty but exciting, because it would so soon be over, present, must she pull herself together and say, "No?" "No" to the sweet brother and sister past and "No" to tomorrow's possibilities, already moving about and forming in her mind, so used were her thoughts to her pattern and technique and waiting only for the subject matter and even the subject matter, if not the doings of the subject matter, anticipated? "No"? Was she then to say just that, "No"? Who did she think she was anyway to give the no to the pleasant monkeyshines of her mind? How like a cop she looked, standing there, holier than thou and those she had herself created, in the sense in which she had already made clear to herself. Besides how silly and trepidatory of her to get frightened now, when she had become so expert; when she had all the material she could possibly use put away in her head, so that if she did not have actual contact with reality again for a long time, she would be busy. And there was so much that she had not finished yet, how wrong to waste it, when as she said, she had become so expert. Here she was, she could carry such a lot in her head, while she waited to catch up, that it was amazing for one who had never been very smart at mathematics; but exciting and strenuous, too, and sometimes positively exhausting. Interruptions annoyed her badly, were really a shock to her mental system, and sometimes when she was especially alert, it was an effort to keep things consecutive and straight, and difficult to a degree to keep in order the loop of events, like a lot of names in a receiving line, when the person next to you was too slow, and the person on the other side, who was presenting the guests, was too fast, at least too fast, not for you, you could manage all right, but the person beside you, who was dawdling, and so the names looped up and so it was in her mind without a moment's respite. But that simply meant how pressing and terrific the business of her mind had become. Really business was good and she could handle it, she wasn't complaining, how awful if it were slow; if supply and demand were unequal in inverse ratio; how really boring if there just wasn't enough material, but demand sent the prices up, and she would do so well financially that she could rest, take a vacation, even retire and go to Florida, go fishing, see a few friends or maybe write a book; do something, make a name for herself. Good Lord, how terrible, what a bore, how really ghastly. That *would* frighten her. And just when she had the whole thing so perfected, how characteristic of her to get restless and want to drop it! Was she nothing but a stupid woman with impulses only, and temporary desires and shifting ambitions, now this, now that, look at me, aren't I smart and the next minute tired of it, fed up, restless, let's go to the theatre, why don't we ask the neighbors in for bridge, I want to flirt and make love, and be sick, have a headache you know and pains, pleasant pains, or maybe have a baby and every-

123

thing stop, stop in its tracks and watch me, love me, cry over me. Is that what she was like? She was not! Thank God for small favors, she wasn't a complete idiot. But was she mad? That was different of course from being a fool. She could be mad and brilliant; brilliantly mad. The beautiful long sentences of her imagination she sometimes spoke aloud, dangerous as it was and disturbing, it took so long to speak and things looped up, slowed her down, so that she had to work harder to catch up, be there, in the very burning center of herself, clear and beautiful and exciting, wordless in the sense that words are spoken, but speaking in the sense that speech is wordless. "Whereof ye cannot speak thereof ye shall be silent." What a waste! What? Was that it? Had she caught herself? Red-handed, bloody? Was it waste that bothered her? New England again, no doubt. Doubtless, without a doubt, indubitably. New England, for gosh sakes. Wasted on whom? Must the activity, the energy of her mind, be given to whom? Perpetual as it was, could it be wrapped up and passed around? In itself there was no waste, there were no leftovers, nothing to be warmed up, no, that was just the point. There was a beautiful lack of waste. The perfect mechanism in her head was adequate to itself and perpetual, if that was what was worrying her. Who screamed "Waste" at her? There was no waste. After all she was not frightened. Not when there was an argument about it, anyway. She was capable of defending herself. Defense of her practice made her strong. But it was her tremendous responsibility that scared her a little. Oh, what a cold, little, shivering, miserable, haunting, shameful, powerful rhythmic, actual, deadly, thank-God-so-soon-over fear! So soon over, that in one's brave hours one sometimes dared to imagine it back, in order to catch it and find out what it meant when it wasn't looking, as it were, when it didn't have the advantage of having got there first. Yes, only the brave ones, not quite gone in terror, had the courage to try and bring it back by the ears like a rabbit, and actually succeed sometimes in doing so, only after giving it the cuff it deserves, to have it come hopping back, weeks later, ahead of schedule, when you weren't ready for it, to say the least, and lie in wait until in your most aware and scintillating moment, there it was, "I am it!" Only the bravest can keep from moaning, "I don't want to die" and only when you are at your best, as she said, does that hateful little beast appear, lit up by the searchlight of your mind, because of course you want to know terribly, even though you deny its existence and don't seem to believe in it at all, but you yourself, without telling yourself, light it up and for an instant, there it is, that nasty, smart, here-I-am-again little brute. "I am going to die." "No! I am not!" and it is gone. Put on the light. What time is it? Where was I? and how annoying to be interrupted by something you are looking for but don't expect! It is the others who shall die and I am sorry but where was she? Oh, yes it was her tremendous responsibility, her daily and hourly expanding business, her industrious, well managed what-was-it, that frightened her, but before she went too far in that direction she ought to state clearly why the fear of responsibility re-sembled so closely the fear of death, so much so, that it seemed to be actually the same thing. As a matter of fact, a phrase she didn't like, but there was hardly time for a better one now, when was it that she had found out that responsibility was so frightening, such a white rabbit of a fear, such a clear-cut, white, shining, gleam-in-the-dark, cold, god-damn-it, really-kind-of-thing-not-to-speak-to-at-all to tell the truth, kind of fear? What was wrong with her now, that she couldn't even accept her own conclusions, knowledge well represented, and proven propositions deduced from previous propositions, and ask herself at this point, with so much to be done, and so much pleasure to have, backwards and forwards, where she had left that little bundle of notes in her head about responsibility? For goodness sake, go on from there; if she couldn't follow herself she was certainly slipping, but she ought not to be irritated. A lot of smart people wouldn't be able to follow her, that is, if she knew a lot of smart people and she didn't, she didn't know any smart people, period. Well, little white beasts, whether or no, and notwithstanding certainly, or sitting either, oh, oh, stop that. The idea was, that the one thing you don't want not to have is, mostly, entirely and absolutely, is — what? Tell me. Why the loss of Free Will. Write it in big letters: Free Will. Now there are two ways to lose your free will: go insane or die. It is only given to a few, comparatively speaking, to go insane, clean off their chump, so we won't talk of their rabbit fears just now, because everybody is afraid of death and I am concerned with everybody. Since when? Well, whether I am or not, I will put it another way: the fear of death is universal: the fear of death is an idea that by its nature may be predicted of many, hence, universal. Is that all right? Very well, go on. By the way, in parenthesis, when I get around to insanity, or I might as well say it now, instead of dropping it and having to pick it up later, an insane person is a dead person, any way, except medically speaking, which we aren't, I hope, that is too much to put up with. You no longer have free will when you are dead, or let us at least say so, if we want to get on with this thing, I really can't discuss scholasticism here, and you are dead when you have no free will and you are dead, therefore, when you are insane because, you see, you have no free will. Even the law, I might say especially the law, in all the States, and American law is based, I suppose, on English law and it, in turn, on Roman law and Roman law must be based on something or other, Moses I guess, and Moses, I would like to bet, on the Golden Bough, holds, maintains, presupposes, and that's-all-there-is-to-it, that an insane person is so dead, so absolutely dead, that you can't hang him. Why hang a corpse? A moral corpse? Moral because, you see, the law holds that if you are insane you don't know the difference between right and wrong and if you don't *know* you can't *act accordingly*. I mean how could you? I mean you really can't *do* a damn thing if you are as screwy as all that. Maybe somebody saw you do it but you didn't *do* it. And if you did it wasn't wrong. Anyway you didn't. And you certainly couldn't be held responsible. Ah, but she was! How very much she was! And that of course was why she was frightened, if she was frightened, because it was natural enough, if she wanted to be natural, that is, not completely isolated and alone in a situation which, for some reason in itself, frightens people, to be afraid of responsibility. Because responsibility, there it was, is the antithesis of Free Will! How obliquely it came to her! There it was, the thing she had put away, that she knew all the time. Now she could go on without that bothering her. Anyway, how pleasant and wonderful! And so it was more than natural or something pertaining to all natures, making it human nature, to be afraid of responsibility, akin as it was to Death. In *esse* and in *veritas* the same, Death and Responsibility. Each being a negation i.e., the loss of free will. And so, each being the same, produced that little bastard rabbit thing. *In exacto.* Now she would like to take time off to talk about it, to enlarge and expand it, to make images and similes and analogies and parables. How nice if she could make parables like Jesus and analogies like Plato, and educate people. Not at all, she wouldn't like it a bit. She wasn't a reformer and she was Space itself compared to Plato, she out-Platoed Plato, as a matter of fact. Besides she was busy, as anyone could see, and there was a lot more to it than making a statement, that she had reconstructed, it is true, in the pleasantest way, which is not by trying stupidly to remember it, which is no such thing, if you think remembering is just pitching into the attic and *coming upon it*, even if you do find the damn thing that way sometimes by unconscious reconstruction, intuitively, as it were, but by conscious effort, by walking away from the answer which she knew, she then had come toward it again retracing, in the sense of again tracing, her steps, until she came upon it, sensibly and logically, not like coming upon a friend and screaming "For gosh sakes where did you come from?" but "Oh, hello I expected you." Wait a minute — wait a minute — wait a minute. She had decided to let it go, don't you remember? Remember? Don't let's go through that again. Yes, she had all right: to put it aside, and accept her own conclusion, don't you remember? Yes, that's true, but her intellectual habits were so good that she had unconsciously, consciously reconstructed the thing. Hmmmm. Nice. Pause. Let's get back to what I was doing, so that I can finish it, and back to what I was doing. She knew she must get on with what she had been doing before, because of what she was doing, she, for some reason had felt, and she didn't yet know the reason, that she had to explain why she was afraid of doing what she was doing that she knew she was going to return to, anyway, after she just, please, finished explaining why she was frightened of what she was doing. That's all it was, *c'est tout*, being the person she was, that she had to do, and it wasn't a question of not doing what she was doing at all. There wasn't any need to say, "I am going back to what I was doing when I finish what I am doing." It was understood. In the meantime it would wait for her; it couldn't exactly go on without her. She simply held it in one hand while she talked with the other, a very nice image, never let your right hand know what your left hand is doing. Inconsequential, aside the point, irrefutable, what was the word? Well, anyway, she knew when she was thinking in parenthesis, and she hadn't forgotten for a second that she still had some things to say about responsibility, although she was getting pretty tired of the word, sick and tired of a word that if you looked it up in Webster probably didn't mean a damn thing: re-spon-si-bil-i-ty. 1. State or quality of being responsible. What about sex? That looked like a jump, didn't it? but it really wasn't. If, by sex, you mean women, and some people, lots of people, to influence me like that, think just that, I don't of course, but do you know of a responsibler sex, I know better than to call women a sex, but do you? I mean do you know of a responsibler sex? I am coming back to sex but not now, I am not going to discuss it now, if you don't mind, put it down there on the table and before you go I'll tell you. Thank you. Women, you know, sex or no sex, some people think no sex, passive as against the real thing you know, which is absurd, passive, latent, dormant being quite capable of, in fact is potential, which in the long run, economically speaking, would be superior to active, because, certainly, activity implies surcease and there really must be an end to activity, whereas, potentiality implies beginning and if passivity, in the sense that it is latent, but capable of being potential, and potential is beginning, in antithesis to activity, which must end, I am certainly not going into all that sort of thing now, although I assure you, in spite of what I have said, which might appear to separate the sexes, as a matter of fact to speak of sex as plural is not correct and extremely misleading because sex is singular and to separate it into men and women, is absurd because sex, after all, if you tried to find out, in case you were interested, what the difference between men and women was, is the one thing, the common denominator that men and women

have in common and what you have in common cannot be the difference between you — can it? Women, as she said, you know, are the
responsible sex, or in view of what I have just said, let us say: Women
are responsible. That sounds weak, which is often the result of trun-
cating a syllogism and not her fault, and besides she was, to repeat
an image, holding something in each hand. What she meant was
clear and sensible: take women; take woman; take a card. All right.
Woman. No not "woman" like that because "woman" like that
might mean man, man generically speaking certainly includes women
and so . . . But women have children and that's what she meant,
although that sounded like a primer of some sort: Whales have
whales, at least she supposed so, except it didn't distinguish them exactly, she guessed what she was thinking of was that whales were
mammals, she mustn't let things like that slow her up, but the animal
kingdom was something else again, she didn't mean that kind of responsibility unless of course maybe she did, the responsibility women
felt for their children being such a terrifying white rabbit kind of
thing, probably because it was so unknown, she meant unknown to
them, women, intellectually, and felt so physically, yes really physically, so maybe it was animal. But it was not and she knew better:
responsibility or the fear of death, consequently the fear of the loss of
free will, being given to man, generically including women, alone. It
was an intellectual thing, that was clear and if anyone wanted to bring
up that babies and dogs behave the same if you hold their arms and
legs down, I mean scared to death, all right go ahead. As far as I am
concerned, babies are dogs: they don't know anything; it's just a re-
flex; it's a dog's world and babies aren't man, anyway not yet. She
wished she hadn't brought animals into it, it only confused the issue,
because maybe women who weren't *conscious* of a thing, the fear of
the loss of free will, for instance, were whales. There must be something wrong somewhere, and she knew what it was all right: it was
language, language being the damndest thing anyway, how could you
say, "Women are whales," well, you could, that was just it. It's an
enthymeme. That makes it easy. Did you ever think of stage fright
for instance? She knew what stage fright was. Stage fright was just

plain pure and simple thinking things had gone so far and you couldn't get out of them and you couldn't say "I'll do it tomorrow when I damn well please" because the curtain was going up. Not tomorrow, but today, not in ten minutes but now, up she goes. "Wait a minute, I've got a headache, death, wait a minute, I'll come when I damn well please, and gladly, but not now. Not now, not this very second. Tell that radio man not to drop his hand. *I'm not ready.*" Terror! Hard alee and ready about. Duck. And what about people who didn't have stage fright? Well, I'll tell you what about people who don't have stage fright, we just plain aren't talking about them. You might as well talk about people who aren't afraid to die, they're just beyond the pale, that's all, they don't even know they are going to die, and they've got pink cheeks all right, but you might as well skin them and hang them up in the living room. And what about artists? She was carrying in her head all about women and babies but she had something to say about artists, not their work, that was understood, understood that it was not understood, what of it? but themselves as people, people who were artists. Other people think artists are having fun, "Isn't it fun," they say. "Aren't you lucky," they say, "it must be wonderful to love your work," and artists don't even bother to answer because it's all just too complicated to explain and it's embarrassing, too, to deny what amounts to being an axiom unless you can defend your denial, and artists mostly, I don't mean to be dogmatic, but they mostly can't express themselves legitimately but just obliquely, as it were, and some of them aren't conscious of it, which does *not* make them whales, but most of them know and are perfectly aware it isn't fun and as for loving it, they are horrified, poor dears, never having done any research on the subject in their heads or ever dared reflect on it at all, because they would do anything to get out of working and it isn't indolence, either, because they do all kinds of hard work to get out of working, don't they dash all over the country and join the Army and have babies and chore after chore beautifully done because it isn't work to them, responsible work I mean, and only their own work terrifies them and if only they could get out of it but they can't. And women, here she was back you see, exactly as she planned, it didn't seem necessary to her to make the statement to herself that women were afraid of their children, it being so clear now that it appeared obvious, just as if there hadn't been any sequence, really she had overdone it perhaps, so much so, that how trite, yes trite almost, it seemed, to say, that mothers didn't love their children, as a matter of fact, she still didn't like that phrase, *disliked* them, because women couldn't help their very natures, could they, in a thing as natural as having children, and love something that frightened them so badly, self-preservation being probably the first law of nature after all, and to love the fear of death would be positively absurd, at least masochistic to say the least, the fear of death being worse than death itself, *in enthymemus classicus.* It was hardly worth while to go on, now that it was finished, and besides she did want to get back to what she had been doing, because she loved it so and she wouldn't give it up even if she did hate it and hate it she must if what all she said was true and oh, that white rabbit! there it was. Her loss of free will! She couldn't give it up, she wasn't her own boss, how awful, oh go *away*. Ahh it always went away, thank God, and weren't we all in the same boat, on the Styx maybe (Bullfinch) but everyone was there, everybody that was anybody, if you want to be snobbish. Men were in it too, don't think they weren't, here she was doing her other hand, not men as man either but men as women, just exactly the same thing I mean, the same fear, but a different manifestation, except that isn't the word at all, unless you want to call love a manifestation. Strictly speaking, taking a short cut, as it were, because I want to get back and it is waiting for me, men do the loving, the kind of loving that is so frightening, love being a man's responsibility, just exactly the same as children are women's. Maybe I don't mean the same. What she meant, she knew she meant, and that was that the fear was the same, and so the men were there, too, in the same boat, scared to death of love and consequently the object of their love, and horrified like the artist and the mother to be caught preferring free will to responsibility. Don't think for a minute that she meant anything but *the* responsibility, in itself, in *esse, in excelsis gloria.* Silly people might misconstrue, because they couldn't think, even, what she had made so clear and confuse *the* responsibility with economic responsibility in a man, and in a woman just not wanting to be bothered with children, but she must be slipping if she thought of silly people's thoughts and wanted to refute them, or else she was just putting off getting back to work, which, everything said and done, was easy enough to see, now that it was all so clear. But, really, if women thought they knew anything about love and the white rabbit terror of it, well, they just didn't, because they weren't responsible for love, not a bit, not a little bit, it's all just plain fun or a nuisance, as the case may be, for them, and it is just so much nonsense for a woman to say "I love you," just as it was just so much nonsense for a man to think he can feel the same about his children as a mother does, because he can't. It isn't physically or consciously or basically possible because there is no rabbit terror for him in the business of it at all, and none in love for a woman and so it is nonsense for a woman to say "I love you." Perfect nonsense. Pluperfect. Ah. How sweet to get back. Look how pleasantly things have looped up. I love you, but I come back smart with my own smartness and yours too. I know that I love you, but also that it is nonsense. It is wonderful and pluperfect nonsense to love you so bravely, and to be so bold, knowing as I do that I cannot love you, being a woman, and it's-just-plain fun to love you because I don't, because I cannot, while you, I understand will not love me because, my dear, you are afraid and who can better understand your white terror than I, who have it, but who am returning to the thing that causes it, can I say willingly, and imply my superiority to you in the sense that I am braver, or in view of what I have said, isn't it clear, darling, that I have no choice?

Aunt Julia's Caesar

IDEA

"My Aunt Julia is descended on her mother's side from the Kings, and on her father's side is akin to the immortal Gods: for the Marcii Reges, from whom comes the name of her mother's family, are derived from Ancus Marcius, and the Julii, the family of which ours is a branch, from Venus. Our stock therefore has at once the sanctity of Kings, who among men are most powerful, and the claim to reverence which attaches to the Gods, to whom Kings themselves are subject."*

— JULIUS CAESAR

History as usual does not give us the reason, motivating cause, of a great man's behavior; contenting itself with dates, results, it leaves us discontented, frustrated, without interest to remember; flunking us all, finally, with its impersonal epic, its "It's true because I say so" attitude. Shakespeare makes of Julius Caesar a gentle, lovable person, mistreated, misunderstood, unequal to his fate, a good man, super-

---

*Through Aeneas, prince of Troy, according to fable, and his son Julius.

133

stitious, weak; beloved by all but his ambitious, variable, envious competitors for power. But historically true as Shakespeare's *Julius Caesar* may be, it is clear that he neglected to state in it that Brutus was undoubtedly Caesar's son (by Servilla), not because he did not know it (Shakespeare certainly read both Plutarch and Suetonius) but because artistically, dramatic situations that prevail in his plays notwithstanding, Shakespeare refused to exploit a situation so dramatic in itself that no play need be written about it. Neither did he wish to handle all the material at hand. As an artist he made the spare choice that all artists make. This play is about Caesar the lover. When one remembers that Caesar was a soldier, orator, poet, politician, dictator, scholar, philosopher, historian, epicure, priest (pontifex maximus) the reader will not take this account of him as a scholarly one or take for granted that it is about the whole man. If, on the other hand, Caesar did what he did with his mistresses in mind; if his occupation was influenced by his preoccupation, or vice versa, a woman's name might well be written after each event in the history Caesar perpetrated, and many a lovely, illustrious woman is entitled to boast "I am Julius Caesar; I crossed the Alps; I refused the crown," viz: Cossutia, Cornelia, Pompeia, Servilia, Tertia, Ennoe the Moor, Cleopatra, Calpurnia, Postumia, Lollia, Tertulla, Mucia. Historians make much of Caesar's prolonged stay, as a youth, at the court of Nicomedes, implying that he prostituted his body to the use of that King and that he never quite lived the rumor down. This, I think, is a conclusion based upon an anachronism; with the Greeks still in the blood and minds of many a Roman boy, I doubt if playing Alcibiades to a King would be considered undistinguished.

Caesar's continuous but changeable love affairs, his violent temporary attachments, gave direction to his life, a meaning to his existence; and his brilliant public career was secondary, hearsay, history, *ex post facto*. Caesar ambitious? No. Caesar was in love. And his death, therefore, in the Senate, a victim of many blows as he was, would be less absurd if the husbands and legitimate lovers of the women he seduced had been his assassins. I do not know of what new love Caesar was dreaming when he absent-mindedly allowed

134

himself to be slain but his "et tu Brute" suggests a temporary nostalgic fidelity to the woman he had loved the best, Servilia. Or gentle Brutus, resembling too much his mother, might himself have been the subject matter of Caesar's uncensored dreams. Is it not possible that Brutus ("All others did what they did in envy of great Caesar"), striking the fatal blow, (It was medically established that the second wound, alone, killed Caesar, and that was the blow that Brutus struck. All the others were superficial as if unwillingly given; without motive; merely malice) may have avenged his mother and his half-sister, Tertia, also Caesar's mistress, or in desperation, freed himself? Else why should Brutus have presented Caesar with the immortality he desired for himself when none other than Caesar had said to him, "What he wants is of great importance, but whatever he wants, he wants it badly"?

Julius identified his Aunt Julia with Venus, which he could not help. At the age of eleven he already found himself less interested in his notorious and ferocious Uncle Marius than in his beautiful and equally notorious Aunt Julia. He admired and feared them both but he no longer, as he had at the age of eight, thrilled with terror and pleasure at the blood-curdling tales, all true, in fact somewhat understated, of Marius. Instead his heart pounded and his ears ached at the approach, always imminent, often actual, of his Aunt Julia. Aunt Julia had, it is true, a very special approach. The female descendant of Kings and one whose brilliant lineage is traceable to the Gods, and of these Gods, one in the hierarchy itself, namely Venus Genetrix, has no affectation of pride but the real thing. Julius wondered if he were a waif, a plebian, when his Aunt Julia approached; certainly he could be no more than mortal.

ACT I

Julius sits alone in a big hall, Greek in proportion, Roman in decoration and furniture; there are both Latin and Greek inscriptions, egg-and-dart designs, built-in metopes, vases of all shapes, trophies; spoils and plunder of various worth, souvenirs, and waxen masks of ancestors; a couple of gilded laurel wreaths are suspended from a peg.

If it were not the year 85 B. C., the place would be described as Victorian rather than hyper-Attic.

Julius is slim with rather large calves, pink hair, not too prominent blue eyes and a dreamy air, a little furtive, temporarily lovable, a lad who will grow into a man unrecognizable at present and vice versa.

JULIUS [*to himself; humbly*]:

I am mortal. [*louder*] I am no more than mortal. And Aunt Julia is a descendant of the Gods. But Aunt Julia is my father's sister. Then so am I descended from the Gods. [*very loud*] I am descended from the Gods. [*whispers*] Venus! [*softly*] Venus is my mother. But Aunt Julia? It is Aunt Julia who looks like Venus, the Venus in the Capitol at Rome.

[*He dreams; holds fast in his mind the beautiful image of Venus. Aunt Julia is imminent. Enter Aunt Julia, an out-sized matron, impressive rather than appealing, of a certain age and corresponding displacement. Julius stares at the thing he appears to have created; his mind returning to the original argument.*]

JULIUS [*to himself*]:

If Aunt Julia is immortal, then so am I. But my mother Aurelia is only my mother and therefore cannot be immortal and consequently I am only mortal.

AUNT JULIA:

Why do you look so sad, Julius?

JULIUS:

I am mortal.

AUNT JULIA:

Not quite.

JULIUS:

I am a mere mortal.

AUNT JULIA:

Mere! Julia's nephew!

JULIUS:

I am mortal, Aunt Julia, my mother is only Aurelia.

AUNT JULIA:

And your father?

136

JULIUS [*contemptuous*]:

A Praetor.

AUNT JULIA:

And your Uncle Marius? [*Julius shrugs.*] Marius has sent more souls across the Styx than the Gods themselves can classify. He has cut the throats of innumerable women and children and crucified their men by the legion. He has entered a metropolis in the morning and left it a plain in the evening. Are you moping because you are the nephew of Marius the Mortal?

[*Julius stares at his Aunt Julia's breasts and lets his eyes wander stupidly to her thighs and then to her knees where they halt as he begins to listen.*]

AUNT JULIA:

Answer me, Julius!

JULIUS:

No, Aunt Julia.

AUNT JULIA:

Where is your tutor?

JULIUS:

I gave him permission to walk.

AUNT JULIA:

A mere mortal gave another permission to walk?

JULIUS:

I am Julius Caesar!

AUNT JULIA:

Julius Caesar? What has he done?

JULIUS:

He is Me!

AUNT JULIA [*gentle*]:

Very well, then, behave like Julius Caesar in whom there may be another Marius.* Listen! A spirit mighty in war, unambitious in peace, superior to passion and riches, greedy only for glory (*Tantum modo gloriae avidus.*)† [*She continues, quoting Marius.*] My hopes are all

---

*This was said by Sulla a little later (Suetonius) but Julia may well have said it first.   †Sallust.

vested in myself and must be maintained by my own worth and integrity; for all other supports are weak (*Iam alia infirma sunt.*) I am taunted with my lot in life, they with their infamies . . . . the bravest is the best born. I learned from my father that elegance is proper to women but toil to men . . . . that arms and not furniture confer honor. Truly, no one ever became immortal through cowardice! [*She whispers in his ear.*] Victory, spoils, glory. *Victoria, praeda, laus.*

[*Julius smiles up into her face.*]

AUNT JULIA [*one more quote*]:

Well then, let them make love and drink; let them pass their old age where they have spent their youth, in banquets, slaves to their belly and the most shameful parts of their body.

JULIUS [*intent on Julia, repeats*]:

. . . *turpissimae parti corporis.*

[*Aunt Julia takes his head in one of her large white hands and presses it to her. He reaches just below her breast. He stands unrelenting. He is not angry but frightened, embarrassed. In her embrace his passionate love vanishes. She holds him close; fondles him. She repeats gently and seductively "I am Julius Caesar." But Julius feels only disgust. "I will get away," he says to himself but he does not dare move.*]

ACT II, SCENE I

With many scenes and many loves; same as in Act I; there is Masintha, a dark slave boy belonging to Uncle Marius.

JULIUS [*same as in Act I*]:

We look like a piece of cake together.

[*This makes Masintha radiant, but he says nothing.*]

JULIUS:

I love you and despise Aunt Julia.

MASINTHA:

Sssssh, don't say it; aren't you frightened?

JULIUS:

Never. [*louder*] *I despise her.*

138

MASINTHA [*whispers*]:
You are betrothed to Cossutia.
JULIUS [*whispers*]:
I am betraying her.
MASINTHA:
I love you, Gai, but we will be caught.
JULIUS:
You are a coward.
MASINTHA [*angrily*]:
You think you are a God!
JULIUS [*contemptuously*]:
I know you are a slave.

SCENE II

This scene is the same as the last, but with Julius and his tutor, M. Antonius Gnipho, native of Gaul.

TUTOR [*reading a letter*]:
This is an arrogant letter to write to one's betrothed and there are two misspellings.
JULIUS:
It will do; correct it and send it.
TUTOR:
Cossutia is a lovely girl, plump and nice. She is rich.
JULIUS:
I must leave. Women disgust me.
TUTOR:
Women?
JULIUS:
My Aunt Julia makes me feel sick.
[*Exit Tutor with letter to Cossutia which breaks a longstanding betrothal.*]
JULIUS [*to himself*]:
Aunt Julia, why am I afraid of you? Venus is my only love whom I approach through you, is that it? How dare I love Venus! Still I do,

while Julia fills me with disgraceful terror. I dream of Julia; she surrounds me and holds me fast but that is at night over which I have no control; it is not my fault, besides, I hate it; my daydreams are innocent; Venus and Julius Caesar walk together hand in hand like Daphnis and Chloe. And then what happens? As night falls it is my Aunt Julia, God damn her! She kisses me; each round eyeball reflects my entire figure, my whole self, my whole day, my every thought, even secret ones (Masintha and I kissing each other's ears). Aunt Julia's mouth encloses mine; gradually, my whole face is in her mouth; her soft hands separate into fingers and the ends leave dents in my flesh; my knees and elbows disappear and Aunt Julia drapes me around her hips as if I were a piece of carpet. [*He jumps up; walks; kicks at things.*] Venus asks for nothing; Julia demands and gets my subjection. When I sit on her knees I feel the quick warmth of her soft thighs (Venus is cool and hard) and I cannot help the turn I make at the waist to find Aunt Julia's mouth. "Good night, Julius!" But she is laughing at me! She follows me to bed and *never*, never leaves the room. In the morning she teaches me to be brave (like Marius) and at night she turns me into a cringing slave (like Marius?). That possessive smile! In me another Marius? Yes, I am her husband! [*He breaks one of the less rare vases, a small one.*] Julius this and Julius that; Gaius, darling! Gaius, my love! She leans toward me even in public and my knees get sick. I cannot stay here; I am leaving. Ho! Guards! Slaves! My things! I am really going.

SCENE III

Julius and Nicomedes are in Bithynia. The royal apartment is square with high windows. Nicomedes reclines upon a royal couch. Julius in a white tunic and sandals, with flowers in his hair, waits upon Nicomedes. His blond skin is lightly sunburned, his nose, the backs of his calves, too.

NICOMEDES:
So you ran from Sylla and slit the throats of pirates. Ha, ha, ha.

JULIUS [*sullen*]:
No.

NICOMEDES:

That is what is said.

JULIUS:

It is true I slit their throats out of pity but I did not run from Sylla. I was fed up with women, not afraid of men.

NICOMEDES:

Was it necessary to crucify pirates to get even with a woman? And did you slit their throats first out of pity for their mothers? You are confused, my Gaius, but much good will come of your confusion and evil, too. All men will call you King, my little Queen. Sit here, eat figs, and tell me again about the pirates; what sport!

[*Julius obeys; looking like a pretty girl, he twists his forelocks with one finger.*]

JULIUS [*authentic*]:

They chased me, followed me, kidnapped me; they tossed me in the air; fondled me; got me drunk; dressed me as a girl; threatened to drown me; kissed me; gave me a sword and forced me to defend myself; and finally demanded twenty talents for my ransom. I was insulted; I laughed in scorn.

NICOMEDES:

Ha, ha, ha, ha.

JULIUS [*concludes*]:

Twenty talents for Julius Gaius Caesar!

NICOMEDES:

Ha, ha, ha, ha.

JULIUS:

Not less than fifty, I said.

NICOMEDES [*delighted*]:

Optime! Go on.

JULIUS:

I dispatched my servant and was left alone with the most bloodthirsty and loving people, those Cilicians. For thirty-eight days they amused me and I them; when they teased me too much or kept me awake at night I threatened to hang them. They laughed but I meant it. Twenty talents!

NICOMEDES:

Ha, ha, ha, ha.

JULIUS:

My servant returning, I paid my ransom. They kissed me goodbye; gave me presents, pearls for my ears, bracelets for my wrists and different colored sashes, girdles, red and blue sandals, bright red lipstick and blue eye-shade, fruit, spices, salves, everything I could take with me.

NICOMEDES:

Go on, go on.

JULIUS [*cool*]:

I manned ships at Miletus; I pursued them, surprised them, crucified them all as I had promised and as you know I have my fifty talents as well.

NICOMEDES:

But my gentle little love took pity on the pirates, it is said; he was merciful and slit their throats himself before crucifying them; baby! *Suavissima.*

JULIUS:

Yes I did but it is of no consequence now. I intend to be a soldier; I am through, as I have said, with women and lust. Tell me of men, Nicomedes. Alexander was a soldier and he conquered the world at 33. I must hurry, but I am ignorant. I have read Plautus, Ennius, Cato, Terence, Naevius; many times my tutor has read out loud the *Odyssey* translated by Livius Andronicus; my father is dead; I am the son of a woman, Aurelia, and the little lover of a super-woman, Julia. They tell me that I was plucked from Aurelia rather than born of her; that I did not experience my mother in the usual way nor she me; and I have thought that that is the reason I have not troubled her with my attentions since nor she me. And so I went to Julia by mistake with Venus in mind. I feel that I am born of Venus and must return to her. But I wish to be with men, soldiers. My books have taught me nothing but happenings, events, which I had no hand in nor do I wish to repeat the things that others have done. What of men? What are they like?

NICOMEDES:

Go back to Julia if you wish to know about Marius.

JULIUS:

Not Marius, men.

NICOMEDES:

Go to as many women, then, as you wish to know men and do not
expect to learn from your soldier comrades anything but news of
women. Lie down now at the foot of my couch and sleep; you are too
ambitious to be lovable; I predict a crown where the rose and myrtle
are and a violent death.

[*Julius drapes himself as suggested at the foot of the royal couch
and there is silence.*]

JULIUS [*cries out in his sleep*]:

Aurelia! [*He awakens Nicomedes by his calls.*] Nicky! Nicky!

NICOMEDES:

What Ho! The guards! My sword! What the Pluto!

[*The room is instantly filled with armed men; Nicomedes is already
looking foolish and Julius, his sandaled feet hanging over the couch,
the flowers still fresh, his cheeks pink, is weeping. Nicomedes tries
to dismiss the guards, waves his hand, says: "Leave us." But there
are a few big fellows remaining, their eyes on Julius as Julius sobs:
"My mother, dreaming of my mother, I lay on her breast."*]

NICOMEDES [*to the guards; stern*]:

Go! [*They leave reluctantly. He turns to Julius, taking him in his
arms.*] Gaius, my lad, my little love, calm yourself. I do not have to
send for my soothsayers to tell you the meaning of such a dream.
Listen: your mother Aurelia represents the Earth; have you not heard
of Mother Earth? Have you not conquered Aurelia tonight? Caesar
shall conquer the Earth. Go to sleep, ambitious lad. Sleep now, my
love, and *vale*.

END OF SCENE

Cornelia, in the meantime, first wife of Caesar, daughter of Cinna,
expected little of Julius and that is what she got (with the exception
of his only legitimate child). Julius's anger followed love scenes, his

143

fainting fits, his principles which seemed to her arbitrary and sporadic, alarmed the child of an illustrious and successful politician who never spoke anything but Latin. Caesar was Greek to her; a kind of Republican and Reactionary, so aware of his superiority and high born ancestry, so preoccupied with Mythology that in times of excitement or crisis he spoke the language of his daydreams, Greek. (His famous "Et tu Brute" was actually *Katsph Teknon*.) Cornelia, proud of her democratic *pater*, four times Consul, felt that Julius was a sissy and a snob; she also knew, via the Roman matrons' grapevine, of Julius' male companionships and loves, and her lip curled at this aristocratic pastime, this ancient Platonic formula. She was not stupid but how could she know that poor Julius disliked her because she reminded him of Julia, whose wanton ways had spoiled his mythological dream of fair women, whose soft warm flesh had suffocated his waking and sleeping hours, who had intimidated and enslaved him at the very hour of his youth when he had wished to please and yet be free. Julius's attempt to free himself from Aunt Julia, this Caesarian, as it might be called, ambivalence which he did not understand, may have accounted for his many loves, and unsuitable affairs, his passionate attempts and quick cooling point, as it were, his almost immediate dissatisfaction with each woman as she resembled inevitably in her love behavior, Julia, rather than the Venus of the Capitol. When he identified and confused his relationships and loves with the Goddess he felt resentment, disgust, revulsion upon his physical capitulation to the Julia in them. And when he was offered the smooth warm breasts of wife or mistress he did not feel the passionate security that men who are less than Caesar feel, but only a pagan wish, a brutal desire to be among men, to be a soldier, be safe, a conqueror rather than vanquished even so sweetly as this; and another lad fed on purely mythological daydreams and given a Julia as first contender might feel the same, isn't it so? Cornelia began to die and Caesar set out to perfect himself in his studies, in oratory, soldiery. His brain easily kept pace with his physical ubiquity and it is said that he dictated to three men at once on horseback, no doubt at a gallop at that. His poetry, his *Analogy*, written as he crossed the Alps, his famous *Com-*

mentaries were praised even by his enemies, who felt free to admire his written word. But these talents were secondary and only Caesarian because he was Caesar. It was with one hand beneath a woman's tunic that he caused the "very towns themselves" to leave "their sites" and "flee for succour to each other." Cornelia's death gained her Caesar's praise and her public eulogy was a precedent which gained for Julius the sympathy of the common people almost as much as that other posthumous gesture, that Will we have heard so much about, enriching simple people 75 drachmas each. This apparent simplicity at the height of power gave Caesar a tricky ascendancy over bigger men and astonished and embarrassed them in the river, as it were.

SCENE IV

The Precious Gardens and the Tiburtine Residence of Gaius Julius Caesar (this side of the Tiber). There is a cupola on the roof, an honor peculiar to sacred temples, impiously granted Caesar by that senate which conferred upon him divinity during his life and made him a present of immortality twice. It is the morning after the alleged fancy dress seduction of Pompeia by Publius Clodius, gentleman and scamp. (Publius Clodius, as an amorous diversion, had dared, disguising himself, to witness the strictly female ritual of Bona Dea. Similar to those honoring Orpheus these rites were initiatory, purificatory, expiatory, including peculiar mysteries; an enthusiastic orgy with sacred explanation.)

Pompeia and Julius Caesar; also eight expensive slaves of superb figure and carriage, whose skin has been lightly oiled and who wear only gold sandals and scarlet, blue, and yellow diapers like children at the Lido and who look rather spectacular and nouveau riche, as if complete with price tags, who appear to support open work ceilings like caryatids. Caesar is discovered admiring his human possessions. Pompeia sits to one side on a stone couch carved in cupids and tassels (plunder). She is remembering the excitement and final pleasure of the night before. She is black-eyed with shining dark curls formally arranged; her skin has an inbetween rosyness which pales in a north-

ern exposure but warms up as the sun sets. She wears green eye shadow, exaggerating the leafy shade of the gardens. Her tunic is by Hattie Carnegie. She is chic but warm; responsive, three dimensional, and next to her Caesar looks a little like a paper doll, his skin a little blue. Julius passes from slave to slave less like a general reviewing his troops than a bibliophile fondling the rare and slippery bindings of his first editions. He strokes the chest of one; gently pinches the high, trembling biceps of another; twists into place the scarlet diaper of a third. He finally comes upon Pompeia; holds out his hand, palm upward, into which she dreamily slides her wrist.

POMPEIA [*quickly*]:
You have come from Servilia.

JULIUS [*lightly*]:
There is scandal in the streets of Caesar's wife and at a very early hour.

POMPEIA [*nothing*].

JULIUS:
They say the little gentleman, Publius Clodius, looked very sweet dressed as a girl. [*He laughs.*] What will they say by night? [*Pompeia blushes but is not disturbed.*] I can imagine our stately matrons taking to their heels, the lady-like screams, the bare breasts, the charming disarray, the feeling of rape in the air and afterwards the stillness, the blushes of my Pompeia as once more [*He raises his voice.*], once more Publius Clodius possesses his wife without troubling to remove his rouge or his curls or to dismiss her maid.

POMPEIA [*pouting*]:
It isn't so.

JULIUS:
I admire his audacity. Passing the sacred portals; looking like a little virgin taking in the secret and awful rites; watching the maids and matrons at their private privileges, spying on bosoms never before exposed; and recognizing the faces of his female acquaintances only after he has stared at their unfamiliar knees and pink thighs. What else did he see? He is better informed than Caesar! He has seen women and girls play and make love under holy auspices after which he has wantonly slept with Caesar's wife! And yet I heard no thun-

der; saw no lightning. Did the sight of Pompeia and Publius in each other's arms like make-believe vestals please them, then? The Gods? No celestial anger? No portents? No evil omens? The day as clear as water? Perhaps Caesar should set out, then, at once; march on Agidineum; sack the place and return with pearls for Pompeia?

POMPEIA [*quick*]:

For Servilia!

[*There is a light peal of thunder.*]

CAESAR:

Servilia is a modest girl and would make Pompeia a pleasant companion.

POMPEIA [*angry*]:

Modest! Ask them in the streets how much you squandered on a single pearl for Servilia! Five million sesterces!

CAESAR [*in the same mood, it appears, as when he upped his ransom*]:

Six.

POMPEIA [*very angry*]:

And where did little Brutus come from? Servilia's modest brow?

CAESAR:

Let's leave the hierarchy out of this!

POMPEIA [*rudely*]:

Your precious ancestors!

CEASAR [*pale, shaking*]:

I divorce you, Pompeia!

POMPEIA:

Gaius!

CAESAR [*calmer*]:

I dismiss you.

POMPEIA [*frightened*]:

You will have Publius murdered!

CAESAR:

On the contrary, I shall have him made a candidate for the Tribuneship, for which he has been striving with less success than for Pompeia.

POMPEIA [*resigned*]:

You insult me once more, Julius.

CAESAR [*gesturing toward the street*]:
You lack discretion for yourself alone, my dear. I wish Caesar's wife to be "not so much as suspected." Well, I am off. *Vale.*

POMPEIA [*frowning; practical*]:
But Publius Clodius is a patrician and may not become a Tribune of the people.

CAESAR:
He is also beardless, licentious, profligate, but Caesar's word is law. I don't intend to tamper with his appearance or his character but I shall have him transferred at this ninth hour (3:00 P.M.) from the patricians to the plebians. And then, Pompeia, I repair to camp and join my soldiers, my comrades. I need relaxation.

[*A soothsayer dressed as a soothsayer enters timorously.*]

SOOTHSAYER:
Caesar, we fear for your departure. Remain at home!

CAESAR:
What now? [*He arranges his laurel wreath.*]

SOOTHSAYER:
A victim offered for sacrifice is without a heart! Caesar may see for himself.

CAESAR:
"The entrails will be more favorable when I please. It ought not to be taken as a miracle if a beast have no heart." Farewell, Pompeia. *Ave atque vale.*

[*Exeunt, as it were, Caesar. There is a second affectionate peal of thunder. Pompeia resumes her daydreaming on the stone couch.*]

END OF SCENE

And in the meantime, between the scenes, much happens; much occurs; history is made faster than it can be taken down; all Gaul is divided in three parts for school children; Caesar's diary develops into his *Commentaries*, and long before his death, if metamorphosis into a flaming star may be called death, historians are taking down the facts, mistakenly noting everything so that in the end we know nothing of Caesar, so contrary become the opinions based on fact of later writers. Plutarch, Suetonius, Sallust, each give us a different Caesar, and myth seems more substantial, more steadfast. Shakespeare makes us weep, but without respect for a gentle soul whom he ignores in favor of the more intense, neatly forensic and glamorous Brutus. Mommsen, not an artist, puts everything down but Caesar, and lesser contemporary names succeed in teasing us for a glimpse of Himself. Roman busts, measured and trustworthy though they be, refuse to leave their pedestals, and Augustus, cleaning up after Caesar, forbade for reasons not translated the publication of Julius's early works, while Julius himself ciphered everything intimate or confidential; and Cicero, *in re* Caesar, "Domitius, indeed, puts his fingers to his lips before he speaks."

But down to an imaginative posterity, nevertheless, troop single file and two by two the names of illustrious women, women of whom I have already spoken, as well as those simpler lovelies of the provinces suggested in the vain and bawdy marching song of the soldiers Caesar loved, beginning,

> Watch well your wives, O Citizens
> A lecher bald we bring.

One imagines a Roman *pagus* as Caesar marches through, hastily boarding up its boudoirs behind which are confined, but not for long, a row of monogamous but pouting wives who in their *a priori* turn imagine Caesar, too. While Julius, holding fast within himself, (just as another brave and Roman but misguided lad did the well-known fox) the small blond descendant of Venus who was his childhood self refusing to scream, seduced them all, in his desperate, continuous attempt to find and destroy, place a soldier's heel on his first love, Julia, that he might return to purer daydreams, Greek ones, of Venus Genetrix. What singular twist might be observed in Caesar's own *Oedipus* written in his boyhood if Augustus had not tossed it out (twice a tragedy), to lighten the intellectual load of Sigmund Freud? But similarly censored was a *Collection of Apothegms*, which none of us miss.

Caesar's success as a hero and his failure as a lover, immoderate in

each, may perhaps be answered or at least checked in his own words
to Metellus, whom he threatened with death, " . . . and this is more
disagreeable for me to say than to do." These words suggest that
Caesar was more sensitive than formidable just as his statement to
the Commons when hailed as King, "I am Caesar, not King" doesn't
mark him as a modest man but, on the contrary, as one highly sensitive and aware of his individual, his unique greatness, special prestige.

Caesar, then, whom we may call the spoiled child of Venus, is discovered in Scene V opposite the spoiled child of Egypt, daughter of
Ptolemy XIII, whose name, Cleopatra, became the name of all sub-
sequent queens, not one of whom but lives in the oblivion following
too much greatness, along with Cleopatra, Jr. and Caesarion, progeny
of the prodigious who play in the shade, and who at seventeen looked
forward to as many intrigues as Caesar looked back on (Cleopatra
solved her love problems by a quick succession of lovers, numerically
Caesar's equal), together a kind of metaphorical Janus, guardian deity
of gates and heavenly porter, after whom, as the queens of Egypt after
Cleopatra, are named the janitors of skyscrapers.

SCENE V

*"Caesar replied that he did not want Egyptians
to be his counselors, and soon after privately sent
for Cleopatra from her retirement."*

—PLUTARCH

*Caesar and Cleopatra. Cleopatra at seventeen shows none of the
signs, any more than she will at 39 as she outstares the asp, of evil
living, egotism, intellectual intolerance, wit, brilliance, insomnia,
excess, forced marches, largesse, pestilent mischief, incest, murder,
generosity, anxiety. In this she looks like any adolescent who, if
inexperienced as Cleopatra was experienced, nevertheless shows nothing in her face of what she has dreamed of or is capable. Her body,
beautiful, pliant, is wrapped in cloth of gold, I suppose, and her gestures for the moment odalisque; her hair is flecked with gold leaf as
are her shoulders and her bosom. Her eyes are so large that it is easy*

to understand why the Egyptian eye in early sculpture appears complete in profile; the lashes and brows are lamp black. Her skin is warm in tone and certain parts of it have been stained to accentuate light and shade regardless of where she is or what the hour, rain or shine: her eyelids, sienna at the outer edges, are sky blue toward the center, increasing the fullness and arch and drawing attention to the pupils which appear elliptical. The inside of the nostrils are painted Schiaparelli pink, the wings lightly veridian which shortens her nose considerably; above her upper lip is a teasing synthetic shadow, laid on with a feathered brush, bringing to a pout her wide, typically Egyptian mouth which is full lipped and rouged in seven colors from coral to lavender and in seven shades from pink to cadmium red. Her arms are lighter toned on the inner side and darkened at the inner bend, and as she lifts them to greet Caesar the armpits are smooth and cerulean, the palms of her hands cadmium violet with bright pink tips. On either side of her, very becoming, making her taller, gentler, maternal, is a slave boy with enormous eyes, the whites pale blue. This duet steps back as Caesar speaks; they lie on the floor and play at cards holding them over their heads; giggle and whisper.

CAESAR:

Did you really come in a rug?

CLEOPATRA:

I don't think so. I was dreaming of you, Caesar, and here I am. Do not underestimate me; I do not need to play tricks but travel in the light of day. I think you are wonderful but do you expect my gratitude or my admiration?

CAESAR:

Caesar expects nothing, believes in nothing, but is capable and dependable.

CLEOPATRA:

And generous? Formidable?

CAESAR:

Yes. No.

CLEOPATRA:

Thank you very much for regaining me my throne and giving me in place of my elder brother, whom I loved, a younger one I despise. I loved Ptolemy Dionysius and we were lovers; it would have been my duty to marry him, as is our custom, and a pleasure. It is your fault that he is dead, fighting your battles for my prerogative, and you make me a present now of a child for a husband who still fondles his nurse. Please do not interfere with my affairs; cross your own Alps and leave me mine. I already have memoirs; I too shall write Commentaries; there are other Gauls, and I am a compatriot of Moses. I do not need Caesar to wage my wars or recall me to my own authority. I was thinking in Syria, not despairing, and I did not ask for help or reconciliation with anyone. Is it my accomplishment when you conquer? Why must we quarrel? Haven't you anything to say? You look exactly like Caesar.

CAESAR:

I am.

CLEOPATRA:

Yes, I know it.

CAESAR:

You are like Venus.

CLEOPATRA:

A conventional compliment from a poet.

CAESAR:

Not from Caesar who no longer writes verses.

CLEOPATRA:

I am Cleopatra, not Venus.

CAESAR [*reflective*]:

I have heard something like that before.

CLEOPATRA:

What?

CAESAR:

I have heard it.

CLEOPATRA [*quotes*]:

I am Caesar; not King.

CAESAR:

You are clever; mischievous, imperious, bold; you are licentious, no ordinary wanton, insolent, outrageous, violent and disorderly; you are illustrious, famous, spirited, witty, voluptuous, bewitching, notorious.

CLEOPATRA:

How is Calpurnia?

CAESAR:

She dreamed that the pediment of our house fell.

CLEOPATRA:

Has it?

CAESAR:

Not particularly.

CLEOPATRA:

And what have you dreamed of?

CAESAR:

I dreamed I shook hands with Jupiter.

CLEOPATRA:

Is that all?

CAESAR:

Caesar does not need to dream; neither does he wait for propitious omens or fear evil ones. He makes his own decisions and celebrates the consequences. Having gained Cleopatra's ear he wishes now to be silent.

CLEOPATRA:

Cleopatra can be silent in thirty languages.

CAESAR:

So I have heard.

CLEOPATRA:

But just think, Caesar, how still I can be. I can be still in Aethiopian, Troglodyte, Hebrew, Arabian, Syrian, Mede, Parthian, Macedonian, Latin, Greek ...

CAESAR:

Sssssssssh. Be still in Greek.

[The stage is blacked out for a change of scenery but above the half-sound of toppling plastic pilasters, creaking make-believe furniture, painted portières, aluminum cups, ersatz cypress, pasteboard

metopes, can be heard the voice of Caesar, who cries out in his sleep, "Aunt Julia!" in the plaintive tones of his childhood.]

Calpurnia, with her endless dreams of Caesar's downfall as the pediment of their house, her anxious preoccupation with his horrid fate, and anticipation of evil, might have accomplished his murder herself if she had been aware of her intentions; as it was, she was the last to see him alive, the last to warn him; the pessimistic, neurotic, insomniac who had had enough of Caesar the philanderer, Caesar the hero, and didn't know it. What was she thinking of as her actions betrayed the subject matter, to us but not to her, of her subconscious? What sort of pastime can it be to search for and always find ominous portents, evil omens and to recall only the dreams that threatened Caesar? And what kind of therapy for the uneasy and barren Calpurnia were sibylline prophecies, unlucky sacrifices, alchemy, beehives in odd places, forebodings and pirouetting eagles? And did Caesar the author of *Analogy* not suspect his wife's innocent desire to be rid of the pain of his presence? Did he go to the Senate as usual, as some men do to their offices, to shake off an unpleasant apprehension, to face and deal with, facts, and the real thing, as Caesar certainly had to that queer morning, *(Idus Martius)*, when birds seemed to fly backwards and doors to open of their own accord to give the look of reason to absurdity and obey the anticipatory Calpurnia, who stayed at home and willed it so?

Let Cimber and Casca, Cassius *et al* rest in peace for the glancing blows they gave to Caesar, "the only man who undertook to overthrow the state when sober," bloodying themselves in justifiable tyrannicide. Calpurnia was the fatal homicide excused only by divine references and evil counsels; and as for You Too Brutus, doubly illegitimate, noblest murderer of them all, well conditioned, well given, Pretty-boy Brutus, tender, esteemed, Plato was at fault, who tutored you, if any fault there was, too good to be true.

154

Now *vale*, Caesar, as we inflict of the countable wounds, this twenty-fourth and ask in closing: What is "the last infirmity" of a noble mind and what is the shape of Caesar's ghost?

In any event it is no myth that the herds of horses which Caesar had dedicated to the river Rubicon when he crossed it and had let loose without a keeper "stubbornly refused to graze and wept copiously."

While Cicero wrote to Atticus, "We console ourselves with literature and the Ides of March."

SCENE: EPILOGUE

Calpurnia is discovered in a small square room lit by tall torches, too small to relieve the tension expressed by her peripatetic in the little squares it allows her. She is talking to herself; composing that funeral oration which, according to Jacques Roergas de Serviez, she resolved to make, and did, at the Tribunal of Harangues. It is clear to the audience from Calpurnia's gestures that there is a frightful conflict: Her first draft is doubtless a terrific denunciation, a passionate recriminatory document, and the torches sputter and quickly burn down announcing the passage of a long and painful night; but the next day in public she will brilliantly and eloquently defend Caesar saying in effect what Mark Antony said and what posterity accepts. And then like that Mary equally humiliated, like that Mary who retired to the home of "the disciple Jesus loved" she went to live at Mark Antony's house.

The child I am going to tell you about had a liberal education at the age of thirteen. We may call her, therefore, precocious. That the subject matter of her diploma was death, rather than the Law, Medicine, or the Fine Arts, and that her education was informal and involuntary, must not at all detract from her erudition but must rather amaze those of us who have graduated in the less formidable subject matters, and whose theses bear the stamp but not the reality, the ribbon but not the wounds of the passage of Time.

Like Caesar, this child died of many wounds, herself her own Brutus and murmuring, "Thou too, Sister," at that time when her friends must lower their heads to hear those last words, always significant, usually poetic, that the dying make. That her own death among the several deaths of her experience was unsuccessful and a feeble climax to a highly imaginative and willful desire does not mean that it was not death. It was death in that it was like death and unlike death; as twin is to twin, the same and not the same. They did not bury her. Neither did her imagination in all its intensity and realism include her burial. It seems clear, as I write this, that that is alone the reason that they did not. Things happened as she willed them, and she did not consider burial, therefore in a worldly sense, she did not die. All things are rational and so she did not die because it could not be explained. Otherwise she would have been buried and she was not. There is no need to write about her life after death. It is true she continued to live with her last words on her lips, "Thou too, Sister," but gradually the last wound, the fatal wound, healed, and she became even as you and I: fairly happy, mildly discontented, a little unreasonable, not very selfish, conscientious, not very good at figures, contemptuous but sympathetic, affectionate, patient with the servants, irritable once a month, enthusiastic about colors, and, naturally enough, forgetful of death. I will say, however, not forgetful of it as her neighbors and friends were forgetful of it, out of transitive or intransitive anesthesia, but unafraid of it and not anticipating it, because it had passed; she had approached it willingly; she had died, and it was over, consequently she felt not fear. She had experienced a voluntary death which is no death at all and she lived. I am going to leave this housewife, this charming woman with healthy instincts and normal interests, however, and return to the child who majored in death and graduated *magna cum laude*, and who might have worn a small gold death's head for the rest of us to envy.

The realization that her parents were dead came to her slowly, and never with an impact that was precise, nor could it be called, therefore, realization at all. It explained why she lived among strangers, and it meant that every cloud has a silver lining, because it would have been awful if these people she lived with were her parents. They were relations, each under the domination of the other, and herself outside the pale. She preoccupied herself with her dead parents, first with one and then with the other; never together. There was no relationship between them; each was related to her, each loved her devotedly, passionately, gently, protectively. As all this began when she was four, she did not know by what short interval she had missed them and no real memory or recollection conflicted with her imagination. No smell reminded her, no vase had been touched, no wallpaper chosen, or jelly on the cupboard shelf been fixed, by her mother. Suppose she had known that her father's fingerprints could still be seen on one of the old barn windows, and on the barrel of one of a brace of pistols in the attic, also. Suppose she had known that a ball gown in the spare room closet retained the shape of her mother's breasts and that a small red mark at the neckline was lipstick from her mother's mouth. Suppose she knew that if she went to a book-shelf in the front bedroom she would find on one of the pages of *Marie B———*, tears, still salt, that her mother in her sensibility shed. What painful joy all this would have caused Sister. And as she, too, did not spare her emotions, it is just as well that she did not know how close she was to them in time, or she might have imagined that she could catch them if she hurried. Or she might have spent her life handling a vase and sniffing an old coat. As it was the vase was simply to be avoided for fear of breakage and she thought that the old coat belonged to her grandfather and so avoided it too. Death, therefore, was something that happened long ago, inevitably, and in the case of her parents not to be so much regretted, because she loved them as they were, and was spared the effort of being brought up by them. This introduction to death was far from harrowing and the only sor-row that could be called precisely sorrow that confronted her at this period was the sorrow in other people's faces when they looked at her, which like a chameleon she gradually accepted in her own fea-tures and all her life she wore this reflected sorrow on her face, which in no way made her less appealing, but which depressed her and made her feel dark and unlike fair children who played in the sun. She did not think about death as such. Death meant gone. Not to a neigh-bor's house, not to the village, not upstairs resting, not a hide-and-seek gone, but just gone; I don't know why she accepted complete disappearance like this without even making a cursory search, but this double disappearance was Sister's introduction to a series of deaths less bearable, more completely severing in character and heart-breaking, and each one filled her with a sense of guilt more powerful than the last. We must conclude that the hearsay death of her par-ents, therefore, was not a great sorrow to Sister, but a gentle pervasive void, a lack of something, a nostalgia, a kind of indirect lighting, sweet and not unpleasant, that marked her, sought her out, and made her start in life not a handicapped one, but a little odd, a little strange, a little to one side. A voice from the sky or a little sign over her bed might have proclaimed, "Watch over this child; she is without bondage." Let us say that this child, then, has skipped a grade and by some lucky coincidence is now placed in a position where every opportunity is hers and that without homework or notes, she has left envious ones behind and is ready to experience a series of deaths which, crescendo-like, shall ring in her small pink ears until her graduation, her own death.

The death of her brother was quite another matter. A death, that if it had been the last on her list instead of the first, she could not have borne (the cumulative effect would have been too much for her), so real it was, so actual, so frustrating in that her young will could do nothing and her *No, No, Noes* echoed through the house that still smelled sweetly of him and flowers. The stupidity of that ancient pair who looked after her, who in spite of the many deaths they had witnessed, or perhaps because of them, still practiced their dramatic sense at these times, striking horror into the child who was forced to kiss the cold forehead, initiated her quickly, and she knew all. Death, now, was not an abstraction, but a thing. And on top of learning this so fast, she began missing her little lover before the service for him was over. He might have been looking through the upstairs bannisters with her and giggling as they had so often in the tension and carbon dioxide of an Episcopal Church on Sundays, because these two were lovers and did everything in unison, like a dance. Neither ever had to explain anything to the other and they shared their bread and butter and their sins. As neither ate or sinned with another, all they lacked of pleasures that grown-up lovers had was confession and forgiveness. Each identified himself with the other; each wanted to stand where the other had stood, breathe the same air, fill the same little space; in a word, they were lovers and if their play was savage and their love inadequate it is because of their extreme youth and their inability to translate ideas into symbols, and not from lack of emotion or imagination.

159

After that it was a sparrow. There were no other children, and she did not take another little lover as some people buy a fresh puppy to mimic their past love and fill a void like filling an empty pitcher. Fever brilliantly erased part of the pain of her brother's loss and when she slid cautiously out of bed and out into space again, she returned to her parents, teasing each with her love for the other, and finding them easier to play with than a dead brother, whose ghost held none of the charm of his factual, warm and savage little presence. It was like giving up meat in one's diet which one becomes accustomed to, and with her quick, bright illness acting as an anesthetic, she forgot her brother, who bore a horrific sign upon his breast, "Dead." The death of the sparrow on the contrary remained with her all her life, reminding her, as it did, of her guilt, and her refusal to take the responsibility of burying it, of conducting a ghastly little sweet-smelling funeral for it. She came upon the sparrow on the garden walk, near the mint bed, on a cold day. Death was in her mind and the bird lay at her feet as if she were looking for it. She gently lifted its small tense body to the flat of the fence, where the setting sun shone on some of its brown feathers from beneath, turning them yellow. She said, "He will get warm and fly away," and that is what she desperately hoped. But she ate her supper and when she went to bed, she slept; a sleep she never forgave herself, a careless sleep, forgetful of that bird death. She even, as if on purpose, slept through the early bird-morning that usually awakened her, ate her breakfast, and only much later returned to the scene, to find that someone else had given the bird the practical attention he had needed and she had been afraid to do. The memory of that neglect, and her horror of something she had loved, because it was dead, stayed with her always, so that she never quite held up her head again, guilty as she was and fearful.

But see how fast she is learning! And from simple addition she is already carrying over numbers, so that each death reminds her of the last, so much so that she was incapable of burying the sparrow as she might have, simple and naive child that she had been before her brother's death. She had long since forgone the poetry of doll funerals and had put away childish things. She may be called precocious at this point, therefore, if not eligible for a Greek letter society.

She did not immediately return to her parents from this experience and never quite loved them as before or felt as loved by them, failing her as they had, it appeared, in not protecting her from this guilty sorrow, this price to be paid, this knowledge, this orphan's knowledge which other children were spared, it seemed. And so, as she advanced in scholarship, her learning was accompanied by some confusion, as is natural, but which troubled the little neophyte, novice still as she was; and as new doors were opened to her, others were darkened.

Almost upon the heels of the sparrow, if one may put it so, and I believe one may, as certainly the heels of a sparrow are the last to be seen on his final flight, came the death of the horse. The series of staccato scenes, or things, or sounds, surrounding the death of the horse, the short story of this event, remained with her as long as the sparrow-death, but with less atmosphere, less conflict, and more logical in sequence and vivid in recollection. It happened more simply, directly; other people were in on it; other people might even be to blame; other people were sorry and whispered about it and looked at her sympathetically, as if to say, "The horse was Sister's friend," but they did not speak out loud. People tiptoed for a horse and in the very center of the human silence came the shot that their silence made so brilliant and meaningful.

Not until night, when she was alone in the dark, and she could faintly smell the stable, did she remember having beaten the horse and the sound of the shot became a sickening, fiery pain that ran across the center of her breasts and down the middle of her, in the shape of a cross, and it came again and again. She cried, "How could they shoot the horse, how cruel, how cruel!" But she was alone again in her guilt as the picture of herself administering a beating to the horse, as if there were two of her (if there only were, that she might share her guilt), one in bed, and one in the stable, came vividly back in technicolor. She saw the sleek red shine of the thoroughbred forehead and the dark shadows of his stall, the yellowish white of his eyeballs, and the scarlet fringe of blood that came into them. When

he avoided the stinging whip in his face by rearing up and breaking
the rope in a frenzy, she had got out of the stable with the same
ghastly slowness and breathlessness as she had heretofore extricated
herself from bad dreams, and the rest of the day she walked lightly,
in terror of something unheard of and noisy happening. The fact
that she loved the horse had absolutely nothing to do with her beating him; it was a separate thing of itself, that had nothing to do with
anything at all, and it was just such an entity that she forgot it; it
had no place in the continued story of her consciousness and she
only remembered it after the horse was dead, so that it was as if she
were beating his corpse. It had come back to her simultaneously with
the unwanted memory of the shot and from then on it was murder,
her first, and she lacked spirit to defend herself or even prolong her
remorse. Even in this she was precocious: she felt the fatigue of a
criminal who has done it again and it is no longer news, no longer
to be denied, no longer fresh or exciting or the end of the world. It
cannot even be confessed; conscience money is for amateurs. She
accepted the murder of the horse and when her governess a week
later took her for a long walk, she laid a bunch of violets and daisies
on that big heap in the woods where the woman good-naturedly had
taken her, instructed by those aging dramatists who felt responsible
for her soul and body. That evening they eyed her solicitously without mentioning the horse any more than they had her brother (they
knew nothing of the sparrow, that sorrow as secret as the bird's own
dark little grave).

The Great Aunt was an out-of-town relative, always strange and
new in spite of their long association, and the sight of her, beautiful
and distinguished, in her white coffin, wrapped in satin and surrounded by lilies, did not upset her very much at the time. Living
for long periods with the lady had accustomed her to terror and a
feeling of very superior unreality. A distinguished Virginian's belief
in ghosts somehow could not be exactly savage and the high-class
dead who inhabited her Aunt's big house would not stoop to calling
"boo" to a child, or rattling. But the place was eerie, and highly intellectual, abstract. The servants were good Catholics and candles were

burned generously in thunder storms and during the Aunt's final
illness. The dog, the only dog that Sister never made friends with,
disappeared, but his disappearance worried no one very much; he
seemed more in his element absent than present. He had never been
seen to eat, he never romped, he walked slowly behind his mistress,
serious and beautiful, who spoke often of him, but never to him; he
avoided Sister and the servants avoided him, circling him as they
approached his mistress at tea time. The only other animal that ever
appeared in this house was a little cat with electric fur which had
once dashed through the immaculate drawing room, its tail on high,
its face a smirk, ears back, as if either it were being chased by the
devil or it, the cat, was chasing the devil himself. Sister expected
a kind of circular parade, continuous and exciting like a merry-go-
round, but it only happened once. It was the cat that she had heard
her Aunt speak of as "that little elemental." And so, all in all, death
in this house was not shocking, but quite *au fait*, in keeping; it belonged. And her Aunt's passing would be more or less literary, a
manner of speaking, an explanation to tradesmen when the orders
diminished, rather than a change in the house. There was no doubt
that the great lady would always remain in its many mirrors, and her
fingerprints on the tea things, her breath in the garden on a cold
day, and a dent in the flesh of the first slowly ripening peach of suc-
cessive summers. Sister watched an old Irish servant, with eyebrows
as high on her forehead as her late mistress's, extinguish the neat,
bright fire on the hearth with a small pitcher of water as usual, gin-
gerly, with dignity; her Aunt who had wished to be, and had this
day been, cremated, had feared fire. And so as the day ended, these
two commands were executed, as all her commands in life were executed, if not lovingly, respectfully, with a kind of natural acceptance
of her superiority. As the old woman left she said, "Good night, Miss
Sister," and then before she quit the room entirely, hesitated, and
looking in another direction, curtsied and crossed herself. After that
there seemed to be a strange Catholic gayety in the direction of the
usually silent kitchen, felt rather than seen or heard, and when the
old girl brought Sister her glass of milk there were bright spots on

her cheeks. This, then, was the only change in the place, where her Great Aunt, dead, was not much different from her Great Aunt, alive, seeming as it did that she had merely attained a high rarified point in her abstracted existence, and Sister felt no further away and no closer to her than she ever had, and this difference was not offensive either, because it was not exactly disobedience, the Aunt having accepted not too contemptuously the queer earthy scholasticism of the Irish servants.

But not until she got home to the old people and the orbit of her unresistingly fading parents did she snap out of it, so to speak, and return to the everyday world of regret and guilt and sorrow, and hug to her small breast that "old Adam" which baptism had no more dispelled than hocus-pocus or balderdash, and which at least kept her company when she had a toothache. And so she became desperately sorry and woke in the night weeping for an Aunt who despised tears and forbade them. And the realization that she had not loved her Aunt and had feared to touch her, when the Aunt had gone so far on occasion, in her childlessness, to call her "Daughter," filled Sister with pity for the dead woman, who had seemed so superior during her life, and this conflict made her toss from side to side, to rid herself of it. The Aunt who while living behaved like a spirit, now in death became a living woman, but beyond the reach of loving care or sentiment, and the frustrated Sister bit her nails and hid in the ice house, and became more and more a funny, rude, speechless child; walking in the shade and feeling, God forbid, different. And being a precise child, intellectually, she decidedly made no attempt to respond to the old people in any way in order to make up to herself for not having loved the Aunt; no more than she could welcome a live puppy in remembrance of a dead one, as we have said before, and with insight beyond her years, she knew that death was a period, and not a semicolon; death to those who were left behind in that death was the end of something, and no energy or will or imagination could do anything about it, also.

The old people died almost before she knew it and without her even looking, except with her eyes. Awakening to the past she let slip the present and was not there to reach them vinegar or ease their going in any way. The old man went first, worrying about the fruit trees and melons and angry that there were people in the room when he wasn't dressed, and then the old lady, who had only continued to live to be there last, knowing the old man's dependence on her, died comfortably, sinking slowly, not hurting herself or upsetting anything, to the floor, and did not get up. They hardly had to do anything about her, she looked so dressed for death in her best clothes and so neat and pleasant. She couldn't have chosen a better moment, the old grandmother who fussed over Sister's appearance because "suppose you got run over in those stockings!" Sister could not help but note in her first lack of any feeling whatever, the difference in these old people's picture of themselves in death, and the Great Aunt's; they only wanting badly to be modest and buried in the earth and the Aunt in a sheath of satin and lilies, the abstraction of fire.

Sister felt the two new deaths with increasing grief, however, and a kind of cumulative terror as if everything was fast being taken out of her hands and that neither tears nor denials ("No! No! No!") could stop the avalanche, or interrupt the parade until it had passed, and then, as it turned out, she too would join it, bring up the rear, alone and not alone, "Thou, too, Sister." The plain physical loss, besides, must not be underestimated; the death of the Aunt, with her books, her pictures, her continental reminiscences and her intellectual appeal, left Sister with no place to go and the loss of her old people left her with no place to come. She absently returned to her grandmother's room again and again, looking for her, expecting to find her, and at night she walked in her sleep searching for the everyday grandmother, the always-there-one who could not possibly be gone. And she suffered from not having done her homework and having failed to anticipate once again that final examination, Death.

The dog, too, is dead, and Sister has known anger. The inexcusable, massacre of the dog by her mother's sister, who had the colossal nerve and so-called unmitigated gall to maintain that it was "for the best," and that the dog was in pain, enraged Sister to such an extent and infuriated her to such a point that for the time being she felt no sorrow. In her indignation she grew tall in the sight of her frightened relative and her blazing eyes and pale face gave her a real priority, a distinct and formidable stature. It did not last long; down to her last love, her only confidant, not including her brother, because they had been lovers and her intuition had taught her not to tell him everything, she felt her great loss come over her, blotting her out, and she cried bitterly, weakly, uncontrollably, for the dog. The dear dog, the dog of many pet names, names that implied relationship, relationship of every sort and degree down to cousins twice removed, and of a tenderness so personal that I hesitate out of sensibility to repeat them. This was the dog who had been all things to Sister; the one who had brought back to her a sense of direction, and with it security and reality, when she woke up at night not knowing whether she was right side up until she sensed the warmth of the dog at her feet. This was the dog who knew certain things and would never tell, not out of dumbness but out of goodness, and who understood that although some of the things she did seemed bad in English and filled Sister with fear and remorse, according to him might be forgotten. Sister violently despised the woman who had done this thing and her loneliness which before had been more or less chosen, now became real. But her love for the dog had been such an affection, expressed as it was without restraint, and her Aunt's brutality had so outshadowed any cruelty of her own, that this last death was almost easy, so without remorse or guilt it was. The Dog had known she loved him, who else had? If she had? But Sister did not think of these things now, she returned to her daydreams, and fortified by her experiences in the subject matter of her involuntary choice, she began to prepare her thesis. The grind was over and now she could create, alongside of her signature placing that bit of rhetoric, that classic *non sequitur*, "I pledge my word I have neither given nor received aid in this examination," invented by the first cheat who employed the first Ghost, no doubt.

Sister's own death was not simple but complicated. It took place in her mind; in consequence, the unconsciousness following it lasted a long time and only with the gentle care of an old fellow who called himself *pater familias* was she persuaded later to return to earth. This return seemed to her more unnatural and difficult than dying, for which she had so well prepared herself, aided and abetted by funereal events, and she felt as queer among the living upon her return as lively ones possibly do, at first, in Heaven. Sister got up early the day of her death and said good-bye to everything and then she died in a number of ways, none suiting her until she lay upon her bed in a white night dress, everything in good order, her feet in pink-knitted sleeping socks because her toes were cold. On the bedside table a light shone on a small transparent glass empty but for the remains of something chalky, and the weight of this little spirit glass was enough to keep in place that sweet-girl-graduate note of farewell the words of which were never clear even to Sister. The tears that beaded her eyelashes and slid down into her ears were not shed for herself but for the others who felt her loss so keenly. Sister was a musician, a great musician who had won a great prize and her death was a loss to the world and of no consequence to herself. She wept for those who stood around her bed as she stood with them watching herself. "Thou too, Sister," she whispered and they bent their heads to hear more of this Caesarean talk from a little girl. This child without parents, relations or animal friends died surrounded by those who knew she was an artist and she was happy, happier than she had ever been and ever would be again and the strange bright color on the high curve of her cheeks and the fullness of her lips belied so the look of death that the music lovers at her bedside must have gone home and discussed the phenomenon.

Well, Sister is gone as I said she would be, not exactly a prediction *accompli* but the fulfillment of a metaphor: in description as well as in sequence, sweet-girl-graduate, *magna cum laude*. Except that she is horizontal rather than upright she might be dressed for her diploma, in a white gown, with flowing hair and pink cheeks, knowing at last all the answers and leaving perhaps under the glass, "No one helped me and neither am I to blame; forgive me for being so smart," which translated into the academic might become that scholarly perjury I have mentioned, "I pledge my word I have never, etc."

You know the rest because it has been written: how she forgot death and no longer anticipated it either with fear or longing, setting her apart from her neighbors in this respect but in this respect only, becoming as she did a normal, healthy and responsive woman, not lazy enough to be very talented and not efficient enough to be entirely wasting her time. She forgot death after her graduation (from it) just as the young scholar forgets his education, partly from having hated it and suffered because of it, as she had from death in its many manifestations, and besides, why leave the scaffolding after the house is built, of what use is your education except getting it? She forgot death and its attendant fears exactly as the student happily forgets the hardest part and fondles his *Phi Beta Kappa* key almost nostalgically, as Sister might the invisible death's head suspended upon her, having forgotten. And having died, it is improbable that she will die again. She does not anticipate it. Farewell, Sister.

The Marriage of Toto

A PLAY

Suggested by a UP report that a female gorilla had been sold to Pell's Circus by Mrs. Sylvia Waterbury, "because she has grown tall and big and people around her were afraid." The circus expects to mate her with Gargantua, the Great, a notorious gorilla.

CHARACTERS

Toto . . . . *a young lady gorilla*
Gargantua . . . . *a gorilla (550 pounds)*
José . . . . *Toto's keeper*
Mrs. Sylvia Waterbury . . . . *female explorer*
200 spectators
3 policemen
A little girl

SCENE ONE. *Phoenix, Arizona. Friday.*

TOTO [*to herself, analytically. Pronounces "Cuba" — "Cooba,"
which has a sweet sound, very appealing*]:
I miss Cuba already. But it isn't Cuba that I really miss. Cuba is
where I was last, just as I am here now. Everything is a sequence and
it is sensible to remember where one has come from rather than be
consumed with nostalgia for a place one can't remember.

MRS. SYLVIA WATERBURY:
Toto!

TOTO [*continues to herself*]:
Much will be expected of me; I must try to think of the future. But
have I a future? Has any gorilla a future? Cuba was a lovely place;
don't I remember dark, warm looks? Thin, fast hands? I really do. I
have never wanted to be anything else but a gorilla and that is why I
am a success, it is true, neither have I wanted to be any other gorilla
except myself—Toto—but the black eyes of Cubans were large and
lucid and they had whites. What has happened that I have no whites
to my eyes with a pretty pattern of silky veins like tiny rivers of blood?
And love, what is love?

MRS. SYLVIA WATERBURY:
Toto! Have you forgotten me? José, José! Doesn't she love me any
more?

TOTO [*politely*]:
How do you do.

JOSÉ:
Chiquita, kiss the señora.

MRS. SYLVIA WATERBURY:
She has grown. Good for you, Toto; you are enormous, simply huge.

200 SPECTATORS:
It's Toto.
It's Mrs. Sylvia Waterbury.
Hyer, Toots.
Hyer, Babe.

MRS. SYLVIA WATERBURY:
Toto, darling. José, make her look at me. What is the matter with her?

170

JOSÉ:
Look, look, never mind, just look.
  TOTO:
Cuba.
  JOSÉ [*to Mrs. Sylvia Waterbury*]:
She is homesick.
  MRS. SYLVIA WATERBURY:
For what?
  JOSÉ:
She is just homesick.
  MRS. SYLVIA WATERBURY:
But she is mine. Didn't she miss me?
  JOSÉ:
Yes, Señora.
  MRS. SYLVIA WATERBURY [*tries Spanish*]:
Chiquita.
  TOTO:
Cooba.
  200 SPECTATORS:
Speak to us, Toto.
Give us a few words.
What do you think of Arizona?
Were you seasick?
A few words, Toto.
Ha, ha, ha.
  TOTO [*to herself*]:
What is love? What is expected of me?
  MRS. SYLVIA WATERBURY:
I can't wait to see her with Gargantua.
  200 SPECTATORS:
Neither can we.
Neither can we.
Neither can we.
We can't wait.
  JOSÉ:
Poor Toto.

MRS SYLVIA WATERBURY:

Send them all away until tomorrow.

JOSÉ:

Go away until tomorrow.

200 SPECTATORS:

It's a gyp.

Give me my money back.

We haven't seen Gargantua.

No fair.

JOSÉ [*quieting them*]:

Listen, listen: Toto is tired; Toto did not sleep all night. Insomnia is bad for gorillas. It exasperates gorillas. Look out for Toto if you add to her exasperation. Much is expected of Toto. Be kind to her. She is nervous.

200 SPECTATORS:

Ha, ha, ha.

MRS. SYLVIA WATERBURY [*with authority*]:

Go at once or you will not see Toto and Gargantua tomorrow.

[*They go. Mrs. Sylvia Waterbury also goes, throwing a kiss to Toto. José and Toto are alone.*]

JOSÉ:

It won't be so bad, Toto.

TOTO:

Much is expected of me. I must pull myself together. At last I am alone with my José, but he tells me nothing. José, José, what is love?

JOSÉ:

You need some rest, poor Toto, tomorrow will be a big day. Here is a banana, please eat it for José.

TOTO:

What is Gargantua? José, José, what is Gargantua?

JOSÉ:

I think she is worrying considerably about that big ape. She is so gentle, sweet Toto.

TOTO:

I shall be as nice as I can; everyone has been so good to me.

172

JOSÉ:

How do people know how a gorilla feels; what my Toto thinks? I am sure she understands me. But can I comfort her? Can I promise her happiness? I don't trust that big Gargantua. Listen, Toto, tomorrow you will no longer be alone. Perhaps tomorrow you will be happy. Toto, listen to José, don't cry.

TOTO:

Why do I feel so sad all at once? Why am I afraid? What is going to happen?

JOSÉ:

Toto, Toto, calm yourself. I want to tell you something. I must tell her; it would not be right not to. Toto, little one, listen to your José and stop crying. Don't cry, Toto.

TOTO:

What is it? what is it? I am afraid. José, José. Help!

JOSÉ [*stern*]:

Quiet, Toto.

TOTO [*frantic*]:

Help. Help. Help, Help!

JOSÉ:

Toto. Quiet! The Whip!

TOTO [*sobs*]:

José beats me and I have done nothing.

JOSÉ [*more gentle*]:

I can't stay with you if you get so excited. Would you like some hot milk?

TOTO:

Yes.

JOSÉ:

Good.

TOTO [*a little hysterical*]:

Hot milk, hot milk, bananas, bananas, but no understanding. Even José doesn't understand. But how can he? Neither do I, neither do I. I feel overpowered. I feel a sick terror. I am shaking. I remember something but it has no shape. It is coming. Here it comes. I cannot breathe. Oh, help me, José. Ahh, it is gone.

josé [*sad*]:

Poor creature, poor Toto.

toto [*calm, sensible*]:

It is gone but it will come back. Thank you, José, for taking it away.
The milk is good. Oh thank you, thank you, José, for everything.

josé:

Now she is calm. Now is the time to tell her, but what is it I am to
tell her? Look at her poise; look at her charm; how innocent she is;
how almost benevolent and almost maternal; how tender and aloof.
Toto . . . more milk? Nice hot milk, Toto, mine? *Chiquita?*

toto:

No thank you.

josé:

Now is the time.

toto:

I must prepare myself. I must think. But where is the subject matter?

josé:

First I must remember my own apprehension. I must feel sorry for
José; then I can help Toto. I remember very well, too well. I wish I
could forget. How all love fled, all freedom, and in its place responsibility. Much was expected of me; how I wanted to run; how I did
run, in my mind, while my body . . . but this is not for Toto. There
must be something else for Toto—so sweet, so gentle, so good. How
awful everything is, *caramba.*

toto:

Have a banana, José, here, have mine.

josé:

See her offer me comfort, She is sorry for me.

toto:

Everything will be all right.

josé:

(1) Love, (2) apprehension, (3) shame, (4) pity, (5) loss of free
will, that is the sequence. How can I talk of love to Toto who is a
young girl? In the first place I am a man and in the second place she
is a virgin. She is innocent; she is the kind who will always be inno-

174

cent; her strong will will keep her mind always innocent; I foresee
that and yet she is humble; she will seem to give in. While I, José,
am not innocent, was never innocent; that is why I desire it so. I love
Toto because she is innocent. I must not take her spirit in my arms; I
must not tell her anything. But I want to! Toto, Toto, listen, listen,
Toto, give me your attention, unbend your will. José will make you a
woman with his tongue, listen!

TOTO:

José is restless; he needs sleep. Quiet, José. José is beautiful, how
beautiful he is. His skin is too smooth, he should not go without his
shirt. (How smooth and yellow Mrs. Sylvia Waterbury is.) I am very
fond of my José but his skin is disgusting, I love it, it is brown and
slippery and really disgusting and appealing. José? Gargantua? Love?
I must think. Will Gargantua be like José? Will he have whites to his
eyes, slightly blue like José's and skin like that . . . skin like José's?

JOSÉ [*confused*]:

I am crazy. But not so crazy that I will rape Toto's spirit with my
crude words. I am ashamed that I have nearly done it. I hate my
tongue, it is vile. Dear Jesu, I have harmed so many but this one I
really love, I pray to Mary that I do not harm Toto. Amen.

JOSÉ [*continues, tries hard to be helpful*]:

Tomorrow, Toto, you will have a life-long companion, perhaps a
friend; you will have a protector, a playmate; someone who speaks
your own language, understands you. He will take care of you in your
old age, too, maybe, and you will share things together: sorrow and
happiness, contentment, pleasure, even fear; when you are afraid it is
possible that he, too, will be afraid and that will help.

TOTO:

What is he talking about? He has a foolish, patronizing expression on
his face which a while ago was so true, so real. I am very tired but I
must not look bored. Maybe it is a story, it is quite long. Poor José.

JOSÉ:

That is no good; I don't mean it and she knows it. We have had long
talks before and she has understood; I cannot fool her. What will I
do if she loves Gargantua? *Caramba!* [*swears*] I'll bash his stupid,

ugly, son-of-a-bitch head in. Jesu, Mary, pardon. Toto?

TOTO:

Yes, José.

JOSÉ:

I will tell you the truth: love is terrible. Love is an act which is rational for the man but irrational, terrible, for the woman: to receive an act! that is crazy, indescribable, indistinct, without form, mad. For the woman it is murder which she has not even committed; she is without subject matter, without object matter, without verb. That is terror. But don't, if you hate the man, your tormenter, your successor, any name you want to call him, think that being a verb is without its terror, its madness. If you want him to suffer, be content, he does. He does not want what he wants, believe me, I am José of many loves, of many disappointments, much shame, much disgust. To be all action, that too is terrible. Love for the man is a false freedom, a pretense of freedom; he may choose his woman, it is true, and the delight and superiority of choosing so fools and pleases him that he does not see until it is over that his act is not of his choice but he only the instrument and he does not like to be used. He does not like to be merely the key which fits symbolically into the lock which in its turn metaphorically shuts the door on his freedom. Do not misunderstand me, woman, he loves your dependence, the trial you are to him, it is his lack of choice in action, his loss of free will, his responsibility of the act, *the* act, *the* responsibility that makes him feel like a dog with his paws held down, a baby tied in his crib. Pity him, pity *me*, José, who loves you, Toto; loves your spirit but in wanting it, wants *it*, even, in symbols. José is man, not a gorilla, but he cannot achieve an abstraction, he cannot love truly because he must think in images, intuition is imperfect in him, he must symbolically translate his love, must eat it, hold it, act. Forgive José, he is a mad verb and the instrument of symbols; without free will.

TOTO:

José is telling me of life, responsibility, housekeeping, maternity. He is teaching me patience, pity, self-sacrifice. He is telling me to forgive, he is asking for my understanding, perseverance. I love him, I am special. He has chosen me. I am disgusting.

josé [*firm, tries to say it with less emotion, better*] :
Listen, Toto. Tomorrow Gargantua will hold you in his arms. Tomorrow you and Gargantua will re-enact a play without words. You
will together demonstrate an idea in order to prove to yourselves an
abstraction. You will come close to reality, close to Idea, itself, in the
true concentration you will both insist upon, but the imperfect sym-
bolization of your act will leave you each discontented and no repetition will prove to either of you anything at all.

toto:
Why is he scolding me? Is it because I have no whites; is there anything wrong with me? Am I not lovable? Am I evil? What are my
plans; why am I a gorilla? Is it wrong? José, tell me a story, it is
nearly morning.

josé:
By Jesu, Toto, you will listen. But how can I tell her of the sorrow,
the disgrace, the disappointment of love, the hatred, the lack of companionship between man and woman; the silences which in courtship
are pregnant, sweet but in possession are barren, filled with regret,
disgust, a time to plan the death of one's love, to think of cruelty,
torment, sarcasm, expiation at most, the want to retract, get out of it,
revenge oneself, regain one's self respect, unity, oneness, to be lonely
again? Poor José, poor Toto, *Chiquita!*

toto:
I am not sad, José, don't worry about me. Have some hot milk.

[*José and Toto eat crackers and milk while it is nearly morning.*]

SCENE TWO: *Same Morning.*

*In a big glass cage sits tremendous Gargantua on a little stool like a
prize-fighter; his great hairy arms are draped over its sides exactly like
a prize-fighter, too. He is vain and looks from side to side at the crowd
and shows his teeth, two of which have been filled with gold; they
shine. He also wears a handsome pair of horn-rimmed sun glasses;
the crowd is delighted, they point. He takes the glasses off, spits on*

them, polishes them on his knee, replaces them. The crowd howls happily. He is without doubt the ugliest of all possible creatures and they can hardly contain themselves when, upon being handed a woman's pocketbook, he takes out a tiny mirror, removes his glasses, and peers at small parts of his great face in its shiny surface; finally he opens his mouth wide and stares at his tonsils. He is much more satisfactory than Toto, a real showman, a credit to his owners, to his tamer, to all gorillahood. What will Toto think?

There is a commotion; cries of "There she is," and Toto is gently pushed into the cage by José, who turns away, saying, "Think of something else, Toto." The crowd is suddenly still; the sun shines brightly; three policemen push through the crowd with Mrs. Sylvia Waterbury and her party; a couple of flashlights are taken of Mrs. Sylvia Waterbury; and all eyes are turned now upon the two animals.

TOTO [*brings herself to look*]:
Oh, my God.

GARGANTUA [*sullen; thinks here is a competitor for favor*]:
(nothing)

TOTO [*critical*]:
He is beautiful but he lacks charm. Can this be Gargantua!

GARGANTUA:
He isn't as big as me, or anything. What are they looking at him for?

TOTO:
Why doesn't he take off his coat?

GARGANTUA:
I didn't ask for company. Phooey.

TOTO:
He has no skin. I prefer José although this Gargantua is disgusting in a different way. But he is not gentle, he is mean, selfish, despicable. Oh, I distrust him, I despise him. Look at his forehead, his ears, his long feet, he is beautiful but bad. He is a bad gorilla. I am lost. José, José! Help Toto!

GARGANTUA:
Cripes, it's a female.

TOTO [*wrings her hands*]:
José, José, I'll be good, I'll be quiet. José, José!
JOSÉ [*appears; worried*]:
Stop it, Toto, he hasn't touched you.
TOTO:
I have a headache, José; please, please let me out; I don't feel good.
Take me back, José, back to Cuba.
GARGANTUA:
Kewbar? What a goofy dame. Hi you, babe, this joint has it all over
Kewbar. What's all the shootin' for?
TOTO:
What a funny accent.
[*The crowd is getting restless; a few indecent remarks are passed.*]
MRS. SYLVIA WATERBURY [*feels responsible; stands apart and makes a
megaphone of her hands*]:
Give them time. [*Then to Toto.*] Toto, see the Nice Big Husband.
200 SPECTATORS:
Ha, ha, ha, ha.
MRS. SYLVIA WATERBURY [*indignant*]:
Don't laugh.
[*Gargantua is pleased at the laughter; takes no further notice of
Toto; starts his tricks. But the spectators, beguiling as he is, are
disappointed. They boo.*]
SPECTATORS:
Boooooooooooooo.
[*Gargantua looks worried; tries hard to amuse.*]
SPECTATORS:
Boooooooooooooo. Boooooooooooooo.
GARGANTUA [*suddenly jealous of the newcomer; in a rage*]:
That goofy dame. I'll kill her.
TOTO:
Help, help, help, help!
[*Gargantua rises with slow fury from his stool and starts toward his
supposed rival. The spectators gasp.*]
SPECTATORS:
Ahhhhh.

MRS. SYLVIA WATERBURY [*claps her hands*]:

Goody, goody.

JOSÉ:

You're all right, Toto, take it easy.

[*Cameramen set up their cameras.*]

CHILD [*in a thin voice; insisting*]:

What are the Teddy Bears DOING?

[*Gargantua swings his long arms like a windmill, first one way, then the other, lifts up his chin, opens his mouth wide and shuts it again, stops in the middle of the cage and jumps up and down in one place, and then with a scream, a long drawn screech, takes off his sun glasses and hurls them at the frightened Toto.*]

GARGANTUA:

Goofy dame, goofy dame, get out of here!

SPECTATORS:

Hu - hu - g-g-g-igh. Heh, heh.

MRS. SYLVIA WATERBURY:

Naughty Gargantua, that isn't the way to please a lady. Be nice, Gargantua, be nice.

[*Toto in her fright presses herself to the glass, kisses it in supplication.*]

TOTO [*moans*]:

José, José, Toto will be good.

[*The spectators see Gargantua, shaken by his unsatisfactory act of fury, in the center of the cage turning his head from side to side, coughing like an old man.*]

GARGANTUA:

Ummpfh, garumpfh, rugpfh. Grmngtfsh. Achgftsh. Ggggg . Ssspff.
[*Recovering, he remembers his precious glasses; starts looking for them; spies them at Toto's feet; edges over, one arm protecting his head as if he feared a blow. This gesture charms half the spectators, makes up for their disappointment; they laugh.*]

HALF THE SPECTATORS:

Ha, ha, ha.

180

[*Gargantua is happy, starts mugging; repeats the successful gesture; outdoes himself.*]

200 SPECTATORS:

Ha, ha, ha, ha, ha, ha, ha, ha, ha, ha, ha.

MRS. SYLVIA WATERBURY:

Ha, ha, ha, ha, ha, ha, ha, ha, ha, ha, ha.

3 POLICEMEN:

Ha, ha, ha, ha, ha, ha, ha, ha, ha, ha, ha.

CAMERAMEN:

Ha, ha, ha, ha, ha, ha, ha, ha, ha, ha, ha.

TOTO [*can't be heard*]:

José, José.

JOSÉ [*kind*] [*neither can he*]:

Come *Chiquita*, never mind; poor Toto. It has been a big day. Do not be humiliated. It is not your fault.

[*He leads her away by the hand.*]

SCENE BEHIND THE SCENES: *Toto. José. Enter Mrs. Sylvia Waterbury.*

JOSÉ:

Toto is exhausted, I am giving her some hot milk.

MRS. SYLVIA WATERBURY:

I am sorry for the poor thing. But wasn't it a scream. I nearly died laughing.

JOSÉ:

It is not really funny, excuse me, Señora, to Toto.

MRS. SYLVIA WATERBURY [*peering at him curiously*]:

You seem to know what Toto thinks.

JOSÉ:

I sometimes know how she feels but no man can understand a woman.

MRS. SYLVIA WATERBURY:

You amuse me.

JOSÉ:

(nothing)

MRS. SYLVIA WATERBURY:

Come here, Toto.

JOSÉ:

Please, Señora, don't worry her.

MRS. SYLVIA WATERBURY [*angry*]:

I worry her? She's mine, I brought her up.

JOSÉ [*placating her*]:

Si, Señora, Si, Si.

MRS. SYLVIA WATERBURY [*continues in the same tone*]:

From the time she was little. I fed her on a bottle; everything. When she got so big, I was the only one who wasn't afraid of her. People thought it was remarkable that I wasn't afraid of her, but I had to sell her because other people were; you know all that, everybody does. I managed her by firmness, character. *Come*, Toto, come this *instant*, come to Mother. *Come*, I say! [*She approaches Toto, who is eating her crackers and milk with a big wooden spoon.*] *Obey* me! Toto!

[*As Mrs. Sylvia Waterbury comes within reach of Toto, Toto sets down the bowl of milk, wraps a long arm around Mrs. Sylvia Waterbury and lifts her from the ground. Before José, who does not hurry, can reach her, Toto has broken the neck of Mrs. Sylvia Waterbury, who dies instantly, without having had time to change her expression which shows firmness, character. Not one hair is out of place; she might still be called one of the eight best-dressed women.*]

TOTO [*picking up her bowl of milk*]:

Don't look angry at Toto, José. I know I have failed. Much was expected of me, but what is love, José? What is love? Cuba. I must think. José expected much of me, much, much, was expected of me. What shall I do? José, José.

The Metamorphosis of Toto

By the way: have you heard the rumor that Toto is a male, after all, and not a female?

SCENE ONE:

A zoo in the Middle West. Toto is alone; moping. Enter José. Toto looks the same; has sustained herself. José, however, has a crew haircut and wears a bow tie; has his first papers. At heart he remains the same José, nevertheless.

José runs in; throws his arms around Toto. Toto hunches her shoulders; disengages herself; doesn't smile.

JOSÉ:
Toto, Toto! It is definitely established that you are a male!
TOTO [*a little slow*]:
Really.
JOSÉ:
Really.
TOTO:
I don't believe it; how could I.

JOSÉ:

The gentlemen say so; the anthropologists voted on it; only one of them held out for acquittal . . .

TOTO:

But they don't know me; they have never seen me; Toto doesn't know these people; I don't want to be anybody else but Toto. Please go away, José. Do you mind going?

JOSÉ:

Toto, listen: they don't have to see you; that would prejudice them and they have to figure it out in their heads because they are so smart and they use statistics. It all adds up.

JOSÉ:

Statistics?

JOSÉ:

There is only one of you, Toto; I'm afraid you don't count in an important scientific conclusion like this. Excuse me, Toto.

TOTO:

This is too much. I can't stand too much even if I am a gorilla. [*She begins to cry.*]

JOSÉ:

Toto! Be a man! Jeepers, *caramba!*

TOTO:

Oh, oh, oh, oh, oh, oh.

[*José, as if for the last time, tries to soothe her, pets her, tickles her ear.*]

JOSÉ:

Laugh, Toto mine, laugh for José.

TOTO:

I don't *want* to be a man.

JOSÉ [*inspired*]:

Just think, Toto, we can be friends now.

TOTO [*between sobs*]:

I thought we *were.*

I thought we *were.*

184

JOSÉ [*shakes his head in disbelief*]:
Toto, baby, you are so innocent; you will have to stop all that now.
  TOTO [*interested*]:
Aren't men innocent?
  JOSÉ:
Oh, no, never.
  TOTO:
But you, José? My José?
  JOSÉ [*angry; sincere*]:
Stop it, Toto. Me innocent? José innocent? Cuba innocent?
  TOTO:
How awful everything is. Why is José so angry and truthful? He has
changed. What has happened to him; he is different; can it be that
it has been definitely established that he is a female? What is he try-
ing to prove? Why isn't he gentle anymore? I miss him.
  JOSE [*pays no attention; laughs; is vain*]:
Me innocent: José of many conquests, continuous love affairs.
Women in his arms from morning till night? Find a woman who
will not give José all she has to give and whisper in his ear her grati-
tude. Eh, *amigo*?
  TOTO:
José, José, how you have changed!
  JOSÉ [*improves a little; looks at Toto*]:
You must know, Toto, the big difference, the historical and psycho-
logical difference between a man and a woman?
  TOTO [*intuitively*]:
José is a Latin but I am only a gorilla. How can I be specific?
  JOSÉ:
It is going to be even better than before, Toto. We can be friends
now; I can understand you; before I was afraid of you, I did not know
how to please you, Toto; quite frankly, between pals, there is only
one way to content a woman, as you must know now, certainly you
know that, and I was at a loss if you don't mind too much, Toto,
amigo. You see now my predicament. Our affection was sweet, it is
true, but I was confused, oh so confused; I could not sleep with you,

could I? There was no end to our relationship, was there? I waited
on you, felt for you, really adored you but it was exhausting. Now I
can relax. I know where I stand now. We will be friends. Listen,
amigo, to what happened to me last night. [*He laughs.*] I went out
as you know to buy us our late supper. I had not gone far when a
blond girl, a pretty one, *caramba*, with bare legs and high heels, a
pretty little tart, *caramba*, Toto . . . are you listening?

[*Toto looks so stern, so aloof, so deliberately uncomprehending that
José is quiet. José thinks, frowning. Toto has no expression at all.
Finally—*]

JOSÉ:

Toto, you exasperate me. You will never adapt yourself to anything.
You won't see that the States can be fun, isn't so bad, and now you
refuse to be a man, when it is as inevitable as the States. I, too, miss
Cuba, of course, but it is fun here too . . . and this is not a bad picture
of you here in the *Tribune.*

TOTO:

May I have the funnies?

[*Toto examines the funnies, looks sadder and sadder, starts to cry.*]

JOSÉ:

Caramba, why do you cry, my Toto?

TOTO:

The funnies are so sad, so sad, so inevitable like the States, José, like
the States.

JOSÉ:

Once, Toto, I tried my very best to prepare you for love; I failed. I
failed because I was not a woman and you were. But I know something I can teach you now, *amigo*, if you will please not be so aloof,
so feminine, so hard to please. Listen, Toto, I know all about women,
listen to me; I am wise. Listen, Toto: play hard to get. A woman,
Toto, must be indispensable, gently, gradually indispensable, but a
man, *Chiquita* (excuse me, pal), a man must be a bad boy, playing at
war, playing at love, a big businessman, a little lad; a wicked, spoiled

child, a drunkard, a liar, a tease, and a hero, above all a hero; a hero in the air, on a horse, in the stock market, and a coward, too, don't forget, who cries in his sleep for his mama and is afraid of the dark, that is very charming. And a big appetite, Toto; eat happily immense amounts, chew hard, smile and fall asleep, wake up and swear and kick things around and go out for a spell, come home late, and make love, Toto, make love like a hero, squander yourself, don't be stingy; make love and do as you please. You can't lose, *amigo*, now **that you** are a man.

TOTO [*has not been listening*]:
When I was Toto I was afraid of love. Now I am *Amigo*. I am disgusted.

JOSÉ:
Why do I always lie?

TOTO:
But I will refuse this honor: I don't have to accept it. I am Toto. [*rehearses*] Thank you very much, Gentlemen, Anthropologists, Scientists, but I cannot, I must not, I will not. Thank you each and all [*bows*], thank you from my heart; Toto thanks the eminent scientists who have spent other people's money and much of their own time, very much; who have aggravated their wives and missed their children's growing up while they counted, subtracted, divided, formed committees, dissolved committees, commuted, etc., in the name of pure science of which I was the temporary symbol; I know I was only the temporary symbol and that is why, please, may I go home now?

JOSÉ [*staring*]:
Toto, what's the matter?

TOTO [*sobs*]:
Please, José, please, please, please.

JOSÉ [*annoyed*]:
Oh shut up, you're a pretty sight I must say.

TOTO:
José, don't leave me!

JOSÉ:
A great big ape, a big gorilla *crying*. Sissy!

TOTO:

José, José, don't accept! And besides they will laugh at you, they will laugh and throw tomatoes at you.

JOSÉ [*uneasy, confused*]:

What is the matter with her?

TOTO [*serious*]:

I won't tell on you if you won't tell on me.

JOSÉ [*gives up; shrugs; takes out a little comb and fluffs his hair*]:

Well anyway, Toto, let us rest; there will be a big crowd tomorrow, a big stupid crowd. There's your milk, Toto, I am going out for a beer. *Adios, amigo.* See you later, pal.

[*Toto is left alone. She looks across at her bowl of milk but does not move.*]

TOTO:

Poor José; he must feel very queer. I must protect him from the big stupid crowd. They will laugh at him. What is the matter with José? He doesn't understand anymore. I am all alone. Poor Toto. But I am still Toto. The anthropologists have made a mistake; they have changed José instead of me and I am sorry because I do not like women. What is the matter with anthropologists, what is the matter with the States? Is this Democracy? I suppose so; José must be content to be someone else, then, not José. He has his first papers and he has signed them. Why did you sign, poor José? [*She is exhausted and sleeps.*]

SCENE TWO:

Same, except a sign has been added: Toto, Gorilla Maximus, Male. Dangerous. There is a crowd, policemen, a Headman and Toto.

POLICEMAN:

Stand back; stand back; remember the lady; this big one is vicious.

SOMEONE:

That's Toto who killed Mrs. Sylvia Waterbury.

POLICEMAN:

Stand back, You.

188

SOMEONE:

Hello Toto. Grrrrrrrrrrr.

CROWD:

Woof! Woof!

TOTO:

Grrrrrrrrrrrr.

HEADMAN:

Quiet, quiet, quiet, please.

POLICEMAN [*swings his club*]:

Stand back, wise guys; keep your distance.

HEADMAN:

Ladies and gentlemen.

POLICEMAN [*to the crowd*]:

Shut up, Youse.

HEADMAN:

Ladies and gentlemen, I have an important announcement.

CROWD:

Sshsshsshsshssh.

HEADMAN:

Due to circumstances, hmm, over which this gorilla, hmm, whom you
have known as Toto, hmm, this gorilla which was a, hmm, female,
due to circumstances over which she had no, hmm, ha! control . . .

CROWD:

Ha ha ha ha ha ha ha ha.

POLICEMAN:

SHUT UP.

HEADMAN:

I refuse to speak to such an unmannerly crowd.

CROWD:

Aw gee please, mister.

HEADMAN:

I say after long and painstaking research, hmm, after much conscientious deliberation it has been definitely established, hmm, hmm, ha!
that Toto [*bows to Toto*] is not a female as we had, hmm, very much,
shall I say, hoped, but is, hmm; it has been definitely established, ha!

that she is a, hmm, male which accounts, which hmm, accounts. I
thank you.

CROWD:

Hurrah! Hurah! Hurrah!

SOMEONE:

It's a boy!

CROWD:

Ha ha ha ha ha ha ha.

[*Enter José, same as Scene One. Someone spies him, notes his crew
cut, his bow tie, etc.*]

SOMEONE:

It's a girl!

CROWD:

Whoo whoo!

[*The crowd instantly switches its attention from Toto, who has
never moved from the back of her cage, who seems more dead than
alive, a miserable Toto, to José . Someone lets fly a tomato; it strikes
José squarely. There is a quarter of a minute's silence.*]

TOTO:

José! José! Oh, oh, oh. No, No.

[*The crowd loses control. It is completely out of hand. The air is
filled with flying fruit. José is scarlet. The policeman runs away;
the Headman has left to announce the birth of a llama. Toto picks
up the tomatoes that drop into her cage and hurls them back with
sustained fury. Sides are taken, and the crowd is so delighted with
the battle of vegetables that they keep coming back with more all
day long. Toto, a huge success, a succès fou, alternately menaces
the crowd and pleads with it.*]

TOTO:

Stop! Wait. Don't. Please. Listen! He cannot help it! José! José!

Les Malheurs des Mannequins

Once there were two Mannequins, derived 1. from Manneken (Teutonic) 2. Mannequin (French), proof of whose modern existence, for the skeptical, may be found in any art exhibit. Artists and art students have always used mannequins whether other models were available or not and they know that a mannequin is a charming person made of wood who can do everything but talk. Any curious person, layman or artist, however, must wonder whether it is part of a mannequin's cleverness to be silent or whether it is a necessity, perhaps a punishment of some sort, or a vow of silence, religious in character, carried to the extreme of *pas un mot jamais de la vie*, fanatically insisted upon, Trappist. None of this is so. Fond of my two mannequins, Quin and Quine, who have lived with me so long, I have pieced together, beginning with the fact of themselves as a premise, their history; working backwards, as it were, into their past, their causes; thinking back into that great abstract void so silent in itself, prehistorical, aboriginal, pre-elemental, even, for the reason of the identical silence which all mannequins practice; saved the interruption at least of variables; neither do I have to prove a mannequin's existence because if you do not take my word you may go to Paris where mannequins are still made in all their original beauty, each an identical image, if not of God, of Mannequin; and each is silent. I am sure no mannequin will ever speak because I know now the powerful reason for a mannequin's silence.

Until I had unravelled the *ex post facto* story of my mannequins I had made the mistake (herein disproved) that mannequins were merely images, at the most symbols, with the intrinsic dignity and everlastingness of symbols, but with that middleness that symbols by definition must have, that definitive boundary from which there is no escape. That my mannequins could voluntarily cease to do something that had been in their past their greatest, even only happiness, raised them at once, in my mind, to the doubtful loftiness of man himself, bearing like him the exciting burden of his originality among the animals, that apple of his eye which he has found so indigestible, free will; that gift from God; that sharing of *His* will; that willful deliberate severance from *His* children; that "will," as it were, disposing and sharing *His* estate, necessitating *His* retirement into abstraction; *His* sacrifice of complete omnipotence; *His* forsworn, "Do it because I say so." Well then, so He hung a painted apple on a painted bough and trusting to His children's natural contrariness forbade that which he in reality willed. I mention Adam and Eve and their pitiful but tremendous expulsion because my story is analagous and the similarity and differences significant. These similarities and differences I need not here enumerate or insist upon because everyone knows the story of Adam and Eve and may compare and contrast it as he reads the history of the mannequins. I should like to point out, however, that the expulsion of Adam and Eve was not, as is generally supposed, a punishment, but the result of a choice; even though that little choice with big consequences resulted in its turn from what looked like a pusillanimous curiosity, a childish contrariness, disobedience. God said "Don't" and man, because God willed him to, said "I will." (Has he ever said anything greater? And yet in his nostalgia he paradoxically prays to God for liberation; plaintively begs to be relieved of the results, spared the consequences of his own godlike [right or wrong] acts.)

The Mannequins did not surrender their Paradise for any of the reasons, powerful though they were, that motivated, it seems, Adam and Eve: not from boredom or curiosity, contrariness, original sin (nor did God, preoccupied with man, bend his glance or huge will upon them), but from sorrow, and of their own accord, mutually spontaneous, the mannequins became still, everlastingly quiet, and for their unspoken motto chose that lovely one, "Whereof ye cannot speak thereof ye must be silent."

Adam and Eve quit their Paradise in shame and continued for uncountable generations, which depended upon it, an act which had become shameful, no longer innocent, while the mannequins, whose only manifestation of the deep love they felt for each other had been expressed in words, forswore at once, words, when they discovered their conversation had not been innocent.

In the beginning mannequins could talk; in fact speech was their greatest joy, a supreme happiness, an exciting perfected act of love. They said beautiful things extremely well; they did nothing else, and they so perfected speech that it existed by itself and did not have to mean a thing. Words, almost by necessity, (not blessed as they were with the senses), were the love medium of this pair of doubly unrequited lovers. Amateurs of love they might be called; Figures of Speech; they were that Poetical Gender, of the subjunctive mood, conditional clauses, I think, and they were a perfect example of the concord of pronouns; qualifying adjectives and phrases, conjunctions of supposition, condition, best describe Quin and Quine: almost, not quite, as it were, hardly, perhaps, maybe, possibly, nearly, *pour ainsi dire*, if not, except, unless, without, otherwise, notwithstanding, albeit.

They had no interest in anything but each other: he did not care for stag parties, and she had no female friends. They had no resources whatever and were not interested in politics. Everything was good insofar as it reminded them of each other. Everything they did supplied analogy and metaphor and simile, otherwise they tired of it. Even the dishes they used drew sighs of recognition: a jug and it looked like Quin, a vase was Quine, arms akimbo, and a little pitcher was Quin again.

Quin and Quine were almost identical, as it turned out, but at first and for a long time in spite of long delightful staring they thought they were the same (*L'image à deux*) and they were very happy in this kind of original sameness which was real to them and which all lovers strive for and feel excitedly happy about whether it is a biological trick or not, pretense or coincidence, incest, satisfactory ultra-monogamy, double indemnity, bifocal, as it were, hermaphroditic. The differences, subtle and engaging in their neatly turned, genuinely executed and pleasingly *articulated* bodies, visible to the artist, were only noted by the mannequins in their speech, a slight and lovely difference of simile, metaphor.

Alike in body with only a variation of line, a teasing visual differentiation, Quin and Quine were alike also in mind and interests. They liked to do the same things, felt the same things, saw the same things, eliminated the same superfluous and unnecessary from the same landscapes; indulging in a kind of perpetual twinship; sighing together, lying together, always in step, a complete understanding existing between them. Almost in parenthesis one might say, so unimportant it might seem it is hardly necessary to note, that each lacked the organs indicating the probability that she might someday have a baby and the lack of which would certainly ensure his rejection by the Army. (The Army's rejection slip was, in fact, couched in such bad English that neither could understand it [it wasn't *good non-sense*], and the gynecologist's weary suggestion that she consider a hobby [sketching? gardening?] made them laugh and cry.) I am not at all sure that their mutual inadequacy affected them in any way whatever that would bear upon this story but I do know that neither, preoccupied with a career and heroism on his part, children and domesticity on hers, grew apart in the slightest or ever became part-time friends as might have happened if they had been united in what is called normal marriage; neither knew that the other was legally impotent, neither felt any inferiority whatever. The pretty things they said, descriptive, as I have indicated, of each other's bodies were only a small part, lovely as it was, of their conversation. The mannequins loved best to tell their dreams. Alike in every other way they recognized with a pleasant, palpitating excitement that their dreams were different. This sweet difference, *their* difference, continuous and cumulative, chameleon-like in its change of subject matter, saved them from the gentle, lovable, acquired brother and sister, twin-like boredom, a contented husband and wife domesticity, a sleepy, lovable existence without pain; they were happily spared, too, he the ticklish remorse, she the uneven felicity, of happily married mortals. Sleeping quietly in each other's embrace, silently, soundlessly, they awoke each morning with strange eyes, sideways looks, anticipating each other's dreams. The pleasure they gave each other early in the morning when everything else was still, when the sky was orchid before dawn, when the leaves were on edge, when the raccoons and the squirrels were catching a few winks trustingly before day, when the rain stopped short and the moon was light blue and the sun waited for daylight is too elusive to describe, too graceful to communicate. Quin, eager to speak, to remember, to please, withheld the words that leaped to his tongue; politely, paternally almost, whispered, "Quine, you dreamed?" and Quine sighing, anticipatory, murmured, "You, Quin, you first." These lover's manners enhanced their pleasure until, interrupting each other, they began, and in great detail, in analytical, diagrammatic profusion, they drew from each other's mouths the intricate double entendre, give and take, dual but singular exchange of subconscious; the intimate symbolism, the complete and passionately desirable innocence of the unspeakable, the final "silence" of the unspeakable. This "silence" the mannequins anticipated, finally enjoyed to the fullest; and then during the day, as in a fifth act, rested; gently withdrew from; walked hand in hand on tip-toe; waited in the sunshine and common sense of day for the thrilling non-sense of dreams to be communicated, the exciting glossolalic, the "speaking in tongues," that ancestral, aboriginal, abstract babel; witnesses, these two, of things unutterable, described by St. Paul (Cor. 14).

Mannequins, being nearly abstract beings, dream especially complicated dreams which are a kind of continuous non-sense, a pure reminder of what was originally a complete existence (their symbolic, jointed bodies were given not so much to them as to us that we might see them). They told and retold their dreams and almost holding hands sighed in nostalgia for that long ago time when they had been absurd. They resurrected in their imagination, using recollection as a blueprint, that *Tower of Babel* where everyone spoke perfect non-sense and chose for themselves the topmost spire to have been born in. They wondered in a scholarly way, sweetly pedantic, when they had first felt the frail desire to communicate; at what moment in glossolalic pleasure the heights had seemed too rare, too thin, too lacking in probability, and mannequins had begun to talk sense, satisfying and prosaic, useful and pragmatic; a descent from the heights, from the Tower to the Crossways. They wondered about music and tried to remember how inferior it must have been when it had merely announced the onset of war, the death of a heathen; and about the plastic arts, three little Indians coming this way, painted on a tree; and sculpture, when it consisted of therapeutic "spitten" images designed by one's enemy or one's medicine man with alternative intention. "Sanity in art, it was called," they said in unison and each laughed; because knowing the Fine Art of Speech did not make them too proud to say things and make jokes, too, when it was appropriate to do so. They loved words, language itself, roots, caesural pauses, extra light syllables, dangling participles, limping iambic, plain iambic, infinitives, dialectic especially, ablatives, syntax, auxiliary verbs, disguised compounds, even gerunds; they respected the trivium; they liked the thrill and mystery of elliptical sentences; they could spot topic, dilemma, axiom, analysis, interrogation, prayer, invective. They lay in the woods not quite intertwined, talking, talking, talking, talking, talking, talking, talking; never having to bother with the frustration of punctuation. Sometimes for variation Quin would sing a strong conjugation like this:

bitten (bit)
chidden (chid)
hidden (hid)
slidden (slid)

and Quine woud tastefully trill a weak conjugation like this:

dipt
shipt

stript
whipt
chopt
dropt
lopt
stopt

When one or both were suffering from laryngitis they enjoyed dia-gramming each other's sentences, but it was partly to pass the time 'til evening, a daytime companionship, cozy and friendly, waiting for the differentiation of their dreams, the consummation of difference with difference, (alike as their dreams were in verb) unlike in subject matter. Quin and Quine were innocent; and changing the subject was enough. They knew that "the knowledge of the gender of a noun is necessary in order to correct use of the pronouns" (Bain) but that is all they knew of Sex. They were never apart, could not bear to be separated (even by a comma), but in order to practice the tiny, peripheral, almost extra-marital pleasure of writing and receiving love letters they would turn their backs and write each other notes. These notes were always strictly non-sensical, classic examples of pre-historic dialectic and Quin and Quine called them, quite properly, "Belles Lettres." Sometimes they were inspired and wrote them fast but sometimes they labored as conscientiously as you and I might over a sonnet. "Sweet Clause" they began and "To a Lovely Pro-noun." This started a sporadic discussion on "The Difference Between Inspired Glossolalic and Intentional Non-sense" but neither was a philosopher and each languorous from dream-telling so that Quin at last put an end to the discussion by saying simply, "Nothing is easy." and wasn't he right.

One day when Quin and Quine were walking smoothly in the woods, their bodies arranging themselves in beautiful composition each to each, functional, his arm encircling her small waist, his hand lowered at a pleasing angle from his wristjoint not quite touching her thigh, their knees bending in unison, straightening out, not quite locking, and bending again, his torso turned a little toward hers, her round head and cylindrical neck inclined toward his, his grave profile on the lookout for flora and fauna to point out to her and analyze and whisper about, their bodies shaded and highlighted, toned, intensified by the woods they lived in, protectively colored but enhanced, they came upon a place in the narrow path of their own making, one of innumerable ones, that had been recently disturbed. Fresh upturned dirt was scattered and there were big careless footprints. They both saw the same thing at once. "This is singular," said Quin. "Or plural," suggested Quine. Quin let go of Quine and bending scraped away the dirt. "Look out," said Quine, "it might." "Might what, little Timorous?" "Might." said Quine. "Please make a full stop." Quin laughed and wrapped one of his smooth arms around the two slim legs of Quine while he continued his explorations in the path. "Hold on to me, sweet twig, perhaps I shall find you a Christmas present, perhaps I shall find you a beautiful new word." Quin soon uncovered from its shallow grave a huge book. Quine cried out with delight, "The word, the word! Oh, Quinio, Quinare, Quinatus! How this! How that! Let me guess." "Watch out for your infinitives," cried Quin as with all his beautiful strength, his lean wooden back arching, his cream-colored biceps leaping and trembling, his pelvis at a right angle, he lifted out the shamefaced tome from its shallow tomb. Quin and Quine read outloud the great title of the gigantic book, *The Interpretation of Dreams* by Sigmund Freud.

Quin and Quine felt rosy all over. "Infinite words," said one. "Innumerable speech," said the other as they glanced at the uncountable words. "Who would have dreamed there could be so many," said Quine, in the midst of her pleasure, however, feeling a little apprehensive. On the flyleaf sprawled and sputtered an angry warning which the mannequins unfortunately did not recognize as such: "This book has cost me my wife; led me into abnormal infidelities, disgraceful conjectures; taught me to dislike my own children; ruined my appetite; spoiled my bridge. I hope it rots." and there followed glossolalic words and dashes indicating unspeakable things unknown even to Quin and Quine. "It is an imprecation," said Quin, "and a very good one." "It has the impact of good invective," added Quine. Quin began turning the pages lovingly as if the book were music and for a while they were both silent. "Listen," read Quin, " 'For nature is really daimonic, not divine; that is to say, the dream is not a supernatural revelation, but is subject to the laws of the human spirit, which has, of course, a kinship with the divine.' " "Listen," read Quine, " 'The dream is defined as the psychic activity of the sleeper, inasmuch as he is asleep.' " "This is not a work of art," they both said at once, "it is clear that this man is trying to say something; let us be patient," and they were. They spent three weeks reading Mr. Freud in the Brill translation so that it was not only that they had to understand Freud but Brill! Quin and Quine read for a long time without any comment, just for the pleasure of reading. Quin and Quine were innocent as I have said. Neither did it occur to them that anyone would write a book about *them*. They were not suspicious, had no infantile or adult feeling of guilt, hadn't a trace of paranoia, didn't think for a minute as they were finally forced to realize, however, that Mr. Freud *was* talking about them. And that all the nasty cracks and insinuating editorial remarks by Mr. Brill referred to them, too! Ahhh, poor mannequins! introduced to evil by means of the so precious words of their own happiness! Dear Quin and Quine who had accepted all things in nature and their own artistic improvements upon it as acceptable revelations of beauty, to be told so brutally that "beauty" itself and in quotes like that, too, was nothing but something very horrid and *that* something something they had never imagined in *itself* was horrid: the pleasure of looking at each others variations, so exciting, so sweet, beautiful; to be told that it in itself was evil, and beauty forever after relegated to quotes in a footnote by an imaginary Mr. Brill!—and the "remarkable" paradox, they read, that what is being looked at is in reality so unbeautiful, "can really never be considered beautiful!" Dear God in Heaven!

Quine put her hand on Quin's and in a husky voice said, "Let us read no more." "But there is more to read," said Quin, and so they read on. "What do quotation marks around Beauty mean?" Quine insisted. "Words are wonderful," said Quin, "please don't interrupt, my little Jointess." "Even when they mean something awful?" asked Quine with tears in her eyes. "Oh Quinio, Quinatus, *quelque chose arrive!*" and Quine for the first time in her life lay down and fainted because in all modesty what else could she do? Quin was not alarmed; but very weary from reading Mr. Freud, he lay down beside her and bending over her, slipping one thigh beneath her and one arm, protected her from the dampness of the earth beneath and the light of the moon above, as usual. But Quin himself did not sleep, did not dream but only thought and wondered about the *Interpretation of Dreams.* When the first bright pinkness in the sky and a restless early morning movement of Quin's awoke Quine, she, without remembering anything preceding her dreams, murmured, "Quin, I dreamed," and Quin said, "What?" sadly. Quine in a flute-like voice accompanied by beloved explanatory gestures related the following dream: "The fur-bearing crab, as soft as a kind of extra-jointed kitten without that feeling of nothingness and intangibility that a cat has when you pick it up; more satisfactory. This crab, it appears, has no need of a mother; it is orphan; a phenomenon, called scientifically 'the economy of the leaves,' attends to the appetites of these little crabs. Growing upon, and tendrils hanging from, the roofs of pastoral cottages a kind of vine which bears blossoms, from the center of which appear small smooth nipples supply the crab with nourishment. There are also books (the economy of leaves refers to the leaves of books) with blank white pages except for a tiny green fringe which either grows from or has been pasted down the edge of the pages about two inches in. This green fringe will grow into hardier plants producing the blossom described and this handy economical method of feeding the fur-bearing crab is recommended. The green fringe growing or pasted along the edge of the pages reminds one of the greenery of pinks or carnations pressed in old scrapbooks (that belonged to one's dead mother.*)" The words in parentheses Quine affixed upon awaken-

---

*The author is well aware that the dream recorded may with reason be censored in that capital where American conscience is situated, Boston; and the list of words murmured by Quin may be written as follows: C—b, e—a, j—d, f-r, u——y, c-t, c——s, e——y, p——e, b——s, r——s, p——l, f——e.)

ing (they were not in her dream), and then added sweetly, still pre-occupied as she was, "And you Quin, what did you dream?" "Quine," said Quin with furrowed brow rather coldly, "it is clear that your dream, superficially at least, has something to do with lack of nourishment, hunger of some sort; it also strongly suggests the need for reality; but the important thing is to look up its meaning, its basic underlying significance in the index of our book," he added, "then all will be clear." "No, no! not clarity!" cried Quine. "It is indicated," said Quin solemnly. "But Quin, what is the matter with you? Dreams don't have to mean anything! They aren't commercial! And it is my dream, an original! Please, *Mon Image*, don't stay in the indicative mood, what did *you* dream?" but Quin was already looking up her dream in the index, murmuring, "Crab, extra-jointed, fur, unsatisfactory cat, carnations, economy, paste, blossoms, roofs, pastoral, fringe." If these highly significant, pregnant words embarrass a normally sophisticated, Twentieth-Century man-about-town or club woman in mixed company after reading Freud, please imagine, dear reader, how shocked, grieved, dispossessed, taken aback, horrified beyond words, eventually speechless were the naive mannequins of whose tender existence, sustained by innocence and beauty, the intellectual exercise of words alone, you have read.*

Quine, watching her beloved Quin, saw his body change color, saw his knees give a little, but saw him bravely straighten up, turn his handsome face that looked like a series of profiles toward her. His expression was grim, his eyes burned with one word only (she saw it written on his look): sacrifice.

"Quin!"
"We must not tell our dreams anymore!"
"Quin!"
"We are subconsciously preoccupied with sex."
"Sex?"
"Sex."
"What is that?"

(If the profane Bostonian is shockable, consider the sensibilities of our pastoral* pair! *p——l.)

"It does not say."

"Then how is it bad?"

"That is the premise."

"Oh." Quine knew logic as part of the trivium they loved and hung her head, at least suspended it as only a mannequin can, expressing the deepest pathos, the tenderest sorrow. When she looked up at Quin she studied lovingly ("*Voyeuse?*" He shivered.) his whole body: he stood with his weight equally distributed on his heels, brave and strong, but he had raised his arms, elbows out, his slim hands hiding and sealing his mouth. Quine, equally brave, finding some small pleasure indeed in mimicking Quin, nevertheless murmured, "*Mon Image, adieu, ma joie.*" and raised her own hands tremblingly to her lips, but before her final and everlasting silence she asked, "Not even in French?" Quin did not reply.

Finis

The Wandering Jew

IDEA

This play shall consist of two parts: the Predicament (metaphysical, theological) and the play itself.

The Predicament (metaphysical, theological) shall consist of the argument: God created man. God sent his son as a man on earth. He was called Jesus. It is understood however that he was Christ. As Jesus he had a soul. As Christ he was God. Jesus died upon the cross. He was placed in the tomb. Three women watched. In the morning the stone was rolled away and he was not there. "He is risen," the women said. Aside from the fact that he returned sporadically three times after this to his disciples and to certain women, no more is known. It is simple to accept in the abstract the "return" of Christ to the Trinity. It is not so simple to understand what became of Jesus the Man, either spiritually or physically. Jesus the Man had body and soul. The placing of his soul in Heaven would be superfluous and embarrassing. Likewise his everlasting stay on earth would be unreasonable and unacceptable.

Conclusion: With no place for his soul in Heaven and no place for his body on earth Jesus the Man became the Wandering Jew.

*The play itself shall consist of the wanderings. The wanderings will
be the uneasy reminiscences and flighty recollections of an old man
whose domicile at the time of the play is an Old People's Home.*
*Description: No description of the characters in this play seems to
me necessary, their description being inherent in what they do and
say. I hardly need to insist therefore that the old man does not physically resemble Jesus.*

*Extra notes: The old man may be referred to in the play as Eli (for
Elijah), Jerry (for Jeremiah) or Abe (for Abraham). He may on the
other hand be simply referred to as J. C. The old man at some time
may explain the necessity of his everlasting presence by the expression
"moral exaggeration." He does not clarify this and I will therefore
leave it to the reader's insight, with the help of my written Predicament, to understand. I would hesitate to be so impudent as to suggest
that God in His desire to impress the followers of Jesus as well as con-
found His enemies, was guilty of an exaggeration.*

SCENE 1

*The Administration: consisting of some men and two women. They
straggle; seat themselves.*

1ST A:
Are we all here?

2ND A:
Yep.

3RD A:
Guess so.

4TH A:
Yes sir, seven.

1ST A:
There's no sense in being formal. He's got to get out.

WOMAN A:
But . . .

1ST A:
There's no sense in being sentimental.

204

WOMAN A:

He's so nice.

2ND WOMAN A:

Nice! He's dirty.

2ND A:

He's awfully funny. I tell my wife about him; he's a card.

WOMAN A:

He's pathetic.

3RD A:

He's nuts.

4TH A:

He's crazy as they come.

2ND WOMAN A:

The nurses are complaining; they say he makes passes at them.

WOMAN A:

I don't believe it.

2ND WOMAN A:

He calls them pet names and Bible names. Ahhh.

WOMAN A:

The old hags ought to like it.

1ST A:

But they don't, though. They think he's making fun of them. He's got a light in his eye. [*He whistles a wolf call.*] Sometimes he laughs himself sick. He's insulted the Reverend Jenkins so often the Reverend says he won't come back if we don't oust the old man. He says he's blasphemous, and impudent; that he abuses the cloth and insults the Church.

2ND A:

He means him.

1ST A:

Well, there are too many complaints.

3RD A:

The other inmates like him.

4TH A:

Yes, those two old lady friends of his and that young feller.

5TH A:

Young?

4TH A:

He's only seventy. He likes the old man. He says he's a combination of Rabelais and St. Paul.

1ST A:

He's a dirty old man and a Jew if that's what he means.

WOMAN A:

As a matter of fact we all know he thinks he's Jesus Christ.

3RD A:

There's nothing unusual about that.

2ND A:

But this old man is positive.

1ST A:

It can't be helped. He's got to go. He's a terrible expense. He's the biggest item on the books. He's always been here. I've been here fifteen years and that old man is the same age as when he came in. There's no record of when he came in even. I tell you he's always been here. As far back as I can make out in those old books we've got, there's items about him: candy, cigars, mustard plasters and so on. I tell you I was looking at an old book there, the date was . . . [*He hesitates and looks around.*] . . . 1852.

2ND A:

That makes him just a hundred; that's possible.

3RD A:

That means we ought not to throw him out; he can't last much longer.

1ST A [*amazed at what they haven't realized*]:

But folks! This ain't no orphan asylum. This is an old people's home! [*He looks scared.*] He didn't come in here as no boy! *We don't take 'em under seventy.*

[*There is astonished silence as they figure it out.*]

2ND A [*foolishly*]:

He's a hundred and seventy.

ANOTHER:

But look here, man, you've made a mistake, that's all.

1ST A:

Mistake nothing. I've got the books here for you. Look here—and here—and here—Item: cigar for J. C. Item: ten pennyworth licorice for J. C. Item: mustard plaster for J. C.

[*They all look over the books excitedly.*]

3RD A:

But that may be a different J. C.

1ST A:

Different nothing. Look here — 1854. Item: fee for Dr. Griswold; examined J. C. again. Report: delusions of grandeur; harmless. Thinks he is Jesus Christ. And the very next line . . . Item: two pennyworth licorice for J. C. It's the same old feller all right. Whew!

[*One of the A's had been taking down old records from the shelves. Some yellow leaves fall to the floor; he reaches down, and picks them up; some books, papers and junk fall to the floor, raising the dust. Those who aren't too old sit on the floor like children in an attic; the rest hang over them.*]

3RD A:

Good Lord! Look here! Be careful, it's coming to pieces. Look! [*He reads aloud.*] 1796—Old J. C. had severe fall out of second-story window. Says Devil told him to jump. Item: pennyworth licorice. Item: mustard plaster. Item: leech. But, good Lord, are we all crazy? What's this? [*He holds an old daguerreotype up to the window.*] Cracky! It's him. And there's the date pasted along the side. Well now look at that . . . 1839. Proof enough—proof enough. That's enough for me; proof that's what it is.

AN A:

What's he doing?

ANOTHER:

He's just grinning.

AN A [*ejaculates*]:

Jesus Christ!

ANOTHER:

Hush, Mr. Welch.

SAME A:

I guess I can *say* it if he says he *is* it. [*He giggles.*]

AN A:

Wait. See here—here *is* something. A copy of an old newspaper notice of some sort and a card attached. I can hardly read it. The date on the card is 1720; the newspaper date is lost. This card shows they were wondering about our old man in 1720.

ANOTHER:

Read the notice.

AN A [*reading the clipping*]:

"An old Jew this forenoon nearly broke up the founding exercises of Harvard College by declaring he was Jesus Christ. The Fellows of the College courteously invited him to partake of refreshment. He attempted thereupon to change the water into wine and laboriously cut his bread into infinitesimal pieces, declaring he would feed the multitude. He arose, called for order and announced that all seven Fellows would betray him before morning, but that he forgave them. He was lodged in the county jail for the night."

1ST A:

When was Harvard College incorporated?

SOMEONE:

1636!

SOMEONE ELSE:

By cripes he's three hundred years old!

ANOTHER:

Came over on the Mayflower I'd like to bet my bottom dollar. Haw!

ANOTHER [*practically overcome with delight at his witticism*]:

Not him . . . *He walked!*

[*They are all in complete disorder by now. From nervous giggling they are now slapping their thighs and throwing themselves about. At this moment the old man appears in the doorway. He is smiling affably and eating a long piece of licorice. "Stand up; stand up for Jesus" they all sing crazily, the tears streaming down their quivering cheeks. They stagger to their feet. The old man calmly raises his hand in benediction. They file past him in various moods and out the door.*]

SCENE 2

It is a semi-public anteroom, a pretty dreary looking place. The old man is reading the Bible. His two old lady friends are rocking, sitting on their hands and staring into space. There are some artificial flowers and an old clock. Through the door can be seen a sign turned partly toward the room. It reads: Visitors Day. Now and then a group looks in at the door; stands back and whispers. Those in the group look as if they might be saying of the old man and the old ladies, "What a charming picture."

OLD MAN [*shaking his head*]:
I just can't remember it all.

1ST OLD LADY [MAGDALENE]:
Readin' your diary again, lovey?

2ND OLD LADY [SALOME]:
Allus is. Allus is. Allus is.

OLD MAN:
Those disciples of mine now; they didn't always get me straight, not by a long shot. I had a good time, too. They make me out pretty solemn. [*He reads on a little to himself; following the lines with a big finger.*] Cracky if I didn't! [*He starts to laugh; he laughs and laughs; he laughs himself sick.*] I scared Hell out of them pigs! [*He slaps his leg.*]

M [*laughing*]:
Them swine, lovey.

s [*laughing, and passing a little bag*]:
Have some candy, Maggie.

M:
Thank'ee Sal.

[*The old ladies munch and rock.*]

OLD MAN [*mumbling and serious, the book closed on his knee, while the old ladies regard him with affection*]:
Chief priests and scribes; chief priests and scribes. Get out of my house. [*He gesticulates.*] Git now. Robbers. Humph. No! No signs today. Git! Go easy with the little doves. Place the little dove in my

bosom. [*His head drops and he sleeps a moment.*]
  M [*whispers*]:
My eyes ain't so good and I keep forgettin' what he tells me; I keep
forgettin' who I am. Dearie me. Who am I, Sal?
  S:
You were sinful, you were. You sinned but you took his eye. It says so
in the book there. You were beautiful and wicked.
  M [*accepting this*]:
I was that. So I was. [*She strokes her wispy hair.*] My hair was black
and long, down to here!
  S:
That's it; you were Magdalene.
  M:
No, no. Abagail. I was Abagail, but my hair was black and long to
here. [*She rocks excitedly.*] And Sal! Come closer Sal. Sin? Sure!
[*She holds up her knotty fingers and starts counting them off.*] Him
and him and him. What d'ye think I think about all day long! [*She
rocks.*] Ah, that one, that reprobate. Don't tell the Holy Ghost there.
[*She laughs vulgarly.*]
  S:
He knows it. He knows everything. Shut up and repent. Where's your
long black hair now I'd like to know.
  M [*begins to cry*]:
Uh uh uh uh uh.
  S:
Shut up, I says—what became of you in the diary there? Nothin'.
Me, I am Salome. I allus stayed with him; allus, allus.
  M [*still weeping*]:
Uh uh uh uh uh. Some candy, Sal, like a good un.
  S:
It's gone. There won't be none till Saturday.
  M:
What's today Sal? What's today?
  OLD MAN [*waking up calmly; then wide awake*]:
"What went ye out into the wilderness to behold? A reed shaken with

the wind?" John! There was a friend! Aye, John my friend. A fine man. And what did they do to you for your trouble. Prison! And that little bitch Salome! [*He suddenly looks furiously at the old lady.*] You fat little bitch—what did you do it for? You gold-headed vampire, you naked wench. John my love. John my darling. [*He sobs.*]

s [*frightened*]:

No, no, I didn't do it.

M:

It was me. God save us.

s [*turning in her anger*]:

It was *not.*

AN ATTENDANT [*appearing at the door*]:

Quiet in there, folks. Visitors.

S AND M:

When do we get our tea?

ATTENDANT [*to visitors*]:

You see how comfortable everything is; and these are three of our oldest guests. Abagail here is—how old are you, Abagail?

M [*pleased*]:

A hundred.

ATTENDANT [*admonishing her gently*]:

Abagail.

M:

Well, goin' on it. Sal here she's only ninety-two goin' on ninety-three.

s:

Good evenin', folks.

ATTENDANT:

That's a good girl, Lucy.

[*The old man has watched all this with disgust and contempt. He stands up and everyone looks at him.*]

OLD MAN:

These ladies are not Abagail nor Lucy. They are my friends, Magdalene and Salome.

[*A visitor titters.*]

ANOTHER VISITOR:

And what is your name?

I am Jesus Christ and I shall one day sit on the right hand of my
Father which art in Heaven. And where will you sit, miserable sinners,
robbers, thieves, Philistines, mockers, pigs and bastards! In the dump
heap! In the ashes; covered with boils. Git now. Get out of my
temple!

[*They go. He sits down exhausted. The old ladies nod with delight.*]

OLD LADIES:

You did it beautiful, Jesus, you did it grand.

OLD MAN:

I ain't got the strength anymore.

M:

Aw lovey.

[*A woman who is searching for her father enters with an unidenti-
fied gentleman.*]

WOMAN:

It isn't him, yes it is, no it isn't.

OLD MAN [*kindly*]:

Sit ye down, 'publicans or democrats. Visitors Day we have all kinds.
Tea's a'comin'.

WOMAN [*tearfully*]:

I am looking for my father, my old father. [*She turns to the old man.*]
Are you my father?

OLD MAN [*sternly*]:

Woman, what have I to do with thee? I have no daughter, only
daughters. These are my daughters [*nodding at S and M*] and my
brethren are everywhere, even in Congress. Sinners and monkeys and
reptiles and little children, republicans and skunks and cockroaches.
Art thou the Syrophoenician? *Talitha cumi.*

[*The woman looks around, frightened. The old ladies look very
pleased and proud.*]

GENTLEMAN [*businesslike*]:

Where were you born, Old Man?

OLD MAN [*quietly*]:

Bethlehem.

GENTLEMAN:

Pennsylvania?

OLD MAN [*roars*]:

No. By God!

M [*quickly, delighted at having remembered some of the Old Man's
teaching*]:

Oh, oh, lovey. Don't swear. Say only Yea or Nay. Allus Yea or Nay.
Yea or Nay. That's it. Hm. Hm.

GENTLEMAN:

Come, my dear, it's no use.

WOMAN:

But it's so awful. My poor father. I promised mother I'd find him.
I have nothing but a picture of an old man. Mother said he was an
old man. Please, old man, did you have a wife called Elizabeth?

OLD MAN [*interested*]:

So you're it! I told her to keep still and be quiet. I told her she would
conceive and she wanted to argue. Go along, old woman, I said—go
home and conceive; funnier things have happened. Mighty funny
things goin' on I said. Haw. Haw. [*He has one of his laughing fits
and the old ladies rock faster and faster with excitement—it has been
a big day.*]

[*The gentleman leads the woman out. She is weeping into her
handkerchief. She moans over and over: "Oh God. Oh God.
Daddy." The old man gets up, slaps his leg, and yells after her:
"Sure! Sure! Right the first time."*]

OLD MAN [*impatiently*]:

Where's my buddy? Where's my friend? Boanerges? [*He sleeps.*]
[*The old ladies rock quietly not to disturb him.*]

SCENE 3

*The resident doctor's office. He has a distinguished doctor calling
and the old man's friend, Boanerges, is present. He is talking.*

BOANERGES:

Yes, Doctor, I am sorry you see fit to remove my friend to an asylum.

He is a remarkable old man and I do not think I shall stay after he
goes.

RESIDENT DOCTOR:

Mr. Boanerges has means.

DISTINGUISHED DOCTOR:

Oh, excuse me but your name is an unusual one, excuse me . . . ?

MR. B [*smiling*]:

It was given to me by my old friend. It means "Son of Thunder" you
know—the surname given by Jesus to his disciples. I prefer it to my
own. I have no family. I like it here. I like being called Boanerges.
Floyd-Jones is common.

DISTINGUISHED DOCTOR [*in a snobbish tone*]:

Long Island?

MR. B [*bored*]:

Possibly.

DISTINGUISHED DOCTOR [*to the resident doctor*]:

Is he in good physical condition? Heart . . . kidneys . . . what about
his tonsils?

RESIDENT DOCTOR [*going through charts*]:

Perfect. He has some sores in the palms of his hands which respond to
local treatment . . . otherwise hale and hearty. Hale and hearty.

MR. B [*quickly*]:

Sores in the palms of his hands?

RESIDENT DOCTOR:

Yes.

MR. B [*a little excited*]:

And his feet—his feet?

RESIDENT DOCTOR:

Feet? O. K. O. K., far as I know.

MR. B [*letting it pass; talks partly out loud and sometimes to the two
doctors who look and listen more or less amazed*]:

He is such a wonderful old man. His knowledge of the New Testament is astounding. He is very old and consequently often confused
but when he is treated properly and appreciated as I appreciate him
he shows an astounding insight. His recollections and reminiscences

214

of his life among his disciples are revealing.

THE DOCTORS [*interrupting*]:

Recollections? Reminiscences?

MR. B [*annoyed*]:

Knowledge then—knowledge. He has pointed out that the stories of the four—Matthew, Mark, Luke, and John—are artistically true rather than factually true. He made the distinction himself. He snorts at John. John was a theologian and used the story for his own intellectual purposes. He likes Matthew the best, calls him a realist. No one of them, he maintains, was an intelligent man or a good historian. They make him out a simpleton and that he was not. They did not understand the parables; not in the least. They misquote him and take him out of context; Luke in particular shows his ignorance by his quotations concerning the parables. [*He pauses, then continues.*] I, gentlemen, shall write a fifth testament; according to my friend, my old friend. [*He hesitates again.*] According to Jesus. [*The two doctors look at each other nervously; they frown but say nothing. Mr. B. looks at them, wondering if they have the wit to understand.*] Jesus—the man you understand—not Jesus God. My new testament shall of necessity be the life and teachings of Jesus and not Christ. Let the Old Testament stand as revealed truth and the New Testament as a beautiful and artistic—but unsuccessful—attempt to combine the life and teachings of man and God. My testament will be based on the truth as this old man has told it to me and it will speak for itself. It shall be authentic—as this old man is authentic!

TWO DOCTORS [*astonished*]:

Authentic!

MR. B:

He is Jesus.

TWO DOCTORS [*foolishly*]:

Jesus?

MR. B:

Jesus, but not God. He is with us and always will be because of a moral exaggeration.

TWO DOCTORS:

But he says he is God.

[*The doctors are petulant; not noticing that they are being asked to accept something very remarkable. They have accepted it and are only annoyed at his saying he is God.*]
MR. B [*to himself*]:

I wonder why he does not know that he is not God, seeing that he was. [*He speaks to the doctors.*] He has forgotten that he is not God. He cannot grasp that he is not. He is a man. He is the Wandering Jew. He recollects the details—he remembers everything. He can easily grasp the abstraction of his being God but he cannot grasp his not being God and I cannot tell him.

TWO DOCTORS:

Why? Why not tell him? You are the person he will believe.

MR. B:

You ask me ... whom he calls Boanerges ... to deny him!

TWO DOCTORS [*seeing the light*]:

Of *course* you couldn't.

DISTINGUISHED DOCTOR [*excited; and talking fast*]:

But this is terribly interesting ... terribly interesting. It's amazing but simple! Look here, Dr. French; look here, Mr. Boanerges. The old man didn't really ever quite believe he was God when he *was* God. Ha! Because look here now, he was a man: and as a man, of course, certainly he doubted. He doubted he was God.

RESIDENT DOCTOR [*jealous, sarcastically*]:

What a predicament.

DISTINGUISHED DOCTOR [*pays no heed*]:

But he had to maintain it ... he had to ... to everyone ... to his disciples ... he had to prove it even by [*He hesitates—he can hardly believe himself.*] miracles. Miracles wasn't it, Boanerges?

MR. B:

Yes.

DISTINGUISHED DOCTOR:

For fifty years he had to prove he was God.

MR. B:

Thirty-two.

DISTINGUISHED DOCTOR:

For thirty-two years he struggled with his doubts. [*To Mr. B*] Am I right? I mean as to facts?

MR. B:

Even on the cross.

DISTINGUISHED DOCTOR [*finishing up*]:

His doubt became his belief; his weakness became his great strength. It is the one thing you cannot take from him; the belief that he is God.

MR. B:

Now that he is no longer God.

DISTINGUISHED DOCTOR [*completely convinced of everything now that he sees the "psychology" of the "case"*]:

Is it clear to you, Dr. French?

RESIDENT DOCTOR [*bitterly*]:

You are all nuts.

DISTINGUISHED DOCTOR [*healthy, distinguished and exhilarated*]:

Shall we have a drink, Boanerges?

SCENE 4

Same as Scene 2. The old ladies are rocking as before and as before have a little bag of sweets. The old man is snoozing and then wakes up.

OLD MAN [*murmuring*]:

Simon, Simon, behold, Satan asked to have you, that he might sift you as wheat. [*The crazy clock on the mantle starts ringing although it does not mark the time. The Old Man is startled.*] What was that! Eh? Sal and Maggie? How many times did it ring?

S:

It allus rings wrong. It's an antique. Have some candy.

> [*The Old Man sits back as if he were tired. Enter without formality the Administration; a person who has come for the old man, and a female attendant. Gradually the old men and women come in until the room is nearly full.*]

OLD MAN [*starting up and excited*]:

I am delivered up to councils! [*to the female attendant, angrily*] Take down your hair and wash my feet.

THE PERSON [*wheedling*]:

Come along nice, Mister.

OLD MAN [*very angrily*]:

Is this a prophet's reward!

[*The Administration whispers to the Person.*]

THE PERSON:

Now you come along nice, Mr. Jesus.

OLD MAN:

Mr. Beelzebub!

THE PERSON [*uneasy, but gradually gaining character*]:

Now you come along nice, Mr. Jesus, and you're going to like it over to our place. We got a nice view. We got a fine modern building and an elevator. And we got some fine folks over with us; just as fine as you got here. Nice and quiet they are and harmless, absolutely guaranteed harmless. What say, Mr. Jesus? And listen, we got a garden, too, Mr. Jesus, so you come right along nice. [*He turns from the Old Man to the Administration as if selling something.*]

OLD MAN [*standing straight and very dignified; seeking for the apt thing to say*]:

Neither tell I you by what authority I do these things.

OLD LADIES:

That's grand, Jesus, that's lovely.

OLD MAN [*starts to cry, shaking his fist weakly at the Person and the Administration*]:

Hypocrites. Dead men's bones. Whited sepulchres and comfort stations. Sadducees and suckers. Gangsters!

M:

Aw lovey, lovey.

S [*trying to stand up*]:

I stayed with him. I followed him.

THE PERSON:

Take it easy, girls.

OLD MAN [*imposing, convincing, speaking gently*]:

I say unto you that the harlots go into the Kingdom of Heaven before you . . . So long, Sal. So long, Maggie. [*He starts to go along. His old*

218

comrades make way for him. They are solemn.]
  OLD COMRADES [*sincerely and spontaneously*]:
Stand up, Stand up for Jesus, Ye soldiers of the Cross.
  M [*trying to get the old man's attention*]:
Jesus, Jesus lovey. I almost got that Solomon song. I almost remember it . . . but I keep forgettin' it. I keep forgettin' it. Uh . . . uh . . . uh . . . [*She subsides and rocks.*] Where's he going, Sal?
  [*As he goes the old people close in on him, singing.*]
  OLD PEOPLE [*singing*]:
Stand up, Stand up, for Jesus, Ye shall not suffer loss.
  [*He is gone and there is quiet. The voices of the Person and the old man are heard in the hall.*]
  THE PERSON:
This way, Mister Jesus.
  OLD MAN:
Let us go out by the narrow gate for wide and broad is the way to destruction.

Soliloquy at Dinner

The woman was so identical with so many others that you wondered that such a gentle soul as her husband could commit such adultery. In loving the one he surely loves the others, I thought, and the undisciplined imagination pictures him fondling a multitude of counterparts cast in a mold that the thoughtless artist did not destroy so that as long as this man lived and no matter where he went he might always lie with his wife; wiser indeed than seeking to sustain by your own frail power the image of a one-and-only peerless one, hand-painted, as it were, and rare as hen's teeth, so they say. A man is not sensible who chooses the apex rather than the base and whose heart turns to ashes along with the unequal one; ever after a priest without a temple; and continent to a T, one might say; and only resembling his brother, the one who has been mentioned, in his psychic inability to be unfaithful, there being only one of her, and she mortal while the gentle soul's lady is infinite, in number at least, and consequently deathless, I should say.

The more I see them together, this man and this easy, effortless image of his, the more shocked I become in a fine ticklish way, at the frieze my imagination presents to me almost without censorship. The gentle soul, the subtle uncontroversial poet, a kind of bas-relief hero passing and covering (only in slightly higher relief than they) an endless row of the daughters of Danaus, touching each, eclipsing each, for a moment, like a bee intent but disinterested; and whose the honey; I ask myself? Does he present it to his muse? But this man, it seems to me, has no right to such poetic license, if that's what it is, and this row of exact maidens appears to me desirable, very, and I am envious. What Ivory Tower is this that he lives in, its only decor a circular Parthenonic frieze of the self-same girl with continuous lips and round breasts divisible by two, an amazing Diana of the Ephesians indeed and more of this sort of thing that makes my head reel. Are they faithful to him I ask myself, does each wait patiently to be revisited in her turn, does she watch his equator-like progress to her right or does he travel counter-clockwise to the left? And how after this sort of thing can he appear in decent drawing rooms among decent people? That gentle soul, that fine distincted poet with heavenly subject matter to his rhymes? Hypocrite! See him so easy, self-possessed, among the decent, remorseful spouses, on whose arms, and hanging on whose lips, one-of-a-kind wives, individuals accept for sex and quips. This is good society, you must understand, no small-town or surburban chatter here and the gentle soul, although a poet in good intellectual standing, is here only on probation, in wartime, and he won't last long; he isn't witty and he is a little too innocent, if you can believe it, and naive; a good man, oddly enough, it would appear, but not well informed and not quick enough to change the subject when it is new to him without changing the meaning of the conversation. His wife, if after my visual experience with her and her infinite ilk I may describe or touch upon without shame, I can not represent in words better than I have already done: her identity is her identicalness. If, upon meeting her, you think or say, "Haven't we met before?" you are right; if you've been around you have seen her all right, seen her and forgotten her, except for the continual interruption of her always being everywhere, a constant irritation, unwanted mushroom of a woman, at your elbow but not in your heart. If the party is a big one and not exclusive there will be several of her there, and even at a privileged gathering like this she has got in in the shadow of her man; and if you know the kind of woman I mean, she's not at all nonplussed in brilliant society, not a bit of it; she draws attention to herself at table when wise and modest ones hesitate in this well-known conspicuous position, when even the servants listen and judge and carry on the conversation in the kitchen pretty intelligently, by saying in a sweet voice something which she cannot sustain and she has not the sensibility to be embarrassed, finding herself hanging in the air like that; she even takes the stares for tribute, and blushes.

And her husband, whom I have not called insensible, lacking in adroitness, (far from it, the old devil) comes to her rescue, of which she is not aware of the need, by explaining but not appearing to explain the content, of which she had no idea, of her remark. Of course this man does not particularly admire this woman but she will do, especially as she is everywhere and with benefit of clergy he may satisfy his polygamous (to put it mildly) nature without any trouble at all or censure; he may lead a libidinous ubiquitous sex life in a little white house, as it were, a disgraceful kind of domesticity, I call it, who cannot even say the peerless woman of my choice is entirely my own either in the kitchen, in the garden, or in bed. And so to the deuce with this evil little-boy poet who seems to have all, in the big sense of all, much, while I have chosen of my own free will a superior woman around whom I may place only the choicest things, in whose ear only the fairest words, about whom I am continually remorseful and uneasy. I would not change her, but that row of virgins in thought and body and sensibility sounds like more fun than for a horrible man like him who whispers the fair things and gives the choice gifts to his A-number-one peerless muse, I suppose, his first and one love, his poet's choice, too beautiful to touch. Can you imagine him choosing his wife! He made no careful study of a bunch of flower-like girls, weighing this and that, love me, love me not, tearing off the petals, or sick with desire begging assent from the only one, no; he absentmindedly but unerringly married at high noon every other woman in a single ceremony but with endless geographical reward, the dog. By the way, did you ever eat whitebait? Innumerable, tiny, white, shiny, inch-like, naked women; not bad. Quite a diet for a gentle soul who has dared, to her innocent and great happiness, to dedicate his poems to my wife!

www.ingramcontent.com/pod-product-compliance
Lightning Source LLC
Chambersburg PA
CBHW061616100726
47898CB00002B/679